JC

FALL OF THE

THE

ORDER

WWW.BLACKODYSSEY.NET

Published by
BLACK ODYSSEY MEDIA

www.blackodyssey.net
Email: info@blackodyssey.net

Library of Congress Control Number: 2023919149

First Trade Paperback Printing: December 2024
ISBN: 978-1-957950-24-2
ISBN: 978-1-957950-25-9 (e-book)

Cover Design by Navi' Robins
Developmental Edit by Kreceda Tyler

10 9 8 7 6 5 4 3 2 1

Manufactured in the United States of America
Distributed by Kensington Publishing Corp.

Dear Reader,

I want to thank you immensely for supporting Black Odyssey Media and our ongoing efforts to spotlight the diverse narratives of blossoming and seasoned storytellers. With every manuscript we acquire, we believe that it took talent, discipline, and remarkable courage to construct that story, flesh out those characters, and prepare it for the world. Debut or seasoned, our authors are the real heroes and heroines in *OUR* story. For them, we are eternally grateful.

Whether you are new to JC or Black Odyssey Media, we hope that you are here to stay. Our goal is to make a lasting impact in the publishing landscape, one step at a time and one book at a time. We also welcome your feedback and kindly ask that you leave a review. For upcoming releases, announcements, submission guidelines, etc., please be sure to visit our website at www.blackodyssey.net or scan the QR code below. And remember, no matter where you are in your journey, the best of both worlds begins now!

Joyfully,

Shawanda Williams

Shawanda "N'Tyse" Williams
CEO & Founder, Black Odyssey Media, LLC

I dedicate this book to my late beloved great-grandpop, John Thomas Kiser. RIP. The times spent on his lap as a young kid watching monster and science fiction movies contributed to this story. I pray I made him proud with this one.

PROLOGUE

THERE ARE THINGS . . . creatures in this universe that you could never comprehend, things that people of the higher powers do not want you to believe. As long as they were considered legendary monster myths and maintained as folklore, those people felt they had done their due diligence. Our governments cover up hundreds of paranormal and cryptic activities every year. The Order, a secret agency, monitored and controlled these activities. It regulated the use of paranormal abilities according to the secretive laws of each land in North America. It also investigated any paranormal, supernatural, or cryptic threats to the safety and security of North America and each country's citizens. Trust me, it is much deeper than that. People of higher powers used smoke and mirrors to hide scandalous tactics. Some of them would be considered inhumane and an abomination.

In history, there were just as many documented monsters and creatures written off as myths and folklore. In most cases, they were used for religion and entertainment to hide the truth, dating back to the days of the cave people and the dinosaurs. Cave paintings of man versus beasts in Egyptian hieroglyphics depicted wars and worshiped creatures and gods that present-day man dissected and redirected the narrative.

One of the most hidden historical events under the folklore tab was the Vampire-Lycan War, which lasted over two hundred years between 1200 and 1000 BC. It was a sociality unknown to many where the enslaved Lycan Clan, known today as werewolves, rebelled against their oppressors, the vampires, who held them captive for centuries. Since the capture of the first Lycan in 1430 BC, the vampires used Lycans' strength and endurance to work as slaves and laborers, such as building massive castles and wall structures, ironworks, and more. Lycans sent assassination missions to any entity threatening their exposure and existence. Sometimes, they captured humans and villages for the vampires' blood thirst.

Two issues plagued the vampires. They could not use the werewolves during a full moon or keep the Lycans' population down to a minimum. In human form, the Lycans had nowhere near the strength of the vampires, but once in a changed animalistic state, they rivaled the vampires in speed and were at least five times stronger. So, special safeguards had to be implemented to protect the vampires. For example, powerful, accurate weapons on roofs and walls would shoot sharp, silver spears at the slaves. A scratch from one of these spears would result in a painfully slow death with no cure. The vampires made their weapons and armor mostly from silver, a poisonous metal to the Lycans' bloodstream. Also, the enslaved Lycans were to be locked up in a bunker surrounded by silver bars before dusk every evening.

They performed cruel abortion tactics when the population hit a specific number, and the vampires either backed off or enforced breeding when the numbers dropped to a particular census.

Over time, some vampires violated their laws and used Lycan people as sex slaves. Rape and sodomy became commonplace. The elders believed this would cause uncontrollable offspring, and with the elders in deep hibernation, many in their society did not fear retribution.

After decades of mistreatment, including beatings, rapes, mutilations, lynchings, and other horrendous acts, an uprising of the slaves broke out within the castle grounds. The vampires the elders left in control lost their power over the people and eventually faded out or became corrupted. Unlike the generations before, the new generation of slaves would rather die than continue to live the life they were born into.

A battle erupted under a full red moon and caught the vampires off guard. Silver spears ripped through fur and flesh before the Lycans overtook the vampires. The claws and teeth of the Lycans ripped chunks from their suppressors' flesh. Many died from both races, but in the end, only fifty of the 220 werewolves were alive and escaped into the unknown and left behind a tremendously decimated vampire race. When that bloody night ended, the war between the two left carnage all over the world through their respective gangs.

Scared, the vampires known as the rebellion tried to eliminate all three elders by burning them in their hibernation chambers because a judgment would be inevitable. A fight broke out between the rebellion and the loyal vampires, who were dedicated to the old ways. The loyal vampires tried to save all three elders but only managed to rescue one as the rest burned in their hibernation chambers. The rebellion captured and slaughtered the remaining loyal vampires. However, they never gave up the hiding place of the recovering elder.

Over the years, a vampire known as Cristian the Elder hunted down and slayed all the remaining rebelling vampires and any offspring in the shadows. This caused a shift in the war and took the upper hand from the vampires. Cristian hunted down the Lycans as well. In the early 1800s, The Order captured Cristian due to the betrayal of a trusted vampire and placed him in a solid steel coffin to rest eternally until they could figure out what to do with him.

Many of the Lycans escaped to Africa and lived peacefully among the people without revealing their true identity, partly due to their melanated skin and features. But as time passed and the Lycans mingled more and more with humans, intercourse led to some offspring, and acts of violence and misuse of power increased. Increased birth rates between the Lycans and the Africans led to many stillbirths for many generations. Although it was rare for those who survived, the ones who did became known as the hybrids, and their bloodline would become something unimaginable and, in some cases, uncontrollable.

The full moon never affected the hybrids, but they retained powers of their bloodline. Several generations later, one young hybrid morphed into a feral state. In this new state, the transformation became triggered by anger instead of the full moon. . After a certain age, every annoyance, displeasure, or hostility the young boy's body morphed him closer to the curses of his ancestors, to the point of being much bigger, faster, and stronger than any of his elders before him. The Order took this boy under their care. Two generations later, Jefferarri was born.

CHAPTER 1
THE MEN IN BLACK SUITS

JANUARY 16TH, 1984, while searching for a missing father-and-son's hiking team in West Hopkinton, New Hampshire, the hikers found a crashed airplane half-buried in the deep snow twenty-five miles off-trail. The search party recovered three mutilated bodies that wild animals had eaten . . . or so it seemed. Several hundred pounds of cocaine were tossed about the plane's cabin, broken from the bands that held them together. Someone smeared and walked fecal matter all over the plane, including overhead. Shredded human skin lay in the chaotic scene that didn't match any of the three bodies. The unexplained, frigid Arctic air baffled meteorologists and the pilots for the twenty-two-mile radius. That area was 20 degrees colder than its surrounding area. The hikers could hear an unknown wailing in the distance grabbing the rescuers' attention through the large trees that dressed the white land.

Back at the coroner's lab, Coroner Jessica Taysom and Investigator Mya Stevenson stood around one corpse, trying to brainstorm any scenario. Guts hung from the bottom of its rib cage. Liquids formed around it on the table as it defrosted from many years of being frozen. Something ripped the arms and heart away. Skin and eyes were also missing.

"The nose appears bitten off. Those are *human* teeth marks. Well, closer to human than any other animal," Mya said, pointing around the nose area. She took a few steps down toward what was left of the

5

torso. "Teeth marks here," she referenced the grooves on the few ribs attached as the rest of the ribs lay in place inside the torso.

Mya grabbed her hanky from her pocket and held it to her mouth and nose.

Jessica looked up and asked, "Do you need a minute?"

Mya had been around many crime scenes during her four-year tenure as a detective constable, yet the stench of the frozen bodies made her want to gag. Until now, the worst she had endured was a pile of burned bodies. She wanted to run out of the room but fought to remain professional.

"Were the legs ripped off?" she asked after lowering the hanky just long enough to ask the question.

"That is correct," Jessica answered. "And he was possibly alive when it happened."

"How do you know that?" Mya asked, always impressed by Jessica's smarts.

"Well, I said 'possibly,' but there is not much blood left in what remains of the body. He bled out of the femoral artery. The heart pumped most of the blood out before it was yanked out."

"What in the world could have done that?" Mya asked, puzzled. "Or was strong enough to do that?"

"I have no clue, but here . . . You wanna see something even stranger? Follow me."

"Oh God, really?" Mya replied as she followed Jessica, bypassing one of the other tables to the last one across the room. The fetid smell from this one was three times stronger than the other. The first body differed from this one in that the second one was fully clothed, but the clothes did not fit its extremely tall stature.

"You see anything strange?" Jessica asked.

Mya examined the body. This body had all his limbs, but something snatched the heart through the shirt. It didn't take long for something to catch her attention. She moved her face closer to his half-deformed face. Then her eyes pinged the details.

"What in the hell?" she looked up at Jessica. "Are those real?"

Four one-inch canines protruded between half-inch jagged incisors and premolars. The skin had eroded around the mouth, exposing the darkened gums and most of the back teeth. The eyes were slightly sunken, and the jaw looked somewhat elongated. Pealed eyelids revealed cloudy eyes as if he had gone blind.

"Look here." Jessica turned her attention to his hands.

The fingers were a little longer than the average human's, and the fingertips seemed to fuse with the long, bloodstained fingernails.

"This is some vampire shit," Mya said aloud.

Before she could utter another word, Jessica pointed to the black boots. Mya walked down to the end of the table. Tiny claws peeked through the front of the leather boots.

"Some type of mutation shit," Jessica replied. "I made a phone call out to—"

The double doors busted open, interrupting Jessica. Two men, one white and the other Black, dressed in all-black suit attire and wearing dark shades, waltzed through the door, followed by three other men. The three men that followed wore black berets and black coveralls with black boots. They holstered a sidearm on their legs. No doubt, they meant business. The two men looked in their late sixties, but their facial structure told the story of two men in great shape.

"Coroner Taysom . . . ah, and Investigator Stevenson?" the white man named Agent Matt Jones asked. "I'm glad you are here too. Now, we can be in and out of your hair in a jiffy and get these bodies off your hands."

Agent Eugene Ware, the other man, slightly taller, handed Jessica papers that she immediately opened. "These subjects are now the Federal government's property," Matt continued.

Moments later, Matt and Eugene sat down with Jessica and Mya inside one of the five black SUVs parked in front of the Coroner's Office. The chilly gusts of wind did not bother the other men guarding the truck as four different men in white Tyvek suits carried the bodies in body bags to a tall black van. Eugene sat in the front passenger seat, and Matt sat across from him in the driver's seat. Jessica sat behind Eugene, and Mya was next to her.

"I am going to cut to the chase," Matt said. "What you and your people witnessed never happened."

"Never happened?" Mya barked. "What the fuck was that lying in there on my table? What's going on?" Her eyebrows furrowed as she whipped her head and eyes from one man to another.

Eugene adjusted the rearview mirror to see the ladies in the back. His intense eyes locked with Mya's. She rolled her eyes and focused back on Matt.

"Is that a threat?" Jessica replied, speaking from the gut with a bit of an attitude.

"Yes," Eugene said calmly as his eyes shifted to her.

"You and your people will not speak to anyone about what you've seen. Someone from our department will instruct you on what to say to the public." Matt continued, "This is not a request."

"This is such bull—"

Matt cut Mya off. "If you disobey these instructions, there will be serious consequences." He turned in his seat to face the women to show his face and the seriousness behind his demand. "Are we clear?"

The two ladies exchanged brief glances. Realizing the seriousness of his words, they had no choice but to comply.

"Okay," Jessica said. "Okay." She rubbed her face in distress, followed by a deep breath.

Matt and Eugene both turned their attention to Mya, silently waiting for her reply. She looked at them as their eyes bullied her, sighed deeply, and then nodded.

CHAPTER 2
THE GUGWE

FIFTY-FOUR-YEAR-OLD CLIFTON HELLAMS, the Korean War Veteran and now a stock investor and accountant, had served his country in more ways than one, with more medals than you could count on two hands and two feet. His biracial lineage came from the Blackfoot Indians on his father's side, and African from his mother's descendants, who were from Ghana.

Clifton's ranch was silent except for the heavy bumping noises that shifted across the roof. His squinted eyes followed the sound that echoed through his large living room at 3:06 in the morning.

"C'mon, you son of a bitch!" Clifton screamed at the ceiling.

"How long before they get here?" his wife, Margaret, asked.

The location of the fenced-in Hellams ranch was on flat terrain just a few miles east in the mountain region of the rolling hills in Tylerville, North Carolina.

Margaret retired as a schoolteacher and was an excellent cook. Shortly after Margaret's retirement, they moved to North Carolina and built the ranch on ten acres of land where Clifton raised and sold horses, many of which won derbies. He also raised other animals like goats, chickens, and cows, just to name a few. He built a nice-size man-made catfish pond on the east end of the property, opposite the horse stable, which rested on the west side. A gated driveway split the property almost down the middle.

Security lights from the house and stable illuminated most of the property at night.

"I don't know," Clifton said, fidgeting with his rifle. The phone lines were down, so that they could make no calls. "We should be safe as long as we stay inside," he said, looking down at his rifle. *Just in case*, he thought.

Suddenly, a hard thud came from the wraparound porch of the two-story home. The thump elicited a fierce, red glow from Clifton's eyes as he made his way towards the right-side window, his limp evident. He saw nothing, but the motion lights were on. It had rained earlier, so a light fog filled the outside. He knew what was out there stalking him. An enemy from the past. The very thing that ended his life as a cryptid hunter and gave him his limp. Now, after all these years, it came back to finish the job.

Chaos erupted from the horse stable, and the sounds traveled into the home. Clifton turned his attention over to the stable on the left, about fifty yards across the field. He hobbled toward the door as quickly as his limp leg would allow.

"Clif?" Margaret called out to him.

"Get Jefferarri and head to the basement!"

"Clif!"

"Now, Margaret . . . Now!" Clifton barked at his wife. There was a noticeable roughness to his voice now. "I'll be all right. This has gotta end. Just do as I say!" Without saying another word, the stubborn old man rushed out toward the stable, leaving his wife on the stairway. The door locked behind him.

She rushed up the stairs as fast as her old bones let her and ran into Little Jefferarri's room. The thirteen-year-old watched from his window as his grandpa hopped across to the stable, anger spreading across his face. He hyperventilated rapidly. With his keen ears, he could hear sirens closing in from a distance.

"Jefferarri!" Margaret said, rushing to him.

Their grandson, Jefferarri, was their pride and joy, and he loved them mutually. His name was a combination of his father's name and his father's love for Ferraris. His mother and father dropped him off one weekend, never to be seen again, as the story goes. A few days later, their abandoned car popped up on a road in Montana. Blood found on the outside of the passenger side turned out to be his mother's. He hadn't been the same since. He wasn't as playful and joyful as before, though Margaret could still tease a smile or two and some laughs out of him.

In his reflection from the window, she saw the curse in his eyes passed down through the generations beyond his great-grandfather down to him. She could see the shine in his eyes like when lights hit a cat's eyes in the dark. The faint red eye shine looked back at her.

"Jefferarri?" she called to him as she crept around the foot of the bed ever so carefully toward him. "Jefferarri, come with me, baby. Grandpaw wants us to go down to the basement."

A low growl vibrated from his throat. He didn't take his eyes off the window as he saw his elder approach the stable in brown pajamas and a tee shirt with no shoes on, his weapon aimed at the door.

Clifton rushed his way in front of the closed stable door. His eyes narrowed at the surrounding silence. The barn emitted no sounds. Police sirens became louder and echoed from a distance. *Did he kill my horses?* Clifton thought as he reached for the door with his shotgun ready. A cool, eerie breeze cruised in from the west, making his pajama shirt wave behind him.

The sound of splintering wood filled the air as a horse burst through the door, sending Clifton flying backward. His weapon slid a few yards across the grass. Burly, a large Gugwe, jumped out, following the horse. He pounced on Clifton, knocking the breath out of him. The pupils in his eyes were darker than the night. The smell of iron escaped the barn.

A Gugwe, also called the "Eater of Faces" was a Type-3 Bigfoot creature with a canine-like snout. Its features were combinations of a bear and an ape. Depending on the clan, the face may vary, but all had oversized heads and broad shoulders. They loved the mountains but would go anywhere for food. Although it rarely happened, they ate humans only when no other options existed. Their skin was callous and bulletproof at a close range, except for the temple area of the head. They were a hundred times more aggressive than any other Bigfoot-type creature.

Burly's nails were as black as tar, combined with a foul stench of cow manure and wet animals. He stood over nine feet tall and wore old animal pelts with markings on them. They hunted in small packs, so coming alone meant this was personal.

"I told you . . . I would get . . . you," spat the Gugwe, trying to speak to be understood, fighting through a stutter. It was a promise he had made almost three decades ago to himself.

The sound of a window crashing and a low, guttural growl from a distance caught the Gugwe's attention. It snapped its head in that direction as it saw little red eyes dancing through the darkness and fog. The flashing police lights cast an eerie glow on the distant trees near the property.

"Jefferarriiiiii!" Margaret yelled out of the broken window upstairs.

As Burly roared, his muscles bulged, and his sour saliva sprayed everywhere.

Clifton pulled a hunting knife from his side and stabbed Burly in the side of his neck, with only half the blade penetrating his thick skin and again in the jaw, aiming for the temple. Burly swiped its claws across Clifton's chest in a defensive reaction before jumping up. The super deep cut exposed Clifton's heart beating as he released a horrific cry.

"It must…be painful to you that…the curse of your lineage skipped you," the Gugwe poked. "Your immortal strength… deserted you with…age and…time. I…the great leader of the my clan…will end your suffering. We…will now have peace."

Jefferarri quickly caught Burly by surprise, clamping down around his neck as Burly turned to finish the job. He miscalculated Jefferarri's speed and moaned in pain as he tossed Jefferarri through the stable wall. A piece of its hairy flesh flew out of Jefferarri's mouth. Burly gave another blasting roar at Jefferarri and scratched at its bloody neck with its claws.

Clifton spat blood from his mouth, forcing it down the side of his face, past his ears to the grass.

The thirteen-year-old jumped out of the hole in the stable wall and stood toe-to-toe, looking up at the towering Gugwe displaying a David-and-Goliath scene.

"I will end . . . your bloodline," Burly said, turning his head to Clifton.

It stepped toward Jefferarri, but suddenly, a gunshot sent Burly off its feet. Margaret pumped another shot into the monster as it wailed. Most of the buckshot bounced off, but some dug into his skin.

Suddenly, with a piercing screech, four police cars arrived on the scene as Burly attempted to make his escape, and Jefferarri's attempts to take him down were once again unsuccessful. He tossed Jefferarri to the ground as flesh and blood flew from the youth.

"Freeze! What the fuck?" one cop yelped, his wide eyes and his trembling gun trained on the action before him.

Six cops opened fire on the Gugwe as it struggled to hop the fence. Bullets pierced holes and chipped the wood on the fence. One cop pursued Burly, shooting and hitting him in the back, only for the bullets to ricochet into the night.

Burly fell over to the other side of the fence and then connected eyes with the cop.

"Fuckkkk!" one cop barked. "What the fuck is that?"

Burly turned to the cops and let out another massive roar that forced them to cover their ears. Then Burly faded deep past the tree line with an awkward laugh. More laughter erupted from the trees, indicating many more of them. The cops freaked out and ran back to the comfort of their cars to put distance between them and the Gugwes. The horse ran frantically around the inside of the fence.

Sobbing, Margaret grabbed Jefferarri's hand to bring him back to the house, but Jefferarri was not budging. Sweat poured down the child's flushed face as he stood in a wide stance, baring his teeth that had become slightly jagged. His squinted eyes stared into his grandfather's eyes with no emotions. He watched Clifton stare into the dark sky as his breaths slowed and became shallower with time. With each breath, the eerie glow in their eyes grew fainter. A tear rolled out of the corner of Clifton's eye as his breathing and gurgling stopped. Jefferarri's jaw clenched, and his body trembled. Then he let out a wail of anguish and pain before he blacked out.

CHAPTER 3
LITTLE JEFFERARRI X GUGWE

THE SUN CRAWLED over the North Carolina trees. Five vehicles rushed from the Hellams ranch crime scene. Dust followed four government Ford Tauruses, with a single black Ford Taurus Wagon in the middle. Jefferarri rode in the backseat of the wagon, with his head resting on Margaret's lap. Tears ran down his face, and she comforted him by rubbing his arms and the top of his head. He lay in a trancelike state, letting his body recoup from the events earlier that night, watching his grandpa get slain by the monster. Jefferarri's weakness was that he had to recover after transformation mode, leaving him in a borderline vegetative state until he completed a full recovery, which left him vulnerable.

His wounds were healing fast. He had a brief memory, only remembering what he saw from the window, and after watching them put Clifton's body covered by a white bloodstained sheet in the wagon. Everything in between was a blur, but his body felt the bumps and bruises of what had occurred.

Eugene sat in the front passenger seat, marinating in the guilt and anger of not getting there fast enough to save Clifton from Burly. He had no idea the storm was coming or that the monster had developed into what it had become. Glancing back at the kid who had to grow up without his biological father and mother and now losing his granddaddy as his eyes bore witness, killed Eugene's soul.

Growing up without both blood parents was a situation Eugene knew about all too well after losing both of his in a car accident on their way from the hospital after giving birth to him. Somehow, he survived the crash.

His gaze wandered over to Margaret, who appeared deep in thought as she gazed out the window, her eyes fixed on some distant point in the vast expanse of space. She was an old, strong woman fighting back any emotions not to agitate Jefferarri. A woman who had also been through so much, losing her son, Jefferarri's father, and now, her husband.

"I'm going to make sure you two are well taken care of myself," Eugene promised.

She glanced over at Eugene, drawing pressed lips in appreciation.

"On God, I give both of you my word."

With a quick look down at Jefferarri, she closed her eyes with a nod before returning to the passing trees. Something in the distance caught her attention. She squinted, leaning closer to the window. What she saw popped her eyes wide open.

"Gene!" she shouted.

"Yes, ma'—" Eugene turned to her.

Bam! Something ran smack into the moving wagon, causing it to tilt out of control. The window shattered, and Margaret screamed, being snatched out of the moving wagon by her hair.

"Grandma . . ." Jefferarri whimpered. Glass cut across his forehead.

The wagon ran to the other side of the road and slammed into a ditch. Gunshots erupted from outside the ride. Shaking off the cobwebs, Jefferarri slowly climbed out of the window.

"Grandma!" Jefferarri called in a distorted voice.

"Jefferarri, get back!" Eugene demanded.

"Grandma!" Jefferarri shouted again, focusing his eyes through the blur.

Gunpowder and death attacked his nose. He sniffed for his grandmother but was unsuccessful. Amidst the gunshots, men screamed before their deaths. The shootings became fewer and fewer as they died off. When his eyes cleared, and the breeze blew the gun smoke away, he saw that it was a slaughter. Eugene grabbed Jefferarri to protect him. Another Gugwe slammed into them, tossing Jefferarri out of Eugene's arms. Eugene grimaced, quickly shaking off the fog of the attack as he put four bullets directly into the creature's chest and back as it grabbed at him. The bullets were just enough to slow it down, giving Jefferarri time to spring back on his feet and rip out the monster's throat. What Jefferarri saw next made his heart drop to his stomach.

From the edge of the tree line, Burly dangled Margaret's decapitated head to taunt the young one. Her face was grotesquely absent with fragments of flesh and blood oozing down. It grinned at them with such pleasurable evil. Jefferarri's eyes shone bright red. The anger escaped him in a thunderous wail. Blood formed from under his fingernails as his body morphed.

Without hesitation, he bolted toward Burly, who turned and took off into the dense woods, only to be followed.

"No, Jefferarri, stop!" Eugene cried after him, knowing it was a trap.

Jefferarri quickly disappeared past the tree line. Eugene chased, but a leg injury slowed him down.

"This is Agent 821," Eugene called into the radio he had taken from his pocket. "They ambushed us just two miles from the Hellams ranch en route to EVEC. Multiple casualties. Requesting road detours and cleanup. I'm in pursuit of subject 0917. He's back. We need lethal and nonlethal projectiles." Placing the radio back into his pocket, he ran toward the trees.

"Copy that, on the way, 821," a female voice responded. "ETA five minutes."

A little under three hundred yards into the woods, Jefferarri lost the blood trail that leaked from his grandmother's head. His canine teeth bled and had grown a couple centimeters since the start of the chase. He sniffed the air to no avail. Still not recovered from the events earlier that night, he struggled to catch his breath. A sudden thump jarred his attention from behind. He turned around . . . to see her head rolling toward him, stopping just a few feet away as it bumped against a tree root sticking out of the ground.

It was so surreal that he just froze. Exhaustion took over, causing his body to shut down again. However, a snarl from behind him gave him a quick adrenaline boost. Before he realized it, three huffing Gugwes surrounded him, towering over him. Although disappointed it wasn't Burly, he was ready to take his anger out on what stood before him.

"Jefferarri," Eugene called from a distance.

The call distracted the Gugwe in front of Jefferarri as it looked toward the voice just long enough for Jefferarri to leap off the ground, leaving leaves flying behind him. Two other Gugwes grabbed at him but were not quick enough before Jefferarri latched his jaws around the distracted beast's throat and tore a chunk out of it. The injured Gugwe swiped at Jefferarri, sending him flying into a large dogwood tree. His head slammed against the tree trunk. The two Gugwes rushed him as the injured Gugwe clasped his hands around its throat to keep its life from escaping.

The sound of two gunshots echoed through the forest, and the closest Gugwe dropped to the ground. The third one stumbled over its fallen companion. Brain matter ran down the tree trunk. A second gunshot hit the third Gugwe on the shoulder, scratching it. The Gugwe made a loud thump as it slammed into the tree next to Jefferarri. Leaves rose from the ground.

"Jefferarri!" Eugene ran toward them from about twenty yards out now.

Heavy footsteps rushed behind Eugene as he squeezed the trigger, popping the third Gugwe in the temple. Its eyes rolled back, releasing its final breath. Eugene turned and fired a shot at the approaching sound from behind. His eyes got big. Jefferarri went airborne, clawing at Burly's face. The bullet meant for Burly struck Jefferarri in the back of his thigh. Jefferarri and the Gugwe crashed into the scattering leaves.

Eugene put two slugs into Burly's chest before it could pound two fists down on Jefferarri ape style. A third shot soared past the Gugwe's face as it turned and ran. Another two bullets flew past before he disappeared into the trees.

CHAPTER 4
THE FEEDING

BARBARA CARTER, A fifty-four-year-old woman with a stout build, stood on her porch smoking a stogie while her ivory-toned hair blew in the breeze. She gazed up at the cold, cloudy sky above, wishing she had brought a jacket. The forecast predicted another blizzard headed her way in the next three hours. She looked at the time on her digital Quasar watch, which she had received from her mother many birthdays ago. The red digits read 2:16 p.m., so she had about half an hour before she headed to the family cabin to meet a couple renting the place for the next five days. Despite the nearly five figures paid to rent the cabin, something didn't feel right to Barbara. She felt a sense of dread thinking about it.

"Barbara! What time you going to meet them people over at the cabin?" Her mother peeped her head from behind the door to shield herself from the cold air.

"Around 4:00, Mama," she answered, rolling her eyes before taking another puff on her cigar.

"Alrighty, you told them about the storm coming?"

"I did, Mama."

"Well, we know what they about to do. The Oochie Coochie," the seventy-two-year-old widow said, not holding her tongue as usual, followed by her annoying laugh.

"At least somebody will get some," Barbara said, letting the cigar roll out of her mouth into the breeze.

"What you say, honey?"

"Nothing, Mama, just talking to myself about this storm coming," she lied.

"It's the government, I tell you. Always fucking something up!"

"Mama!"

Her mom shrugged her shoulders and twisted her lips, then went about her business, closing the door behind her.

The two-bedroom cabin near Hopkinton, New Hampshire, was once their home many years ago before an insurance settlement for their father's accident at work paid out a healthy amount. Her beloved father got injured when Barbara was only nine years old from a falling tree crushing his pelvis. The company he worked for did not have the proper equipment and inspections regulated by law. He would never walk again; mentally, he was not the same.

The usual trip to the cabin was strange. Normal wildlife that flourished during this time of year in this part of the land was nonexistent. She felt a sense of unease as she drove down the path to the cabin. Only the crunch of the ground beneath her tires broke the silence. Something did not feel right to her. She stopped in the middle of the road to examine her surroundings. There was nothing but silence except the little noise from her diesel 4-engine in her Volvo. She looked around, and the sight before her seemed surreal. She took a deep breath, trying to shake off the feeling of dread that had settled over her.

Barbara arrived at the cabin about half an hour early to crank up the heater that was installed a few summers ago. There were some logs next to the fireplace in case the people wanted to use them, and more logs piled up next to the cabin outside.

The chill surrounding the cabin had a different kind of cold to it. Much, much colder than back at the house or that the forecast has predicted for the area, but she paid it no mind and ignored it.

Finally, she heard a vehicle pulling up on the gravel. She checked the time on her watch and the clock on the wall facing the window. The wall clock was accurate. A little early, meaning she can get back home a little faster. She walked outside to greet the couple who were getting out of the black Tesla.

"Hello," Barbara called, waving and walking out the door.

"Hey," Stephanie spoke with a jolly smile, closing the passenger door behind her. She wrapped her arms around her body as the unexpected chill hit her.

Michael, a tall Caucasian man with an athletic build, had been coming to the area for the past sixteen years since he started with his father. The second year, he brought Stephanie, a petite Caucasian with a slender build, with him, and he'd planned on making it one to remember. After meeting in college, they had been together for the past three years. This was the first time picking this cabin because the one they usually rented was unavailable.

"I hope your trip was enjoyable."

"It was okay. I'm sure this will be worth it," Stephanie replied with a grin.

Michael looked upon the small pond off to the side of the cabin about one hundred yards as he slipped his hand into the pockets of his gray pullover hoodie with matching pants. An owl flew into view from over the pond, and Michael's eyes followed it until it landed on the roof. A gust of wind picking up was the clue Barbara needed to return home.

"Just to give you a heads-up," Barbara got the ball rolling, "and to be clear, there's no way out of here once the storm hits. The snow could get as high as the top of the windows." She pointed toward the cabin windows. "The snowplow could take up to a couple of days after the storm to reach you." She gave them every chance to bail out. "The weather report said it was going to be bad. And cell phone signals are not reliable."

They pulled out their cell phones. Their faces said it all.

"One bar," said Stephanie.

"No bars," Micheal said disappointedly.

"We'll be fine," Michael said, followed by twisted lips looking down at his lady. "Besides, if we leave now, there's a chance we could get caught in the storm, anyway. And we brought enough food to last well over a week."

"And I don't wanna be trapped in a storm on the road," Stephanie added.

Barbara tilted her head in an okay gesture, then walked onto the porch. "Follow me then," she suggested, waving her arm.

Stephanie hugged and smiled at Michael, then kissed his cool, reddish cheek. They followed Barbara into the cabin, and she instantly fell in love with the place. Michael's eyebrows lifted at the place's good condition.

"This is niceeeee," Stephanie said in surprise.

"My father had some work put in on the place over the years," Barbara explained. She continued to show them around and explained the details of the contract.

They upgraded the cozy interior to modern-day standards despite the old-school look of the exterior, which was well-maintained. Slated rocks framed the fireplace to the left. Decorative pendant lights aligned the ceiling. A brown leather sofa stood in the middle of the nice-size living room directly in front of the large, remodeled single window with a suede maroon throw blanket folded on the headrest. They placed another matching chair catty-corner in the corner to the left of the window. A floor lamp with a reading light angled over the chair stood beside it. A small kitchen was adjacent to the living room with simple, matching, white appliances on marble-designed countertops.

The master bedroom ran parallel to the living room and kitchen to the right. A slated woodgrain, queen-size bed with matching dresser and end tables stood with two regular windows dividing the bedroom from the porch. The master bath with a small walk-in closet was on the opposite side of the room.

Walking out of the bedroom, straight ahead and up the stairs to the attic, dubbed a second bedroom. A window looked out from the roof. Off the right of the master bedroom, there's a half bath.

As they followed Barbara down the stairs, she saw the owl through the window sitting out on the windowsill, stalking them like an evil omen. As they reached the living room, Barbara gave them another chance to reconsider.

"Last chance to reassess if you want to be here," she said, holding out the key with a smile. "There is a nice motel on the edge of town to wait out the storm."

"We're good," Michael said, taking the key. "Thanks for the concern."

"Okeydokey," she said as she turned before pausing. "Have a great time during your stay." As she cranked up the Volvo and put it in drive, she glanced at the cabin one last time. That owl was still on the windowsill.

After glancing back at Stephanie, feeling thankful to have such a beautiful woman in his life, Michael stared back out of the large window, hoping this trip would be the one to set the future perfect for them. The couple had been trying to get pregnant for over a year. Nothing could complete their lives more than having a baby. It frustrated them when their doctor declared them both healthy, Stephanie in particular, even though she tried to hide it with vocal optimism. A baby would be the perfect life addition to happiness until the end of time.

The central heating and the fireplace kept the cabin cozy as it got late while the minus-18-degree wind whistled against the structure. The thirty-five to forty miles-per-hour wind made vast mountains of snow dance violently. Stephanie sat on the far end of the couch facing the large window in the living room, reading *The View*, a novel by the author Untamed.

"That book must be excellent," he said with a smile. "You've been in it for a minute."

Suddenly, he saw a figure outside standing in the middle of the storm, fifty yards facing the cabin. With all the swirling snow, it was hard to get a good look at it. *There's no way anybody could stand still out in this stuff.* His heart sank as a moment of dread washed over him.

"What'd you say, honey?" Stephanie asked, still keeping her eyes glued to the pages before her.

"What the hell?" he reacted to the unfamiliar figure out in the elements.

"Huh?" Stephanie finally brought her head up for air to acknowledge him. "I'm sorry. What was that?"

Michael turned his head back to her, pointing out the window. "Looks like someone is standing out in the middle of this shit. Creepy."

She hopped out of her comfortable space to see what her future husband was speaking about, but when Stephanie took a couple of steps to the window and Michael whipped his head back around, the figure vanished.

"Wow, *really?*" He reacted to the figure not being there anymore.

She snuggled up against her man with a sigh. All she could see was a blanket of snow as the wind calmed down slightly. "Hmm," she shrugged, then grabbed him by the hand, pulling him to the couch. Placing her book on the armrest, she straddled him.

"You owe me something, mister," she joked in a romantic tone.

"Oh yeah?" he responded. "And *what* exactly do I owe you, woman?"

She laughed and kissed him on his lips. It was time for Michael to put in some work on that baby.

Darkness fell on the cabin. In the bedroom, Michael woke up with Stephanie secure in his arms, but he had the urge to pee. He eased up, slipped on his blue robe, and marched to the bathroom. The digital clock read 2:38 a.m. His arm hurt from Stephanie laying her head on it through the early night, so he shook it to get out the kinks.

After washing his hands, he returned to the bed, but the overwhelming dread he had experienced earlier returned, causing the hair on his arms and neck to stand on end. He stopped in his tracks and looked at Stephanie, who was sound asleep, then glanced at the closed curtains on the window. He crept out of the bedroom and moved to the living room. The curtains on the big window were closed. He continued to the curtains and peeked out from the side. It was so dark that he couldn't see anything other than the snow that accumulated at the bottom of the window. The outside light switch didn't work, so he concluded that the light must have blown.

"Michael . . . Michael," a woman's voice called from the other side of the front door. The voice flowed like a whisper, but he could hear it. "Let me in out of the cold." He recognized it as his grandmother's voice, though distorted. She passed away many years ago, so he knew it wasn't her, but instead, it was something very sinister. Despite knowing that it wasn't his grandmother's voice, he felt compelled to open the door. His heart thumped in his chest. Regret overcame him, wishing he would have never come there.

"Please let your grandma in, baby. I'm freezing to death out here."

Light scratching played on the door. The blizzard angrily beat up the cabin while the windows shook violently. Lightning crept around the curtains, bright enough to light up the room. Then a moment of silence followed the voice.

He was jolted back to reality by the sound of a brief, sharp scream, followed by breaking glass from the bedroom. He shook the daze from his consciousness and pivoted to the bedroom, where a foul stench that smelled like roadkill and urine crept into his nose.

"Stephanie!". Fear made him hesitant at first, but his manhood made him pick up the pace and rush to the room. He turned on the light switch. What the lights had revealed buckled him to his knees.

Blood painted the walls in random patterns around the bed over to the window. They looked like claw marks. Stephanie's severed hand was about four inches away from her arm and lay on the floor between him and the bed, surrounded by bloody glass fragments. Parts of her scalp with hair still attached rested on the center of the blood-soaked bed.

He squatted, speechless, with a knot in his throat, and screamed out her name. But before he could finish calling her, the voice spoke to him again.

"Help me!" The voice flowed with the gusting wind and snow through the window. It sounded like Stephanie, but he knew it wasn't.

His vision blurred, and a feeling of vertigo suddenly overcame him, causing him to drop to his hands and knees. As he looked, he saw mutilated body parts, primarily bones, scattered all around him. Now, the storm picked up again, with snow and ice beating through the window.

Only pieces of flesh hung from the gnawed-on bones. What remained of the vertebrae was only a few bones, muscles, and tendons attached to the hip bone, with half of Stephanie's intestines wrapped around them. The rest ... *gone*. Whatever did this did it fast.

Suddenly, the drywall cracking echoed through the room as the razorlike claws gripped each side of the window frame. An ear-blasting screech rattled Michael's bones as the creature stuck its head through the window.

CHAPTER 5
THE HUNT

RUNNING THE SECOND shift on the snowplow attached to the front of his old Jeep Wrangler, Jacob ran late clearing the roads at his end of the town due to the storm. He turned off the main road to head to the Carter cabin. Barbara called several times to remind her cousin not to forget the two-and-a-half-mile wooded shoulder stretch to the spot. Now, he fought to beat the sun going down. They wouldn't usually rent out the cabin during a major storm like the one that just passed.

He stopped to sip his spiked coffee a little over a mile. As he turned up his coffee thermos, an owl flew and landed on the snowplow, catching Jacob's attention.

"Hmmm." He praised the owl before taking another sip. "You going to keep me company, buddy?" He saluted his cup to the owl.

As he shifted his jeep into gear, something caught his attention to the right. The swaying tree limbs, moved by the wind, created an eerie atmosphere. Squinting his eyes, he strained to make out the details amidst the tangled branches. *Was that a face peering through the foliage?* His fingers absentmindedly scratched at his tired eyes, the faint scent of pine mingling with the crisp morning air. His glasses slid down his nose, requiring an adjustment. Suddenly, a soft whoosh cut through the silence, as an owl took flight from its hidden perch. Startled, his focus jolted back to reality. With a quick blink, he refocused his eyes, only to find the area where he thought he saw the face was now devoid of any presence. "Don't start that shit," Jacob said to his drink.

Placing his foot on the gas pedal, he finished the job. The closer he got to the cabin, the harder the snow fell. Branches swiftly moving to the left caught his attention. Goosebumps pimpled his skin as his instincts prompted him to turn around and leave before it was too late. *Fuck it*, he thought, remembering the promise he made to Barbara. Looking back through the rearview mirror at the snowy scene, he thought he saw a human figure standing in the middle of the road. The amount of snow and wind that came suddenly from nowhere made it hard to get a good look at it.

"Fuck this," he said to himself.

As he neared the cabin, the creeping sense intensifyed with every passing moment. Nothing had felt right since he turned off the main road. Still covered with snow, a car remained parked in front.

The snow, soft and powdery, reached a height of just over two feet, blanketing the ground in a pristine white. Despite its grip on the landscape, the window on the side of the cabin revealed dark-spotted stains, marring the lower half. "What in the entire hell?" he said as he stepped out of the Jeep into the knee-deep snow. He focused on the broken window. Standing outside the Jeep, he could see reddish stains soaked in the snow and what were chunks of body parts half-buried in the snow. Chills ran through his body, but not from the negative 5 degrees nibbling through his thick, bubble jacket on top of layers of clothes. He high-stepped through the snow to get closer, fighting the random wind's gusts to keep his balance until he heard skidding from the trees to his right. Looking in the direction of the noise, he thought he saw the shape of a face camouflaged high up amongst the trees and the branches . . . the same face he thought he had seen moments ago.

"Shit, naw!"

He retraced his steps through the white terrain towards the Jeep, the crunching of snow beneath his boots reverberated as loudly as the howling wind. As he glanced downwards, his eyes locked onto something that seized his attention. A mangled, torn-off arm protruded from the snow, sent him tumbling backwards onto the frozen ground. The piercing shrieks grew louder, drawing nearer with each passing moment. Panic surged through his veins as he desperately crawled back into the safety of the Jeep, slamming the door shut with a resounding thud. His lungs heaved, greedily inhaling deep breaths as his face flushed crimson, beads of sweat forming on his brow. Frantically, his eyes darted around, surveying the ominous surroundings. Time was of the essence, and with a surge of urgency, he swiftly shifted the Jeep into gear, ready to make his escape.However, something slammed into the back of the Jeep as he spun away, causing the vehicle to rock to the left. Thankfully, the plow on the front kept the ride upright. Once Jacob gained control of the Jeep, he wasted no time hightailing it out of there. He reached for his radio as his heart threatened to beat out of his chest.

"Hey, there is something terribly wrong at Carter's cabin," he blasted into the radio.

Bam! Something rammed into the back of the Jeep again, causing it to lean on the two wheels of the passenger side this time. The radio slid out of his hands and landed on the passenger floorboard as the back passenger window shattered, filling the vehicle with an ear-deafening shriek. The sound blasted through his ears and made his face squinch in pain, and his shoulders rise.

"Come back," a male voice sounded from the radio. "Please, repeat, over."

Jacob managed to turn the Jeep back to the road he just plowed. Survival told him that was the best plan to get out of there, so he hightailed it back out the way he came.

"What the fuck is that?" Tears from fear formed in his eyes.

He looked down at the radio, but before he could reach for it, his peripheral vision caught a pale figure dashing off into the tree line. By the time he got his focus on it, it was already in the trees. He knew something out there was big . . . and fast.

Fuck that radio right now. He placed his attention back on the road. Another glance through the passenger-side window, and he could see the figure keeping pace with him, dashing and weaving through the trees.

"Come back," the voice over the radio said again. "Over."

Jacob knew the main road was near and hoped whatever it was didn't give chase once he reached it. He didn't see the creature anymore, but he still was not going to take a chance, even though he knew he had to slow down to make that right turn onto the main road.

As he slowed for the turn, an ash-gray figure *slammed* into the Jeep, flipping it upside down. The vehicle slid across to the other side of the main street.

Hours later, police lights danced across Carter's cabin. Blood and gore painted a picture of a gruesome death that was amplified by the police lights. No one stood a chance at that cabin overnight.

Smack dead in the middle of it all, trying to figure out how so much snow fell in this area compared to the less than one foot of snow elsewhere around it, was a young investigator named Bruce Dixon. Now, the weather was calm as he stood in the two-foot-deep snow.

Originally from New York, Dixon, as a young, nineteen-year-old white kid, moved to the Hopkinton area because of gang activity. His mom shipped him to his father because she could not do anything with him. Twelve years later, he became an investigator, partly because of a significant turnover ratio. People stayed on the job for a few years to get some experience, then moved to an unfamiliar area for the city life and a better payday, or just disappeared, never to be seen again. Now, four years later, looking across the carnage, he regretted coming here.

"Animal?" asked a scruffy male voice. The chief of police, Ron Fletcher, a former high school pretty boy quarterback with the light blue eyes, had let himself go over the years. Well, over four hundred pounds now, the six foot two, tall, white man's popularity from his high school glory days was enough to get him elected by a landslide with only four years on the job as an officer.

"Didn't the doctor tell you to rest?" Dixon said before facing Fletcher. A plume of white mist rushed from his breath. "I'm sure that blood pressure hasn't come down yet."

Fletcher chuckled, followed by an uncontrollable cough as he stood beside him.

"I need the fresh air," Fletcher said, gazing across the yellow crime scene tape. "Besides, being home listening to my wife yap yap yap all gotdamn day and night will put me six feet under faster than any aneurysm would."

Dixon grinned, always enjoying the 24/7 jokes about Fletcher's wife. "She just loves you, that's all."

"Yeahhh, I know. So, anything new since the update given to me over the phone?"

"Other than no tracks were found anywhere in the snow for a quarter-mile radius."

"Well, the storm could have easily covered them up," Fletcher gave his veteran opinion.

"Logical," Dixon said, shaking his head. "But there were prints inside the cabin that painted a crazy picture."

"Prints?"

"Like none I have seen before," Dixon responded.

"Not bear?"

"Definitely, not bear. I haven't even seen a bear around here in a while. Even before hibernation season began. It's like they been chased away . . . or extinguished."

"I know," Fletcher continued. "I agree with you there."

"Anyway, I wish I could tell you more, but I didn't have time to investigate the hand or footprints before those guys in black showed up to shut us down," Dixon complained as he nodded to the men off to the right in all-black attire. "But there is one thing. They found Jacob's body a mile from the crash. Our men in black over here won't let anyone near that crime scene."

Several men stood around the big, black RV and three SUVs, casing the scene to ensure no one entered the kill zone. The men were using tablets to log their reports. Two towering men, seemingly identical twins, emerged from the RV, their attire clearly unadapted to the freezing 19-degree weather. The other men wore black trench coats, cargo pants, and boots. However, for some strange reason, those two only wore a black tee shirt and shorts—with no shoes or coat.

Fletcher put some gum in his mouth and glanced at the men with Dixon. "I remember growing up, and those guys used to be around here all the time. Not as many, though. My mom used to call them the 'mean men.' The only thing that has changed is the suits. They disappeared for a little while."

"I've heard the stories," Dixon said. "My question is, after all these years, why are they back? And then this happens, and *poof*, here they are. What are they hiding, Ron?"

"Whatever it is, it's bigger than us." Fletcher nodded at the crime scene.

The two men, clad in black tee shirts, swiftly dashed into the dense woods, their hurried steps leaving a trail of snowflakes swirling in their wake. "Them fellas are going to freeze to death out here," Fletcher said before coughing again.

Dixon's voice filled with amazement as he pointed and said, "Just look at how they move!" "It's like they're running the hundred-meter dash on dry ground in this snow."

CHAPTER 6
NO LONGER LITTLE JEFFERARRI

THIRTY-FIVE YEARS LATER, after the death of his grandfather, Jefferarri woke up from the nightmares of that past. His eyes opened to a faint red glow upon the white and blue walls as he sprang up in his twin-size bed. Heavy panting sounds filled the frigid, dark room. White mist formed on the window with each breath. As Jefferarri realized it was all a dream, the panting slowed, and the room dimmed back to dark. The digital red clock on the left wall read 4:19 a.m. After a moment of getting himself together, he sat on the side of the bed, rubbing the palms of his hands against his face.

The nightmares are happening less as I get older, Jefferarri thought. *But they are no less violent. Feels more like I'm back in the moment than ever now, physically and mentally.*

He clenched his fists as anger and thoughts of revenge consumed him. His pupils illuminated again but quickly calmed after taking a deep breath. The strong Lycan trait in him made his eyes glow. He knew they had never caught the monster that had taken his loved ones. To him, that was a good thing.

Jefferarri walked to the bathroom to empty his bladder. After flushing and washing his hands, he observed himself in the mirror. He rubbed the dark birthmark that covered his right eye. He stared as his six-foot-four pecan-tanned body in the mirror before opening the medicine cabinet above the sink. There were stacks on top of stacks of pill bottles with no room for any more. Before he could reach for a specific bottle, he felt an unusual presence in his home and turned his attention to the door as his senses heightened. His eyes started to glow slightly. He sniffed the air at the bathroom door, taking in the familiar scent. He *knew* the smell.

He opened the door to a different bedroom. He could see his girl beneath the covers in the queen-sized bed through the darkness. The warmth from the room hit him in the face like a furnace, causing him to feel itchy. He closed the door quickly but quietly.

The upstairs had three bedrooms side by side that faced the balcony, which was an open view of the first-floor living room and part of the kitchen. Jefferarri did not need lights, so the house breathed total darkness except for some small devices downstairs that illuminated a tiny area. He noticed a pair of reflecting eyes across from him below. Jefferarri jumped over the balcony and landed on his feet down below in a squatted position.

"Anna," he said in a raspy voice. He stood up and slowly turning, looking for another before facing the pale-skinned witch sitting on the stool next to the bar.

"Nice tat," she said, noticing the large, black, gothic-style cross that covered his entire back. "From our past conversations, that would be the last thing I thought I'd see on you."

"Lights on," Jefferarri commanded, and the lights illuminated, causing him to squint.

With her towering height of six foot five and curves in all the right places, Anna was a stunning Amazonian Witch from the Wiccan tribe who harbored a secret crush on Jefferarri. However, Jefferarri had as much feeling for her as his heart would allow . . . which was minuscule. She'd always tried to find a reason to come around, so she acted as a go-between for Jefferarri and The Order.

There was no room for doubt - Jefferarri possessed an unwavering fearlessness, with the mindset to destroy any foe before him. However, when it came to Anna, he refrained from cornering her. The reason behind his caution became evident the moment he witnessed the overwhelming power she concealed, a force that emanated a palpable aura of awe and respect. Jefferarri's gaze shifted to the corner of the room where Kang, his black Cane Corso puppy, was attentive, with his tail wagging on his cozy little bed.

"What good are you?" he asked, rolling his eyes away from the puppy.

The gray-eyed puppy with the shiny black coat tilted his little head to the side, looking up at his master as his tail wagged. Jefferarri decided to keep Kang's tail intact while clipping his ears.

"Tell me what I wanna hear, Anna," Jefferarri said. He took a step toward her. His wide, muscular frame commanded the space. "I'm not with the shitz-n-gigglez."

"It's not Burly—"

"Then you're wasting my time," he barked. "Plus, I'm not due for another assignment for several weeks now. Protocol. Send somebody else." Jefferarri made his way toward the stairs.

"There is nobody else. A Flesh Eater killed the Twins."

Her words stopped him in his tracks like a brick wall. He turned to her with startled eyes.

"Or so we think," she added.

"James and Jamie?" he asked apprehensively. His eyes were wide open and stiff now.

"Yes," she replied, standing and walking toward him.

"The Flesh Eater? The one we could never—" His dialogue tapered off.

"Don't think so, but not out of the question."

The emotions welled inside Jefferarri. Anna could see radiation-type waves flowing up from his eyes. A grunt rose from the pit of his stomach and escaped his mouth. Thoughts of him, the Twins, and several other children playing at the recruitment camp many years ago played in his mind.

When Jefferarri was first processed into the school by The Order after the death of his grandparents, the Twins, a pair of Lycans, were the first he connected with. They were born from a woman who died from a Beta Lycan attack shortly after giving birth to them due to complications from the attack. She never even had the chance to hold them. Their father had his throat ripped out during the attack, trying to defend her. During the Twins' young teenage years, other Lycans who worked for The Order called "Cryptid Hunters" developed a mental breakdown and went AWOL. They killed dozens of people before being hunted down and killed by fellow hunters. After that, all Lycans were given a device called the "kill switch" to control them and prevent those incidences from recurring.

"What happened?"

"About three days ago, a blizzard rushed in out of the blue and overtook Hopkinton in New Hampshire. The biggest storm they have seen in decades. Tourists, campers, and people of the community disappeared left and right. At first, people blamed the weather for the disappearances. But later, people discovered mutilated bodies of animals and individuals that appeared to have been consumed, along with bones that had been chewed on. About a week ago, The Order sent the Twins and some agents to check out a Flesh Eater claim. The last notes received from them were they found evidence of at least a possible level 10 Flesh Eater. Jefferarri, that was nine hours ago."

"An Apex Predator," he whispered solemnly.

After a deep breath, Anna continued. "After that, they disappeared without a trace. We found blood and skin tissue in the snow that belonged to them, where there seemed to have been some fighting. Their vehicle was located by local authorities on the side of the road. All agents were asked to leave those grounds immediately."

Jefferarri balled his fists. His breathing became more labored before he let out a hoarse yell toward the ceiling. His blood boiled as revenge coursed through his veins.

The puppy whimpered from the vibrating mix of a human scream and an animal howl.

Octavia, Jefferarri's lady, ran out to the balcony, looking down at the first floor to see what was happening. Even in her sleep, she could feel Jefferarri's emotions.

"Jefferarri!" she called.

Octavia had powerful spiritual and manipulative powers she conjured through vodou, or what's now known as voodoo. Octavia's mother was a high-ranking priestess who introduced her to voodooism when she was ten years old after her family migrated from the Afro-Haitian communities that arose during the Atlantic Slave Trade. Her family was involved in the Haitian Revolution from 1791 to 1804, which overthrew the French colonial government, abolished slavery, and transformed Saint-Domingue into the Republic of Haiti.

Many generations later, Octavia continued the tradition of learning from verbal teachings. Octavia had two younger siblings who also studied alongside her. Her mom found out by age twelve that Octavia was special and had unique abilities like none other. Octavia's powers were more powerful than the religion itself.

One night as Octavia and her sisters slept, a crash awakened them, and yelling came from their parents' room. Her sisters started crying and calling out to Octavia as she crept toward their bedroom door. She shushed them and told them to hide under the bed before she opened the door. As she turned to her parents' room, eerie smoke and the smell of sulfur crawled from under the rattling door.

A thump against the door made her nearly jump out of her skin as she reached for the doorknob. She thought about grabbing her sisters and running out of the house and down the street to the neighbor's home, but instead decided she couldn't leave her parents in possible danger. After she opened the door, what she saw would haunt her for the rest of her life.

Her stepfather was floating in midair like Jesus nailed to the cross. His clothes were ripped off, and he was helpless.

"Run!" her mother yelled, running toward Octavia in the room. However, without warning, a powerful force pulled her mother into the corner, leaving her dizzy and disoriented.

"Mamaaa!" The brave little girl rushed into the room toward her mother . . . and that's when she saw it. She stopped dead in her tracks.

It was tall with white skin. Smoke expelled from its body. His elongated pointed ears were similar to those of elves but more pronounced, and an orange hue burned in its evil eyes. It had long teeth, no lips, and two holes where a nose would be. The height was high enough to where it was just inches from the high ceiling. Invisible wings fanned the violent, hot air, moving it around the room, causing the wall and pictures behind it to sizzle and scorch. Long, pointed fingers with equally curved claws could easily wrap around a man's head with no problem. Long, black toenails scraped the floor as it floated. Three baby skulls hung around its neck from a leathery rope.

Suddenly, her stepfather's torso burst open, blasting all his guts out on the bed below, followed by his lifeless body splattering on top of his guts. She saw his soul leave his body—only to be sucked into the demon's mouth. His warm blood splashed onto her face.

The priestess jumped in front of her daughter and chanted a spell to cast away the demon but to no avail. Her body rose from the floor into the air with her arms spread out and her legs shaking.

Urine flowed from underneath her mother's flowery sundress to the floor as she wailed in pain.

"Mama," Octavia cried, trying to hold onto her mother's leg.

The demon laughed at the suffering it caused them. Octavia stepped out between her mother and the demon to continue the chant. The demon looked down at her for a split second and laughed even harder.

Octavia suddenly went into a trance as she began to seize. Her eyes rolled back, displaying only the whites of her eyeballs. She jerked and moaned in place, and the demon's laughter ceased. White foam poured from her mouth, and she involuntarily began the dance ritual.

Her mother fell to the floor, trying desperately to catch her breath. What her daughter was doing shocked her when she noticed it was working.

"Octavia," she said quietly, still in shock.

The demon was clearly distressed, letting out a violent screech. It took a step toward Octavia, but her mother stepped in front of her to continue the chant, causing the demon to step back. Eventually, the demon vanished with a painful wail as if it sucked into a black hole. From that moment, her mother knew the power of her daughter.

Her mother died shortly after that, leaving Octavia at the age of eighteen with her sisters. Eugene heard about her mystical gift and kept tabs on her. Once he got word of her mother's passing, he had Octavia's sisters placed with their grandparents, and got her to join The Order.

This is where she met and fell in love with Jefferarri. Octavia was the calmer soul of Jefferarri. After every assignment, it was Octavia's charms that subsided the beast within. Octavia ran down the stairs barefoot in one of Jefferarri's long, white tees to check on him.

"Jefferarri," Octavia called.

"I'm good," he assured her, trying to control the rage inside as David Banner battled with The Hulk.

Octavia placed her hands on his cheeks and lowered his head to hers, touching foreheads.

"Breathe, baby, breathe," she said, taking deep breaths for him to follow. She glanced at Anna, realizing she must have brought some terrible news with her visit. There was nothing new about that.

Octavia never had any animosity toward Anna, and they worked well together when they had assignments to take down and abolish paranormal and ancient spirits. The only other thing that brought them together was their shared dedication to Jefferarri's sanctuary.

"That's it, Jefferarri; deep breaths," she coached as she went through the motions with him.

His eye shine faded, and his breathing slowed. She repeatedly ran her fingers back and forth from Jefferarri's cheek to the back of his neck. Their eyes closed, and they began to rock side to side slowly until Jefferarri was calm.

"I've got a trip to make," Jefferarri told her.

Octavia nodded in understanding.

Unfortunately, Anna had more bad news. "There's . . . something else."

Jefferarri and Octavia slowly turned their attention to her.

From the large living room window with her arms folded, Octavia watched the mini-helicopter lift off the ground into the darkness between the stars. It outraged her that Anna had intentionally come in the two-seater instead of something bigger or just made a phone call. Then she remembered that Jefferarri shuts down all outside communication while on Therapy Leave.

Despite feeling sympathetic to the situation, she couldn't help but feel selfish for wanting to go with him. All she could hope for was for him to keep his cool. She was confident that this time around, they would be well-prepared, especially after the last incident where he caused destruction and harm to many. Then again, *she remembered they hadn't learned from the last time before that with his father.* Killing Jefferarri was out of the question because The Order Document of Laws, which was more complicated than trigonometry, protected them all. However, there were situations where deadly force was acceptable. With the mindsets in The Order's hierarchy, someone could wipe all that away with a pen or a simple command.

Many people in Washington were unaware of The Order and its composition. Unaccounted tax money and places like Area 51 were a distraction. They put so much effort into concealing The Order because, if the truth got out, people would condemn the program, and the hunters would be in trouble. Many people would die trying to hunt these predator-minded killing machines for trophies. Not even the power-hungry military knew about the happenings in The Order. They would want to experiment on the hunters for their own benefit. Even force a takeover with the help of Congress to do whatever they wanted . . . or try.

"We have two entities that are public enemy number one and number two," Mr. Haskins said to his eleven constituents known as The Lead Councilmen in The Order Chambers. "Burly of the Gugwe and the Flesh Eater in Hopkinton, New Hampshire."

Mr. Haskins was an old white man with a receding hairline. His hair was white. Nobody knew his age or where he came from. He moved like a young man, with prominent gray eyebrows and white, hairy nostrils. It was easy to speculate that he was as old as hell. As the oldest living councilman and head of The Order, no

45

decisions were final until they crossed his desk for approval. Fair, but like all people in power, he had personal agendas.

In most cases, the leading councilman always made decisions for the betterment of humanity. According to the written records, some beings attempted to murder Mr. Haskins thirteen times in the last one hundred years, but all attempts were unsuccessful. And none of the assassins lived to talk about it.

"We are down to one tracker now, and we're still using his biomatter to create more. However, it has been unsuccessful," Mr. Strickland said. He was another elder and second-oldest member of the all-men constituency known as The Order. "If we lose him, it's over with. And still no word on the Twins. It's been over 24 hours. We can't put the witches out in the field and lose them."

Mr. Strickland was ninety-seven years old, so the records say, and he seldom ever went against Mr. Haskins's suggestions and decisions. However, he would question things he did not understand.

The chambers had an Old English feel. The highly guarded large room had a huge oak wood, cherry-finished square table in the middle of the first level. A large bookcase held ancient books that went back to the fourteenth century. Some were dated back before the Medieval Times. A giant marble dragon statue guarded each side of the large bookcase. A heavy-duty wooden floor that matched the heavy wooden door ran from wall to wall. Next to the chamber's entrance was an old vintage elevator. The type where you had to pull the gate closed.

On each side of the room were two stairs that ran up to the first balcony level that overlooked the bottom floor. There were three balconies, with each floor containing six offices, and Mr. Haskins's office occupied the third floor. A library was also on the third level.

"We have no real control over the hunters. If we did, we'd still have all of them," Mr. Anderson said. His record said he was sixty-eight years old and was the sixth-ranked member of The Order.

Like Mr. Strickland, he was stuck up in Mr. Haskins's ass too. "They have too much freedom for slaves."

"If the monster is too much trouble, I may have a solution to that problem," Bill Hawk said. He was the newest and youngest member of The Order at forty-seven. He stood up at the end of the table. "I just need a few seconds to explain, please."

"We're listening." Mr. Strickland gave him the floor.

"We can euthanize the animal," Bill caught himself before continuing. "Or maybe if he dies, we can clone his organs."

The sun rose from the east as a helicopter came into view. Jefferarri leaped out of it seconds before it touched the landing pad on top of the eight-story hospital building. The aircraft couldn't land fast enough as he sprinted toward the double doors ahead of him. Armed with Glock sidearms, two guards in black camo gear stood at the large black and purple double doors to greet him.

"Sir," one guard called.

Jefferarri raced past the men who barely saw him. He was just a blur from his white tee and black joggers. He squeezed past the small opening of the door without missing a stride.

"He's on the way," the guard warned through his radio.

While bypassing the three elevators through the exit to the stairs, Anna had already informed Jefferarri about the room where Eugene was hospitalized.

The Compound where the hospital was located was in an unknown location. They built the shadow government like a small military base, including a school for the gifted, training facilities, housing, and an armory. The hospital was right in the middle, among other things. Jefferarri, Anna, Octavia, the Twins, and a few others were raised and groomed in this government facility. Jefferarri burst through the fourth-floor doors. He looked on the

walls for the room directory, quickly found it, and then searched
for the direction of his destination. After pinpointing the room,
he jogged to the area. People there were nervous and quickly got
out of his way.

All the rooms had two glass panes with white blinds between
each pane for privacy if necessary. The corridor immediately
cleared over a fear of what was possible to come.

"Jefferarri," Matt called from in front of the room, waiting for
him. "Wait, wait a minute."

Jefferarri stopped in front of Matt, but his attention was
focused on the glass. He was breathing rapidly.

Two nurses and two doctors there all turned their attention
to Jefferarri. One nurse started to panic, but the doctors quickly
talked her down.

"Jefferarri, look at me." Matt placed his hands on his shoulders.

A grunt escaped Jefferarri's gut as he looked down at the
floor. He fought the emotions that would give everyone a bad day
at work. Over the years, The Order had put extensive therapy and
coaching into teaching Jefferarri how to control his emotions . . .
or, in other words, how to control the beast within.

"Control, Nephew . . . control," Matt said calmly.

After Clifton's death, Eugene stepped up as a father figure
and, because of his close friendship with Matt, earned the
nickname "Unk." Jefferarri fought harder to control himself. After
a few seconds, he nodded, indicating that he was ready, then
looked back to Eugene.

Matt stepped to the side to let him pass. He glanced and
nodded toward Anna, making her way toward them. Jefferarri
took a hard swallow and then walked into the room.

"Where's Octavia?" Matt asked Anna.

She gave a heavy sigh. "We left her."

Matt whipped his head to Anna. "Another selfish, dumb-ass move."

"Don't worry," Anna raised the tranquilizer gun from her side.

"Just one?" Matt asked.

"One is all I need."

"You ever wondered why you've never been up for promotion, Anna?"

As Jefferarri slid into the room, the nurses and doctors swiftly slid out. He walked to the right side of the bed but did not initially look at him. Instead, he focused on the nervous people looking at him from the hallway.

"Son," a faint voice said up to him.

Jefferarri looked down at Eugene. He tried his best to crack a smile but could not muster the energy to fake it.

"It's good to see you," Eugene said.

Jefferarri could hear the slur in his voice, hoping it was the medications making him talk that way. It was very hard for Jefferarri to assemble the thought that the eighty-year-old always had a youthful presence. Unlike Jefferarri, who aged slowly, age had finally caught up to the mortal, who was possibly lying on his deathbed.

"Where's Octa . . .via," Eugene struggled to get her name out of his mouth. Jefferarri knew why Eugene asked about her, but he decided to remain calm, even in his mental turmoil.

"She's at my place, sleeping," he replied. "She doesn't know the details . . . yet. We were in the two-seater."

"Y'all's bond is unbreakable. Some will not like that."

Those words made him look out the glass wall at Anna and Matt. He knew why Anna selfishly flew the two-seater helicopter.

"She knew I would want to get here quickly, and her flying the two-seater meant Octavia had no room."

"I'm glad you're here, son. I love you," he said before his eyes closed.

Jefferarri looked at the machines to make sure he did not flatline. "Nooo," he said to himself.

"He's just resting. He's fine," a voice came from the barely opened door.

Jefferarri snapped his head around to see the nurse with her head in the doorway. He relaxed and took a breath. He did not hear the door. His super hearing failed him, being so caught up in Eugene's condition.

"You don't have to be afraid of me," Jefferarri said in a low, crackling tone. "Please, come do whatever you need to do . . . please."

She looked at Matt, who gave her the okay nod to go in, and she did so hesitantly. The brave young woman attended to Eugene but glanced over to Jefferarri every few moments. He could smell her fear.

"You're good. I'm not going to hurt you," he reassured her.

"Is it that obvious?"

He felt nervous energy but did not respond to her. He pulled the lounge chair closer to the bed, grabbed his father figure's hand, and held it.

"I'm sorry," she said. "I knew there was a reason for the nice-ass salary when I signed all those confidential papers when I first got hired. Later, some people told me why."

He dropped his head on the bed and closed his eyes. Fighting his emotions to keep the beast inside had drained some of his energy.

"They told me what you did some years ago here," she continued. "When your girlfriend was here. All I'm saying is you can fuck up some shit if you get pissed off, sir."

CHAPTER 7
CHAOS AT THE HOSPITAL

"Every time I see him . . . the hairs on the back of my neck stand up," a voice said behind Matt as he nibbled on his thumbnail. "And it makes my throat hurt." Knowing who it was, Matt took a deep breath, closed his eyes, and ignored him.

"Well, if it isn't the asshole," Anna looked back at Anthony Moody, the fifty-nine-year-old Black commander of The Order's task force, which consisted of all humans. At six foot one, with a medium build, the ex-army man was not short of words when it came to the ones with so-called special abilities and pushed for The Cryptid Project to be scaled back or more funding to double security. It had become so bad that The councilmen had threatened to snatch The Cryptid Project away from him if his selfish and reckless actions continued. The cryptid hunters fell under that umbrella.

At one point, Moody found Jefferarri's canine teeth sunk into his neck, and he shook Moody like a rag doll when Jefferarri was only seventeen. Thanks to quick thinking by Anna, who always wore the tranquilizer gun on her hip, she got to Jefferarri just in time to save Moody. Three of Moody's loyal soldiers died that day. By the end of the day, it took three surgeries to repair and fix his neck. The scars on his neck reminded him every day of the incident. The councilmen of The Order concluded that Moody overstepped his bounds. They took The Cryptid Project from under his umbrella and let Jefferarri off the hook under particular conditions. Moody felt like The Order put more value into *those things* than he or the staff. And he was correct.

"I'm surprised you still come within one hundred miles near him," Anna giggled. "You're just as dumb now as you were then."

"I promise you it won't be like that again," Moody threatened.

"For your sake, I hope you're right," Matt said with irritation. "What do you want?"

"I just came to see the world's greatest future weapon. I mean, it's been a minute since he has been on the Compound." Moody cracked a smile, referring to Jefferarri on the Compound.

"You wanna go poke the bear? Kick him out?" Anna teased. "Go ahead on in there. Oh, wait. Do I have my tranquilizer gun?" she asked, patting her pockets.

"Hahaha, very funny," Moody mocked. "You wouldn't tell me if you did. But you know that's a ticking time bomb in there. You both know that's not your normal Lycan. He has the blood of his father in his veins. Not Eugene, but his *real* father—"

"Why do you care?" Matt interjected. "The Cryptid Project is no longer your concern."

"This needs to be everybody's concern," Moody blasted.

Everyone in the hall looked at Moody for a brief moment. Then some returned to their business.

Matt stepped nose to nose with Moody. "The Order has already made their ruling. Now, get the fuck away from me before I have Anna break the house rules and eat your ass."

"I'm hungry too," she said with an evil grin. Dark circles spread around her eyes.

A fake smile stretched across Moody's face as he stepped back. He looked at Anna, back at Matt, then panned over to Jefferarri, who also had his eyes fixed on him. Moody swallowed his spit and held his hands in front of him in submission.

"Okay, okay. I'll say this, and then I'm gone. He is already at level three. You saw what he did to this place years ago. Once he gets to level five," he tapped the left side of his chest. "Be strong enough to squeeze the fucking trigger."

"That's *my* problem, *not* yours," Matt reassured him. His brows creased.

"I'm sure The Order is going to do it anyway once his samples produce something they can control," Moody said before he walked away.

"He's jealous of Jefferarri," Anna said.

Matt remained quiet, feeling the burn of the truth passing through his ears from Moody. *Moody could be right that The Order ends him once they can clone something they can control,* he thought.

"You know Jefferarri is going to want to go after this Flesh Eater in Hopkinton," Anna said. "And let's be honest. Jefferarri is the only one who can do what needs to be done there. They will not want the task force to do it with him. And with all that, chances are he'll return a level four, or five, at worst . . . *if* he comes back at all."

Matt walked into the room, leaving Anna out into the hallway. He stood on the opposite side of Jefferarri, over Eugene's bed. Jefferarri said nothing. He just watched Eugene rest. Like Jefferarri, Matt was not used to seeing his partner and friend down and out like that.

"How are you holding up, champ?"

"I'm going to save him," Jefferarri grunted, his voice magnified above its usual baritone.

Matt quickly raised his head to look across at Jefferarri. He could see the pain and anger on his face. The shine in his eyes flickered with his signature glow.

Matt recognized Jefferarri's temperament. The once-settled rage was now bubbling again. He couldn't allow him to do what he'd just declared, but at the same time he knew he had to tamp down his emotions before he was forced to control them for him.

Speaking calmly, Matt reasoned, "You know that's forbidden under The Order. Plus, you know Eugene wouldn't want that." Matt sighed, then continued, his voice pleading. "You know, less than one percent of people survive that bite."

"Fuck The Order," Jefferarri said calmly. "I'm tired of losing the people I love. And I'm tired of being under lock and key like a fucking guard dog." He stood up.

Matt held his breath while giving Anna "the look" to be ready. "Nephew, I need you to calm down. You and I both want what's best for Eugene for the monster who did this to him to pay. But you know Eugene would never survive the bite."

Jefferarri's breathing was ragged as his eyes began to glow brighter. A clear indication of his burgeoning rage. "If I can't help save him, I want this Flesh Eater," Jefferarri demanded.

"You shall have your wish. Just got to confirm it with the higher-ups."

"Fuck the higher-ups!"

Knowing Jefferarri, Matt knew better than to respond right away. He watched Jefferarri as he began to pace the floor. He feared he was losing the battle against the flair of his rage. It was in this moment he saw the importance of having Octavia by Jefferarri's side.

Matt held a hand out to slow his pace, finding the words that might resonate with him before it was too late. "Easy champ. You're going to give the old man a heart attack."

"I heard the conversation through the glass," Jefferarri said.

Matt's eyes widened. He wanted to kick himself in the ass, forgetting about Jefferarri's superb hearing. The old man dug deep to find the best response.

Jefferarri looked up at him. "This doesn't end well for me no matter what, huh? I'll lose my father, still remain a cursed slave until I'm disposable."

Backed in a corner, Matt took a deep breath and answered. "I don't know, Jefferarri. But Eugene and I protected you—"

"Protect me?" Jefferarri shouted loud enough for the people in the hall to hear.

They directed their full attention through the glass that separated them from the unstable time bomb. Anna reached for the door, but Matt gestured to her to stand down. Jefferarri's eyes brightened, and his face twitched. Anna quickly directed people out of the hall.

"Let her in," Jefferarri's voice became rougher. "We'll set this bitch off. Let's see if she can do to me what she did to the Goatman. I'm a different muthafucka."

"Jefferarri, please, please, relax," Matt pleaded.

Jefferarri's shirt tightened around his shoulders. He kicked off his shoes and then continued pacing.

Matt's heart tried to jump out of his chest, but he strained to remain calm. He put his hand up, demanding Anna stay. They knew he was the most dangerous thing in the building at a level three transformation—not to mention if he jumped to level four.

Jefferarri glanced at Anna, then snapped his neck back around to Matt. "You ready to pull that trigger?" he said in a distorted tone, stepping in Matt's direction.

Heat radiated from Jefferarri's body. Odd sounds came from him as if someone was popping bubble wrap. Claws pierced his fingernails and his socks. He grew more dangerous with every second. Canine teeth appeared in his mouth, and his grunts became louder and more frequent.

"If you do this, Eugene will die. You will kill us all," Matt spat. "Control it!"

Jefferarri dropped to one knee grabbing his head as if he were trying to cover his ears. "Go away!" He looked up at Matt and then stood up again.

"Stop, Jefferarri!"

"I can't!"

After all his demands failed, a tear flowed from Matt's eye as he reached into his cargo pants pocket to grab the trigger. The device was the shape and size of a 25-mm button cell battery. All Matt had to do was twist the top and bottom into the arm position and squeeze.

Jefferarri ripped off his shirt and took another step. A low guttural sound escaped his throat with his eyes fixed on Matt. His nose flared. The top of his ears began to point and grow. "I can smell your fear." His voice drove deep bass from his gut.

Anna stood out into the hall with one hand on the door and the tranquilizer in the other. As her skin cracked and peeled, a light green tint began to wash over her fading complexion, while the veins in her body darkened, and crawled up from her neck into her face. Fear didn't even come close to describing the racing of her heart. Her heart sank as she saw Matt reaching for the trigger, realizing now the importance of having Octavia by Jefferarri's side.

"I told you!" Moody rushed past her from out of nowhere, rushing to the door and bumping her to the side.

"Wait!" Anna said, drawing her gun from her hip holster.

"Squeeze the trigger!" Moody yelled releasing his gun from his holster.

Jefferarri leaped into the air at Moody with his arm back in a swinging motion to rip Moody's throat from his body. Mucous trailed from his mouth. The sudden movement startled Matt, causing him to drop the trigger. In midair, Jefferarri grabbed his head and crashed into the glass wall, cracking it.

"Drop it!" Anna said, pressing her gun to Moody's head.

"We need to end this now!"

"Drop the fucking gun," Anna demanded again. "I won't ask a third time."

Covering his head with his hands, Jefferarri froze in a crouched position. "Get out of my head. Get out of my head," Jefferarri repeated in a demonic tone. Each time, the tone became more human as he repeated the chant.

Matt snatched Moody's gun. "You son of a bitch."

"What's happening to him?" Anna asked.

"Octavia. She's in his thoughts, saving our lives," Matt said. "Tranq him."

Anna holstered her gun, then pulled the tranquilizer gun and shot Jefferarri in the neck. He scratched at the projectile for a few seconds before falling asleep. She turned to Matt. "What just happened?"

Matt looked at Jefferarri and then at Anna. "I think he just attempted suicide."

"Or he's going rogue," Anna said.

A blood trail ran from the bedroom to the bathroom at Jefferarri's house. Sobs could be heard throughout the home. Octavia held onto the rim of the toilet, spitting as blood poured from her nose. Her eyes teared up. She's always been able to connect with Jefferarri on an emotional and somewhat physical level. She often felt his distress from a relatively close proximity but never from such a great distance. However, this time was different. It took a lot more energy and was extremely painful for her. She felt what he felt and could tell he did not fight it like he usually would.

Sounds of blood dripping into the toilet water echoed in the bathroom. Once the bleeding stopped, she reached over to the shower knob and turned the water on cool. Using the side of the tub to stand, her blood-spotted pink cotton PJs made their way to the floor.

He's losing it, she thought to herself after feeling his mindset. She stepped into the shower, letting the water run all the sweat and blood down the drain. *I should have been there*, she continued with the self-torture. She always put her soulmate first to protect him and others from him.

Jefferarri has never been the one for being contained and treated like a slave, Octavia thought. Her thoughts drifted back to their time growing up under the rule of the academy with The Order.

Some overseers back at the academy used to treat them like they were in a prison. They shoved them around and talked down to them like they had no rights. Herded them like cattle, depending on which administrator was nearby. The bad ones overshadowed the good ones, which was just as bad to them because they did nothing. The overseers were in charge and made sure that the young up-and-comers in The Cryptid Project behaved, or more like obeyed.

One day, Jefferarri and Octavia were being bad, just being teenagers and staying out late, way past curfew. As they sat on the bench under the tree, kissing time away, time got away from them, and Octavia was trying to convince Jefferarri that they needed to go before they got in trouble.

"Let's run away," Jefferarri commanded. "Let's do it right now."

Octavia laughed and said, "Yep, right. And go where?"

"Anywhere but here," he answered, looking more serious than ever.

Octavia smacked my lips and replied, "Jefferarri, if you don't get your ass to your room, you know there will be hell to pay."

"Aren't you tired of this shit, Octavia?"

Her answer was yes, but she remained silent.

After a few seconds of silence, he grabbed her hand, and they stood up. He kissed her on the forehead and said, "See you tomorrow."

"Jefferarri and Octavia," a voice called from across the yard. "I guess you two are going to do what you want to do, huh?"

The voice belonged to man the students called Beefcake jokingly for the way he carried himself. He did not like that at all. He was the biggest and meanest overseer of them all, and Jefferarri couldn't stand the smell of him. He hated him worse than all the others. The brown-skinned tyrant stood every bit of six foot eleven and weighed all of 380 pounds solid.

Jefferarri cut his eyes at me and said to Beefcake, "We apologize. Time slip—" Jefferarri had a slick mouth when he wanted to and knew how to push anybody's buttons.

"Shut your little ass up, boy," Beefcake blasted. "I'm sick of your mouth."

"I'll see you tomorrow," Jefferarri said to Octavia with a half-cocked smile as he walked toward his dorm.

Octavia started to walk off to her dorm, and that's when she felt it. At first, she was feeling anger and had thoughts of killing Beefcake, but she was confused because she swore she was more nervous than angry, and there was no way she would do anything intentionally that would cause her to hurt Beefcake. That's when she figured it out. She was connected to Jefferarri. She could feel what he felt.

"Don't hold your breath, sugar," Beefcake told Octavia. "He's going to be on lockdown for a very, very, very long time. But I can come to see you tonight if you want. I'll bust that little voodoo hole of yours wide open."

Jefferarri turned around, and his eyes were as red as Octavia had seen them in a long time. And for the first time, she saw his fingernails were black. She instantly felt what he was going to say next. Before she could beg him to just go to the dorm, he had already said it.

"I'll fucking kill you," Jefferarri said in a slightly different voice, deeper than usual.

By this time, three other overseers ran up, surrounding Jefferarri, ready to use their Tasers.

"You're threatening an overseer, boy?" Beefcake said, quickly stripping off his clothes as he turned.

Beefcake grew taller. His skin darkened, and brown hair sprouted from it. A long, thick snout formed from his jaw. His ears moved near the top of his head, shaping like a wolf's ears. The sound of his knees popping backward thundered while he rose on his toes. Even more impressive, he did all this in about ten seconds or less. His transformation turned Beefcake into an eight-foot monster. Long teeth with sharp, fanglike canines, eyes like black pearls, and large raccoonlike hands that could easily wrap around an average person's head.

Jefferarri was just fifteen yards away from it. He squatted in place and a huge grin on his face showed his new growth of canines. The monster charged Jefferarri without warning. It was quick, so quick. Dust and dirt kicked up from behind its feet before it lunged at Jefferarri.

Jefferarri tried to dive out of the way but was not fast enough as the werewolf's claws pierced Jefferarri's chest and tossed him across the yard like a piece of trash. Octavia felt a little sting on her chest, but it was not painful like what happened to Jefferarri's chest. At that moment, she knew they were connected—no doubt.

Jefferarri rolled back on his feet. His shirt was bloody and ripped at the chest, and the smile on his face was gone. Dark spots formed circles around his eyes. Beefcake kept charging at Jefferarri, who was better prepared this time, ducking under the huge, swiping claw and moving behind the raging beast. It turned toward Jefferarri, looking down at his own rib section. Claw marks and missing hair were visible in Jefferarri's hands. He shook the flesh and hair from his hands and then tasted the blood.

The monster let out a growl that could be heard for miles before rushing Jefferarri again. Jefferarri charged in return, only to be met with sharp claws across his chest that ripped deeper than the first time.

The force sent Jefferarri flipping across the grass, whimpering—a blood trail followed from his opened chest.

"Jefferarri!" Octavia hollered in fear for his life. A slight burn grazed across her chest.

Beefcake looked over at Octavia with a sinister grin. Her heart fell into her stomach, and she found breathing hard.

All eyes turned to the dorm as howls flowed from a distance and were getting closer by the second. It was the Twins running in their direction about seventy-five yards away, closing fast as they transformed into their Lycan form.

The three overseers ripped their shirts off and changed as well, busting out of their pants and shoes, waiting on the Twins, and stepping between them and the fight at hand. They were nowhere close to the size of Beefcake but still towered over Jefferarri.

Beefcake pounced on Jefferarri, grabbing him by the neck and holding him in the air with one hand for everyone to see. This was the lesson on display. He repeatedly began to pound the ground with Jefferarri's limp body.

"Nooooo. Stop!" Octavia pleaded again with tears running down her face.

He tried to bite Jefferarri's face but was not ready for the claws that opened up his throat. Beefcake stumbled back, trying to breathe and feeling for his neck. Jefferarri flopped to the ground nearly on empty, but he mustered up enough energy to leap up to Beefcake's face, clawing out his eyes. One eye hit the ground, and the other dangled out of the socket by a nerve. He fell on his back with blood popping up out of his mouth and throat.

With no mercy, Jefferarri ripped, bite after bite after bite, of flesh from Beefcake's neck. Chunks of flesh and blood fell all over the ground. The Twins pulled up in full Lycan mode, ready to go to war with the overseers. Both sides postured and taunted one another. That was . . . until Jefferarri let out a victory howl behind the overseers that *sounded more like a man screaming than a howl. They turned around in Jefferarri's direction.*

Jefferarri stood straddled over the decapitated and mutilated body of Beefcake. His head dangled upside down from Jefferarri's hand by the stump of his neck. Blood dripped from every orifice. He tossed the head in front of the overseers, who looked confused. The organization's alpha overseer was dead! It was now three on three, and the three overseers, now Lycans, had defeat in their eyes as Jefferarri let out a deafening noise. His chest and shoulders rose and fell with each breath he took. Blood painted from his mouth down to his ripped belly. Huge, defined arms were out to the side, with bloody, one-inch claws in ready mode.

Whining interrupted the raging beast. As Octavia directed her attention to the change in his emotions, Octavia saw him scratching at a large dart in the side of his neck. Although fighting it, he quickly succumbed to the powerful sedative, backing up with his head hanging low to the ground.

The overseers suddenly got newfound confidence and let out their snarls, ready to take advantage of the new situation and rip Jefferarri and the young twin Lycans to threads.

"Enough!" Anna came out of nowhere and jumped between Jefferarri and the overseers. She dropped the dart gun. "It's over! Stand down."

The overseers looked at one another, then dropped down on all fours and, just like that, took off until they disappeared behind the buildings across the yard. The twins sneered at them as they passed by. Octavia had never seen Anna in her true witch form, but she had heard she was one badass bitch.

Anna bent down next to Jefferarri to massage his head as she observed the carnage. Something caught her attention, and she started examining his teeth.

"Octavia, come look at this," she said.

Octavia slowly walked over beside her, stepping over blood, bones, hair, and flesh. Seeing blood and ripped-up bodies was nothing new to her, but watching how it happened tested her stomach.

"Look," she commanded. "What do you see?"

Octavia looked down to find out what she recognized. It didn't take long for her to find it. Her eyes widened at the sight of the answer. "Level three?" Octavia asked for confirmation.

"Passed three but not yet four."

"Did you see what he has done to that?" Octavia pointed at Beefcake's headless body sprawled over the ground.

Anna remained silent, and Jefferarri escaped trouble because the video camera showed that despite not following the rules, they found Beefcake to have used excessive and deadly force from an authoritarian. The overseers ran off and were not seen for a long while. This forced The Order to devise ways to control and track them.

Octavia snapped herself out of memory lane. She grabbed a water bottle from the refrigerator and then sipped before closing the door. It was just enough to coat her raw throat. She grabbed the Samsung Note 20 from the kitchen island to check for messages she knew were not there. Firmly, she put down the phone and walked around to the opposite side of the island. She took another sip before checking her nose for more blood. A text alert from her phone got her attention, and she wasted no time grabbing it. It read, "ETA half an hour to take you to Jefferarri."

CHAPTER 8
HIS SOUL IS MINE

HOURS AFTER THE melee that occurred in Eugene's room, Jefferarri lay down in a special room in the hospital, locked down on a stainless-steel bed, snoring like a baby. The hospital staff removed all his clothes and put stainless-steel cuffs around his neck, waist, wrists, and ankles. An IV ran directly into his arm that contained a sedative, and several EKG pads lined his body to monitor his vitals. This room was much darker than the one Eugene rested in, with a little red spotlight dimmed across the top portion of Jefferarri's body. Another difference is that the glass wall was two-way glass, meaning you could only see through the glass on one side. Here, you could see into this room but not out of it.

Two security guards posted outside the room sat in chairs against the opposite wall facing the room. They were armed with the DP-12 with Dragon's Breath shells for self-protection only. The squeamish soldiers nearly jumped out of their seats every time Jefferarri twitched. A panic button was on the wall between them.

An elevator dinged about twenty-five yards down the end of the dark hallway, indicating it was about to open. Only the light from the digital floor-level sign was visible in the dark. The guards stood at attention, looking toward the elevator.

"How much longer he's going to be in here?" Octavia asked, exiting the elevator and not waiting on anyone.

"I gotta be honest. The higher-ups are starting to get more nervous. Moody continues to make the case—" Matt admitted, trying to keep up with her.

Two men in black suits followed behind them from the elevator.

"Moody can't win a vote with these people. Why does he still have a job?" Octavia asked.

"I don't know, but regardless, the decision-makers are retiring or dying off. These new, fresh faces might see things a little differently, and Moody knows it."

Seeing the guards, Octavia decided not to say anything else around them. She made a mental note to continue this conversation another time.

"May I?" she asked the guard with an attitude, gesturing to go into the room.

"Ma'am," the tall, young, brown-skinned guard nodded before opening the door.

Entering the room, Octavia noticed a blood pressure reading of 289/184 with a respiration rate of 62 and a pulse rate of 164. These were much higher than usual for him, but Jefferarri's regular readings were a death sentence for an average human.

"Baby," she said, interlocking their fingers. Not caring what the guards may see through the glass, she continued, "maybe I need to take you up on your offer. Let's get away from here."

As she glanced over his body, she observed the changes to it. For starters, he looked bigger, taller, and bulkier than she remembered. The hair on his chest and face had many gray hairs. Jefferarri always went back close to his usual self after a transformation. The only difference before was it took longer to get back right each time after an episode.

Maybe he has not finished reversing back yet, she thought.

The door opened, and a white male caretaker walked in with one guard who was posted outside. He rolled a tray with some vials, an IV bag, a syringe, and a tablet.

"What's this?" Octavia asked.

"An angiotensin," the caretaker answered.

She moved to the foot of the bed to let the caretaker handle his business. The caretaker's energy seemed a little out of place, but she concluded he was nervous around Jefferarri like everybody else.

"You okay?" she asked the nurse.

"Yes, ma'am."

The caretaker played with the monitor briefly, then entered the readings onto his tablet. After entering the information, he replaced the half-filled bag with a new one. He glanced over at Octavia, then filled the syringe with the medication. Never a fan of needles, the enormous size of the needle made her skin crawl. He injected the drug into the medication port under the IV bag. Yet again, he glanced at Octavia as he slowly injected the bag.

"Are you new around here?" she asked. "I haven't seen you around here before."

"Yes, I started . . . started yesterday," he tripped over his words.

"Hmm. Big task for a newbie. I mean, working with a superspecies such as this," she said. "You seem a bit nervous. Hell, you seem *very* nervous."

"I guess they're testing me out of the gate," he said, dropping the empty syringe on the tray. "His vitals should come down within the next couple of hours. I'll be back to check on him in a while."

He almost forgot his tray, trying to get out so fast. The security guard backed out, keeping his eyes on Jefferarri until he exited the room.

"Our boy almost lost his grip here this morning," Matt said to Eugene. Matt sat in the same chair that Jefferarri sat in just under 24 hours ago. "He's okay now. Nobody got hurt. Octavia is here now with him in the Medical Lockdown Room."

"What happened, Matt?" Eugene asked in a shallow voice.

Despite the dark circles around his eyes and discolored skin, Eugene looked much better. His vital signs and spirits had greatly approved since earlier. Someone raised the head of Eugene's bed slightly and hung his oxygen mask off to the side of his face.

"Your son almost made pieces of Moody."

"Damn. I would've loved to have . . . seen that," Eugene cracked.

They chuckled before a quick cough escaped Eugene's mouth. Eugene struggled to get in a comfortable position.

"Easy there, my friend," Matt said as he helped his friend slide up the bed. After Eugene got situated, Matt continued. "I was telling Octavia that the faces of the board are changing."

"We may have to take the kill safe out of him now."

"What are you saying, Gene?" Matt asked, concerned. "Set him free?"

Silence filled the room before a *beep* from the vital monitor broke the silence.

"You know it's the right thing to do," Eugene said. "You know it needs to be done."

"Even if we succeeded," Matt silently raised, then toned it down to resume, "he could kill hundreds, maybe even thousands. And God forbid if he reached a full-blown werewolf. He leveled up close to four today." Matt grabbed his friend's arm. "He's safer here. People are safer with him here."

"I doubt he's in good hands under these people," Eugene said. "But I guess you're right."

"That kill safe won't be a piece of cake to remove. We will have to find someone who knows the devices, is brave enough to do it, and is around Jefferarri. That's a tall task. Got to trust them to keep their mouths shut when the shit hits the fan. If The Order found out we were planning something like this, they would have our heads on a platter."

"I know someone," Eugene replied.

Before Matt could have asked who, movement out of the corner of his eye through the glass wall caught his attention. A nurse and a doctor walked into view and went to the room. "We'll finish this conversation later."

"Just think about it," Eugene said.

Sitting next to Jefferarri in the black leather La-Z-Boy recliner, Octavia's eyes grew heavy, reading her Kindle app on her phone. Not to mention, she'd been sleep-deprived since Anna came with the bad news about Eugene. The connection when her soulmate went into mayhem earlier took a major toll on her body and mind.

Her head fell back against the head of the recliner, followed by a quick sigh. A yawn escaped her mouth as she stretched. Her eyes traveled from head to toe at the sleeping carnage that lay in front of her. Underneath the innocent flesh on that table roamed a sinister curse.

A rumble in her stomach reminded her it had been a long time since she had eaten anything. She looked at the time on her phone, which showed 8:30 p.m. and the room temperature of 70 degrees. Although preferring several degrees warmer, spending time at Jefferarri's place made this feel like heaven. She thought about running down to the café to grab one of those smoothies for a late dinner, but she remained glued to the seat.

Just five more minutes, she thought to herself.

As she drifted away, a cool air draft jolted her from out of nowhere. She had felt that feeling before but could not remember from where. After placing her phone on her lap, she crossed her arms over her torso, then looked back up at the clock. It still read at a temperature of 70 degrees. This made her rise out of her seat.

The room had darkened to a reddish hue. Whispers reached her ears. The hairs rose on the back of her neck. She could hear Jefferarri's heartbeat as loud as a bass drum in a parade, and it began to slow down. Looking over at his vital signs on the monitor, she could see all of his numbers drastically dropping right before her eyes, and she noticed no alarm alerts. Confusion invaded her thoughts as she tried to figure out what was happening and causing this. It didn't take long before she got her answer.

A dark, shadowy figure emerged before her eyes, hovering over Jefferarri's bed. The figure's body was made up of a dark gray, smokelike texture that moved and flowed into a hooded figure from the waistline. Inside the front of the hood, where there would typically be a face, there was nothing but a dark, black void.

It is here for his soul, she thought. The chill in the room had become unbearable, and frost formed on her skin. She glanced over at the guards sitting outside the glass wall, unable to see them on the other side.

"Soul Eater!" she called it as she spun back to the Grim Reaper.

It quickly snapped its head toward Octavia and then glided closer to be face-to-face. Even though she knew he could not do anything to her because she was not dying, her heart was about to beat out of her chest. Running over to the guards was a waste of time. Time was ticking, and she needed to use that time to think with no time to panic. She knew it was not his vital signs because they were nearly normal.

"You can see me," it said, whispering like a severe case of asthma accompanied by the sound of wind. Octavia could hear the whispers of the rest of the hundreds of souls in the background. "Voodoo Priestess—"

"You can't have him," she snapped, with her body shivering from the cold that gripped the room. Its following words spewed from the darkness under the hoodie made her heart drop to her stomach.

"Ooooh, you have no idea, my dear. You don't know of the wars being fought in the darkness for his soul. Judgment will be made once I have his soul, dear child."

"It's not going to happen today!"

Her eyes, wide with determination, rolled back, their vibrant color fading into the ivory depths. She could feel the energy building within her, ready to be harnessed from the very core of her being. But before she could tap into her powers, an invisible force struck her with an unexpected blow, knocking her fragile body to the ground. A grunt escaped her lips as the sheer power of the unseen force sent her hurling across the polished floor, the sound of her movement echoing through the air.

"That won't work on me, dear child!" he said, his voice resonating with the echoes of a hundred souls. "I'm not some petty demon from another dimension. I am the deliverer of souls to the afterlife, for judgment."

Slowly, she stood up, feeling a sharp pain shoot through her back. "I said you can't have him!"

All the whispers laughed at her statement, patiently waiting for his demise as she hovered over Jefferarri.

She felt helpless. Then it dawned on her. *The IV bag*, she thought. She jumped over and ripped the needle out of his arm. This finally grabbed the guards' attention, causing them to turn and investigate through the glass. Blood splashed all over her and Jefferarri. She waved to the guards, and after a moment, the two rushed in with confusion.

"Lock this bitch down!" she blasted at the guards. "Lock the whole compound down. And find that damn nurse that came in here."

The guards looked bewildered. They could see the cold vapers escape her mouth, even though it was a controlled climate.

"Now!" she shouted, turning her attention back to The Grim Reaper.

One guard called into his radio, and the other sounded the alarm.

The Grim Reaper turned its hoodie toward Octavia, then quickly back to Jefferarri. Its movements told her it was not happy. She looked at the vital signs on the monitor, and the declining numbers started to slow down.

"Come on, come on, Jefferarri," she cheered. She wanted Jefferarri to fight death, even though he couldn't noticeably hear her.

The alarm lights flashed throughout the space with blaring sirens. A doctor and two nurses rushed into the room.

"What's going on?" the doctor demanded.

"Poison," she pointed at the bag. "Somebody came in as a nurse and added something to the bag."

He rushed over to the table and observed Jefferarri's vital signs on the monitor.

"Do you know what it is?" the doctor asked.

"I don't know."

"Let me get a fresh IV bag stat," the doctor commanded.

Octavia looked up at The Grim Reaper, that only she could see. It was still hovering above the room, meaning Jefferarri was not out of the woods yet. She closed her eyes to get into Jefferarri's head but could not find him. The alarm was possibly too noisy to concentrate, but she had to try harder. Suddenly, darkness surrounded her mind.

"Jefferarri," her voice echoed into the dark space. "Jefferarri, I need you to—"

As if someone were choking her, her throat tightened. Red eyes appeared before her, followed by a menacing grumble. Every time she attempted to speak, her neck tightened. She was finding it hard to breathe.

She fell back into the real world and landed on the floor, coughing and struggling to catch her breath. A guard and a nurse helped her into the recliner.

"Ma'am, are you all right?" the guard asked.

She tried to speak, but her coughing was taking over. She raised her head over the nurse's shoulder at Jefferarri. He was vomiting and pissing all over the place. Then she looked up to see that The Grim Reaper was gone. She relaxed back into the recliner.

"Water," she struggled to say.

"Ma'am?" the guard replied.

"Water, please," she said.

"Water," the nurse said. "She wants some water." The nurse left to get her some.

Matt rushed to the door with wide eyes and jogged up to Octavia. "What happened? Are you all right?"

"Someone tried to poison him," she said in a raspy voice.

"Fuck's sake." Matt stood up with his hands on his hips. He looked at Jefferarri and then at the room full of people.

The nurse returned with bottled water, which she opened in front of her. "Here you go," she said, putting the water to Octavia's lips to drink.

After a few sips of water, Octavia grabbed Matt's hand. He leaned over and used the chair to prop against.

"We need to get him out of here," she whispered.

Matt nodded in agreement. "I know."

CHAPTER 9
THE GIBSON FARM

THE GIBSON FARM sat just on the northern outskirts of Ashville, North Carolina. The workers of the eight-and-a-half-acre farm consisted of people from Ashville and the surrounding communities. It was a sanctuary for animals, plants, and people. Chickens, rams, sheep, and goats roamed between their wired fences. Every vegetable you could name, from broccoli to garlic and many in between, was grown to be sold at farmers' markets across Ashville. Many farm workers, including families, also camped on the property, residing in the second house on the property.

Grandma Etta ran the farm. The little, fair complexion, seventy-eight-year-old, hard-nosed, pudgy woman was as sweet as can be. If someone did not double-cross or lie to her, she would give them the shirt off her back. That seldomly happened, but if a person did any of those things, she would immediately be done with them. The farm had been in her family since the turn of the century. It had survived through many recessions and inflations over the years and numerous racial attacks.

"Ed, when you finish with those cabbages, go on ahead and settle down for the evening and get ready for dinner," Etta said. "It is about to pour down out here."

Ed, short for Edward, was home from winter break from college, helping his grandmother with some chores and earning some money for his pockets for when he returned to North

Carolina State. Studying agriculture, Ed already had big ideas for changes on the farm soon.

"Okay, Grandma," he said.

Thunder rumbled from the mountains, making Ed step up the pace more. It was not long before the heavy droplets pounded the ground. He was lucky to be heading toward the house. He quickly stopped next to the goat pen to pet his favorite nanny-goat.

"Heyyyy, Essie," he said as she hopped over to the fence.

Essie was a beautiful, young, black-and-white goat with light gray eyes. She was the only goat that came up to him at the pen and was the first stop he made every time he stepped outside or came home. As the rain got heavier, Ed ran to the porch.

The main house, also called the old house, was a two-story home with an attic. It had two windows on each side that was dubbed as an extra bedroom. The tin roof kept the attic warm in the winter but very hot in the summer. White paint chipped away from the wooden exterior. The foundation left about two feet of crawl space.

The second house, also known as a rooming house, was set about forty yards away from the main house and had six rooms, two bathrooms, and a kitchen. It was also two stories high. A pigpen was about twenty yards in front of the front porch. Like the main house, the white paint chipped, exposing more wood than paint.

Standing on the backside of the wraparound porch at the top of the wooden steps, Ed admired the torrential downpour. The beauty of it fascinated him. Crops were planted in the rolling, hilly countryside, and the Great Smoky Mountains were in the backdrop. He took in the fragrance of the rain and the sound it made as it cascaded to the surface.

Etta walked out behind Ed with a smile and stood beside his tall, slender, six-foot frame to block the chilly wind penetrating through her wool sweater. She knew exactly what he was feeling at the moment.

"The rain has always hypnotized you." She wrapped her short arms around his arm, hanging down his side. "Even before you took your first steps. Your mother was like that too."

Ed dropped his eyes, turning his head slightly in her direction, remembering the few moments with his mom sitting on this same porch looking out into the rain. His mother conceived him at the young age of seventeen. One day, when Ed was only four, his mom and her boyfriend took a jog on the trail near the base of the mountain . . . and never returned. Both of them disappeared without a trace. Shortly after that, one of his cousins claimed to have seen a large, upright, walking humanoid roaming in and out of the hills. When he reported it, authorities took it as a black bear sighting despite his argument it was not.

"C'mon, baby, let's eat."

"Deer meat?" Ed asked.

"Deer sausage, stewed okra, and tomatoes over rice and corn bread," she answered.

"Oh, yeahhhh," Ed said excitedly. "Now, Grandma, you know I love me some deer sausages."

She giggled as she followed him into the house.

"You trying to keep me here, I see. I'm not falling for it," he joked.

After dinner, Etta and her grandson played cards as the rain continued beating against the house. A full belly and the white noise of the rain had Ed fighting to stay awake, but spending time with his grandma was precious. Lightning brightened the windows in flashes, and thunder rumbled across the dark skies.

"Grandma, do you know that every inch of rain here on the property equals about 1,808,000 pounds of water?"

Etta laughed and said, "You learned that from that place you at?"

"I surely did. And one billion tons of rain falls on earth every minute of the day."

"That's a lot of rain," Etta said, proud of her grandson's knowledge.

Lightning crept into the window, followed by a large crackle. Ed heard the goats sounding very agitated through the rain.

"Wow, that one scared the goats," he said.

His grandma stood up and looked out of the kitchen window at the goat barn. It was hard for her to see through the heavy downpour and the glare on the window from the kitchen lights. Plus, the floodlights on the pen were not on. She had forgotten to replace the light today before the rain came. The porch light was not bright enough to pierce through the thick rain to the goat pen. Ed stood up and walked next to her.

"Yeah, this storm got them riled up," she replied.

Lightning lit up the dark, cool sky, and Etta swore she saw a dark figure moving around the goat pen about fifty feet away. Waiting for the next set of lightning strikes, she squinched her eyes and stepped closer to the sink to get a better look into the yard.

"Wassup, Grandma?" Ed asked, then stood up and walked next to her. "You acting like you seen something."

She remained silent, knowing she saw something big and tall that completely towered over the goat pen. Another flash of lightning lit up in sequence long enough for both of them to see what was staring back at them. Burly stood in front of the pen, holding two dead goats. One was on his left shoulder, and the other was under his right armpit.

"What is that?" Ed said before looking closer. "Is that Essie?"

The black-and-white nanny was propped up on Burly's shoulder. Then the outside went dark, and another bolt of lightning struck . . . and the Gugwe was gone. Ed rushed and grabbed the double-barrel shotgun from over the fireplace and mantle in the living room. Next, he grabbed some buckshots from the drawer on the old-fashioned wooden end table.

"Ed! Ed, come back in here," Etta begged. Her cries escaped his ears as his focus was on the yard. She picked up her wall phone and called 911.

Remembering the lessons taught by his uncles, Ed loaded and charged the shotgun. Placing the extra shells into his pocket, he jogged through the kitchen to the back door.

"Wait, boy," Etta stopped him. "Don't go out there. Yes, hello …"

Ed stopped at the door. His breathing became sporadic and deep as his nerves got the best of him. But his upbringing held him at the door, respecting his grandma's wishes.

She hesitated on how to explain the situation. She knew telling them the truth would not get her anywhere.

"Yes, someone's trying to break into my house at the Gibson farm!"

Wamp! Something slammed into the house. A shriek escaped her mouth as she dropped the phone. Dust and paint fell from the rusted-colored ceiling and light fixtures. Kitchenware rattled in the background. They heard things falling to the floor.

Bam! Another bump against the house was even harder and made the kitchen table shuffle this time. The light flickered like the lightning from the windows. Etta gasped again, falling against the sink, and Ed wobbled onto the table. Suddenly, a growl vibrated from the outside through the walls of the house.

A gunshot crackled between the strikes of thunder from outside. Heavy footsteps pounded the mud outside the house.

"You okay, Grandma?" Ed asked, crouching down next to her.

She held him tight as she began to sob.

"Get!!!" a male voice yelled outside.

"Mr. Hawkins," she said to herself. "That's Mr. Hawkins," she said to Ed before trying to get up.

"Stay here," Ed commanded. "I'll be right back."

"No! No!"

"I got this, Grandma. I need to check on Mr. Hawkins," he said bravely.

He pulled away from her grip and went to open the door. Before he could grab the doorknob, someone—or something—tossed Mr. Hawkins through the door, knocking Ed to the floor. The door shattered into a million pieces, exposing the outdoor elements. The shotgun fell out of his hand.

Mr. Hawkins was a white, sixty-three-year-old retired marine from Sardis, North Carolina. Etta met him at the market in Ashville. Every week, Mr. Hawkins would come to the market begging to do work for food and not necessarily money, and that intrigued Etta because most beggars would rather have money and not be nice, but Mr. Hawkins was different. Most beggars in the market sold food for money, but Mr. Hawkins always ate near or under the market stands when leaving. After some time, and in need of some help on the farm, Etta took a chance and proposed that Mr. Hawkins come to join the farm. It was a perfect fit for what she desperately needed. After learning the ropes and earning her trust within a few months, he became the farm foreman.

Etta jumped and screamed as wood splinters landed on and around her as she sat on the floor with her back partially against the cabinet door.

Ed's eyes stared through the opened door frame into the darkness outside until a continuous lightning strike lit up the darkness. The swirling winds and chilly rain during the strikes made the outside portal ghostly. As the storm grew in intensity, the rain pounded the porch harder. The cracks of the thunder rattled the house, causing the lights to flicker again. He just knew something would be standing there during the strike or running toward them.

A groan escaped from what remained of Mr. Hawkins's mouth. Ed's attention turned from the door over to him.

Something had ripped off the man's top lip, and half of his bottom jaw was missing. He never had many teeth, to begin with, but the few yellow-stained ones up top were now splattered with blood. His tongue hung out where the portion of his jaw used to be. Blood poured from his mouth as he tried to catch his breath. His eyes rolled around in a panic.

"Shit," Ed said before he scrabbled backward to the china cabinet behind him.

Ed wanted to help him but was clueless about what to do. Lightning flared the darkness again, making Ed snap his attention back through the door. The noise came quicker with each lightning strike. What had just happened left Etta shaken and scared stiff. She knew there was little she could do for Mr. Hawkins. A grunt from outside sounded too close to the house for comfort now. In fact, it sounded like it was right outside the shattered door. Even with the heavy downpour, the smell that followed was worse than a hog pen not being cleaned out for over a week.

The lightning struck with a roaring *boom* again, and then nothing was there. But once the darkness returned, he saw three sets of shiny eyes that stood tall in the tree line. Pieces of something flew into the doorway from the darkness. One piece landed in front of Ed, sliding against his hip, and the other flew a few feet before him. It was Mr. Hawkins's rifle broken into two pieces. More grunts flowed in through the storm from the darkness but sounded further away this time.

The eyes were gone now. Ed came to his senses and reached for Mr. Hawkins to grab the shotgun pieces. Then Ed took another look at Mr. Hawkins below him and saw his lifeless body with his eyes wide open, staring up at him.

"Damn!" Ed sprang to his feet, rushing over to his grandma in a crouching movement. "I think they are gone now." Trembling, they embraced each other.

Lightning and thunder made their presence known again. An infant child wailed from a distance.

"My baby!" a female voice yelped. "Help!" the voice continued in agony.

"Oh my God," Etta said, remembering that the worker who lived on the property in the other house had a baby girl.

Ed slowly walked onto the porch. Etta followed in his hip pocket. Both trembled in fear.

"Nooo!" the voice cried out.

With his shotgun pointed, Ed swiftly turned to the sounds. As lightning flashed, he saw a Gugwe running away from the boarding house, chased by a young white woman. The woman slipped in the mud. They saw people filing out of the house behind her, illuminated by the porch light.

"April," Etta called out to the young woman.

The storm eased up a little, but it was still pouring down heavily. Desperate, the woman stood up and continued across the slippery yard. Another Gugwe rushed toward her from the opposite view of Ed and Etta under the lightning strikes. The people on the porch also saw it and called out to her in fright but stopped dead in their tracks.

Etta and Ed saw it too and also halted. The rain beat on their faces, blurring their vision as the cold rain soaked Etta's bare socks. A series of lightning strikes showed the Gugwe closing in on April, and she disappeared behind the hog pen. The people on the porch reacted with fear to whatever happened in the darkness behind the pen and rushed back inside. The only sounds heard after that were the muffled sounds from within the second house, the rain, and the distant thunder.

"Let's go back into the house," Ed said.

They backtracked to the house with police sirens closing in from the distance. At the end of the night, Mr. Hawkins was dead, and the young mother and her newborn were missing, along with three prized goats. The authorities chalked it up as a normal bear attack since it was raining. They justified the heavy downpour for the decline in the occupants' vision.

CHAPTER 10
MATT & ANNA

"THINGS ARE GETTING out of control out there, Anna," Matt said as he paused Norman's video on his computer at his desk. He dug his thumb and pointed fingertips into the corners of his eyes. "It's getting harder and harder to keep a lid on shit."

"You need help," Anna said as she sat on the couch against the wall to the right of the desk and the door. "How is the new guy doing?"

"I'd rather have my old partner, Eugene, back. At least I know my back is covered. And I am too old and don't have much patience to teach anymore. But to answer your question, better than expected. He will make The Order proud." The sound of his voice was not nearly as confident as his words.

"I don't want to make people disappear anymore. That job sucked ass," she said, playing with her black fingernails. The color matched her body-fitted attire.

Matt stared through the paused frame of Norman on the monitor in front of him. *I'll be seeing you soon . . . if you don't get yourself killed first*, he thought. "Anna, give me a crash course about the Flesh Eater. I'm getting old and forgetting what these entities' characteristics are."

"I'm here for it," she said. "But first, let me have a shot of that 1856." She mentioned the premium-aged whiskey in his dusty bookcase behind him. "You look like you can use a shot yourself."

Matt grabbed two shot glasses out of his desk drawer. "Okay, but there is no chaser around here." He placed the glasses firmly on his desk, then reached back, grabbed the fifth off the shelf, and filled both glasses before passing her one.

"To The Order," she proposed a toast, lifting her full glass to the air.

"No, I'm not toasting to that."

Anna let out a short giggle. "Okay, old man."

"Please don't call me old."

"Okay, to a speedy recovery for Eugene."

They touched glasses and turned them up. Matt made a bitter-looking face as he placed his glass back on the desk. Anna smiled and slid her glass next to his.

"Tastes just as good as it did back in the late 1800s."

"And you got the nerve to call *me* old."

"Watch it," she said jokingly. "The Flesh Eater as we call it is known to the world as the Wendigo. It's a Native American legendary creature that comes in two parts."

"The spiritual and the physical." He swiveled his office chair to face her.

She nodded in agreement, then continued. "The spirit of the Flesh Eater lurks in the wilderness. It's always among the cover of trees, but when the carnage begins, it gains strength. This is usually evident by dead or dying trees, the absence of animals, overwhelming darkness, and a large, noisy owl.

"It gains strength through the weakness or wickedness of man. At its weakest point, cannibalism and the psychological effects that come with it are what draw the spirit of the Flesh Eater to inhabit the body of anyone that took part in the act."

"The plane crash many years ago," he said, staring into the glass. He poured another two drinks and passed one to Anna. "One more for the road. We don't want to get to feeling too good."

He turned up his shot and held it in his mouth this time, swishing it around his teeth before he swallowed it. "Eugene and I were sent to Hopkinton once we read the report. We were put on a plane before we could even brush our teeth or wash our asses. We sent trackers out, but the heavy snow was too much for them. No dice."

"Yeah, I've read the report." She took her shot to the head just like the first one. Then she handed him the empty glass and continued. "As the report said, I agreed with the possibility of the Flesh Eater infecting the humans involved in the crash, causing them to eat a dead body or someone who was injured and unable to defend themselves."

"Not to mention the bodies that had frozen over time that they could not eat," Matt contemplated, taking another shot, but decided against it. Instead, he tossed the shot glass and the bottle into the drawer out of his sight.

"Exactly. Until there was no one left besides each other. By then, the spirit had completed inhabited them and the physical changes had already begun so they attacked each other until only one was left. Can you imagine how violent that scene was?"

"And the long, painful transformation and the poor victims losing their mental faculties. Their bodies grew long and gaunt. The skin was just not able to keep up with the growth spurt and the bones trying to bust through the skin," Matt said, then continued, "It was worse than death."

"The body turns an ash gray of death and deteriorates. Their teeth grow sharp and jagged. And the long claws are sharper than the teeth. To make matters worse, the spirit of the Flesh Eater infects their body with the hunger for human flesh. Like a terrible drug addiction."

"This is much, much worse," Matt said. "These bodies used to be human, either good or bad. There are still certain human aspects that remain. While none are of the remaining human qualities like love and reasoning, they are good at recreating human voices, like those of loved ones, and cry for help to trick victims away from others. They move quietly and quickly in stealth mode. And by the time the victim knows what is going on . . . it's too late."

"The more souls get infected, the stronger the spirit will be. It can get to the point where the spirit is so strong that you don't have to eat human flesh to be infected with the demon. If your mind is weak or has experienced some terrific harm or is mentally in an awful place, you can get infected."

Matt could not take it anymore. He opened the drawer, put the two shot glasses back on the desk, and poured the liquor. "Just one more for the road," he said, passing her a glass.

She took the glass and asked, "If you had to do it all over again, knowing what you know now, would you still take the job?"

Matt looked at his glass for a second to contemplate the question. Without saying a word, he tossed the drink to the back of his throat. Suddenly, a notification snatched his attention, and he reached for his cell phone from the desk. "This late can't be good," he reacted.

"You read my mind."

He sighed, followed by a tight-lipped smile. "I got to go. The Gugwes must be bored."

"Fucking pests. You need company?"

"Nah, hang around here in case something goes down." He stood up, letting his knees pop, then grabbed his Ruger off the desk and placed it in his shoulder holster. "Get you some rest. Something in my spirit tells me we will have a long week ahead."

"You sure?"

"Yep. Keep an eye on Eugene and Jefferarri for me. I'm going to take one of the youngins with me."

"Makes sense," she said, hopping off the chair and feeling the effects of the drink. "I'm going to bed. I'll check on them in the morning."

"Thank you," he said, grabbing his black trench coat.

The two fists bumped. Then Anna opened and closed the door behind her. Matt took a long look at the bottle on his desk. *I don't know how much more of this I can handle.* He grabbed the bottle and poured another shot. His eyes closed as he savored the taste.

As dawn presented itself over the Gibson farm, so did the men in black suits pulling up in three SUVs just outside the yellow crime scene tape. The rain had subdued for the moment, but the forecast had predicted more storms later in the afternoon, so the authorities were trying to gather as much information as possible. The men in black suits exited the black SUVs. Matt stepped out of the passenger seat of the second truck, wearing his shades. He felt naked. It's been a long time since he has been in the field without his partner in crime, Eugene. He did not want to come, but Eugene insisted. Plus, no one was ready to go out into the field, which needed to be addressed. It took a special kind of person to overlook the needs and feelings of others. Someone who could lie and intimidate people to force them to do what the authorities wanted. People feared the men in black suits, the company men of the government.

A slight breeze blew in from the east. Matt buttoned up his coat as he walked toward the front of the vehicle. Looking across the hood, he could see some of the mayhem that transpired some hours ago. The roof of the goat pen to his right had been torn off, and the top half of the left side was crushed into the mud. Familiar footprints were scattered around it. He stopped and shook his head, watching two goats trample through the evidence. The way

Matt figured, that was a good thing for helping hide the truth. He showed the officer his credentials, and he then raised the yellow tape for them to pass.

"Come with me," Matt commanded. He pointed to one of the men to follow him.

He smelled the stench of the Gugwes still lingering in the air. *Do these things ever bathe?* he thought.

It was horrible, and no other cryptids smelled worse than the Gugwe species except a Flesh Eater. The foul odor lingered for hours and, in some cases, days.

To the left of the path, more police tape protected an area on the opposite side of the hog pen. The path split in two directions. One to the right and the other to the left, where they proceeded. The path continued between the hog pen and the rooming house, where several people gathered on the small porch with two police officers interrogating them. The fidgeting woman on the porch was furious and in tears. Her legs were shaking, as were the others, and the officers tried to calm her down.

The hog pen was intact, but as he continued on the path, stained puddles of water stood in large and small footprints. The smaller footprints disappeared as the two larger sets ran into the tree line. It was easy for Matt to figure out what might have gone down there.

They about-faced to the right path. Across from the goat pen stood the main house on the opposite side of the path. The scene on the outside was much different from the first house. Etta could be heard wailing from within, where the back door was torn down. They stopped in front of the porch as Matt listened for a moment.

"We'll start here," Matt said. "I'll do all the talking. I need you to look like you mean business. Put your training face to work."

His temporary partner nodded. Zedrick Coby, a young, Black, twenty-eight-year-old prospect, got in The Order under the "Who You Know" umbrella. He was just two years in.

The steps creaked as they walked up to the porch. From the porch, Matt looked over the land before him to the tree line. The rolling mountains were staggered in the distance behind the horizon, and it was a gorgeous sight, but danger lived there, and danger decided to come visit last night.

CHAPTER 11
THE GUGWES, ROUND II

LITTLE JOEY HAD been waiting for weeks to go hiking with his father. So, it was no surprise to Brandon that his son was up before sunrise, too excited about the trip to remain in bed any longer. When Brandon's alarm sounded, the nine-year-old jumped between his father and his mother, Suzanne. His excitement was motivation enough to get Joey's parents moving.

The white, All-American, middle-class family was well-liked amongst the people of the suburbs in Charlotte, North Carolina, and loved to be in the spotlight. Suzanne was an award-winning teacher with accolades such as Teacher of the Year and many Teacher Appreciation medals.

Brandon owned three gas stations under a major franchise. He stayed involved with many community activities, and he and his wife always donated to different nonprofits and charities. He even teased about running for a city public office.

Suzanne made sandwiches and put them into their backpacks with water, juice, chips, and cookies. She even made a bag for Joey's best friend, Charlie, and his father, Daniel, whom they would pick up along the way. She did not dig the nature stuff and had no interest in battling the cool, windy woods, insects, or animals, undoubtably because she grew up in the big city of Seattle, Washington. Then she headed off to Duke University in Durham, North Carolina, where she met her future husband, Brandon, nearly ten years ago.

She had no problem with Brandon taking their only son into the woods, trusting his hiking knowledge and that they would be with others they knew. Plus, it was only a day trip, so it was no big deal. It was safe to say she would not join them on the trip despite Joey and Brandon begging her to do so.

After picking up Charlie and his dad, Daniel, in their blue Ford Bronco Wildtrak, they headed to the Pisgah National Forest. They passed the bags of food to the back so they could slide them into their backpacks.

The grown-ups talked petty politics and some Hiking 101 since Daniel was new to hiking. Daniel was an average, ex-high school football player and a gym buff, and he loved being a part of powerlifting competitions where he always placed high. He excelled at talking sports along the not-so-busy road to their destination.

The excitement in the backseat was evident. The conversation went from stuff that happened in school to video games and animals in the woods for about ninety minutes, then silence as sleep crept upon them.

The crew pulled up to the parking lot from just under a two-hour drive. After a few minutes of stretching, the excitement returned outside the car. After a quick restroom run and checking their backpacks and devices, the foursome stepped onto the trail. Brandon looked at the downloaded map of the trail on his phone and directed the way.

"Are we going to see a bear?" Joey asked his dad.

"A bear?" Charlie said nervously. "Will they eat us?"

"Hopefully not," Daniel said.

"We should be good as long as there are no cubs with her," Brandon said confidently.

In anticipation of the unlikely scenario, Brandon and Daniel had already talked and prepared themselves. Both had handguns, and Brandon had bear spray stuffed in the outside pocket of his backpack.

The first trail was the Northern Red Oak. The weather had eroded the trail of trees, but groves of hazelnut and tall, shady red spruce dominated the landscape alongside azalea and hawthorn bushes. Even in the cooler weather, they could still hear birds singing and spot a few flying from limb to limb.

Two miles of the beautiful scene continued into the Fryingpan Gap path. A communal frying pan hung in a tree used by mountain herders back in the day.

"Who's ready to climb the fire tower?"

"Me, me, me," the kids shouted.

The fathers smiled and laughed at the kids' excitement.

"Are we going to see fires?" Joey asked.

"Like big fires?" Charlie followed up.

Brandon chuckled and said, "Probably not today, son."

The path turned into a gravel road, and kids played and walked between five to ten feet ahead of the men, giving the men time to talk.

"How are things at home, Daniel?"

Daniel seemed surprised by the question. After a brief pause with no reply, Brandon started to apologize.

"My apologies—"

"No," Daniel interrupted. "Things are better. The counseling is a big help. I appreciate you turning me on to her."

"Aww, you're welcome, dude. No need to thank me," Brandon said sincerely.

Daniel lost his wife, who was Black, in a mass shooting a little over a year ago at a church. Daniel broke the brief silence after a few more quiet paces up the trail, asking, "You told Suzy yet?"

Brandon chuckled, "Not yet."

Brandon referred to moving out into the country by the end of the coming summer. His wife would not want to leave city life.

Suddenly, out of nowhere, eight deer of different sizes rushed from the right to the left just a few feet across the front of the children. Several leaped high in the air, jumping over the path into the underbrush. This caused Joey, who was a shade ahead of Charlie, to fall back on his butt from being startled. Charlie let out a shriek as he stopped in his tracks.

Brandon and Daniel ran to their sons in protection mode, looking toward the deer. Brandon removed his backpack from his back, then unzipped it in case he had to grab his firearm.

"Wow," Daniel said. "What the heck got them so excited?"

Brandon was looking in the direction in which they rushed with concern. He responded, "I don't know."

"Wow," Joey said stunned, his eyes wide with excitement after realizing it was nothing serious. "That was close!"

"C'mon, guys," Brandon said briefly after getting his senses together. "Let's go to the tower." He played off his concerns but kept his eyes to the right of them.

Moments later, they finally reached the Fryingpan Fire Tower. The tower was restored so visitors could safely visit the historic structure, even though it is no longer used for lookouts over the rugged, rural terrain.

The foursome fell into the short line and started up the seventy-foot tower to the top. Many people were walking down the stairs. One couple toted their whining German shepherd, bringing him down. The little brave souls held onto their dads' hands past the halfway point as the wind pressed and whipped around them. They wanted to keep going. Neither Joey nor Charlie wanted to show fear in front of each other on the tall, wobbly metal structure. At the top, they had to crawl through a tiny steel opening to get to the observation deck, which was even scarier than the stairs behind them.

They found a spot on the tower that overlooked the rolling landscape. The view from the top was a beautiful eye-pleaser to Brandon and Daniel. They took plenty of pictures with their cell phones. The different shades of green were interwoven with a little mix of winter's yellow and brown. For Joey and Charlie, it was a different type of excitement. That exuberant vibe from the boys was the pinnacle of the entire experience.

After a while and the many promises to the boys that they would be back here again soon, they headed back down to solid ground. They returned to the trail. Soon, the foursome stopped at the picnic area for lunch. There were not as many people in the area. Another couple was also having lunch, and three people passed through. Other than the boys talking, all natural sounds of nature were absent.

"You hear that?" Brandon said to Daniel.

Daniel sat back, looking around with his ears at attention. It was hard for him to grasp what Brandon was alluding to. His eyes wandered into the woods just beyond the couple as they got up and left and headed back up the trail. "Yeah, it's time to go," Daniel said.

"Come on, kids," Brandon said. "Let's head back to the ride."

"Something stinks," Charlie said, pinching his nose.

"Somebody farted. Ewwww," Joey laughed.

Brandon tossed his unfinished sandwich into the trash can and finished his water. Daniel rewrapped his sandwich and stuffed it back inside his backpack. The kids quickly finished up and tossed the wrappers in the trash.

The silence kept Brandon and Daniel on high alert, but they remained calm for the sake of the children walking back down the trail. Brandon kept his unzipped backpack in hand in case a wild animal threatened their space. Daniel held on to his knife, keeping his gun in the backpack. Now, the boys were tired and less talkative.

Suddenly, a life-threatening scream rang from behind them on the trail before everything went back to silence. They glanced back at the trail that curved to the left but saw nothing.

"Let's move," Brandon said, touching his son's back so he could continue walking.

"Help me!" a woman cried in fear.

They looked back again and saw a woman frantically running toward them. Blood covered most of the front of her body. It was the woman sitting in the picnic area who had left with the man. The man was not running back with her. They heard some movement from the brush behind her as she got closer. The trees and the brush started moving toward them. It was apparent to Brandon and Daniel that something was chasing this woman. It was definitely time to go. They took off in front of the frantic woman.

"Run!" Brandon ordered, picking up his nine-year-old.

Daniel followed suit, picking up his son. Terrifying roars soon followed, and the sound was *not* too far away. It was a no-brainer that some predators were fast approaching from both sides of the trail. Charlie buried his face in his dad's shoulder. Meanwhile, Joey kept his eyes on the woman who tried to catch up with them.

Shockingly, a giant claw reached out from the underbrush and snatched her midstride, pulling her into the harsh bushes on the left side of the trail. She did not even have time to scream.

"Dad!" Joey shouted after the woman disappeared.

Brandon glanced back quickly and saw the woman gone. Massive dark bodies were moving about in the woods. He moved the backpack to the side that held his son and grabbed the Glock out of it. Something was burrowing through the thicket to the right. Brandon aimed and fired into the underbrush, hoping to hit anything moving.

Suddenly, a Gugwe jumped from the open tree line from the right to the left side, ripping Charlie out of Daniel's arms. Daniel fell to the ground. Dazed, he got to his feet. Blood poured from his broken nose.

"Dadddd!" Charlie squealed from a distance.

"Charlie?" Daniel called out.

Brandon stopped and looked back. He watched Daniel stagger between the trees. There were not many bushes in this trail area, primarily trees.

"Charlie?" Daniel called out again.

"Daniel?" Brandon pointed his gun but hesitated. "Daniel?"

Joey started crying, "Dad!" The tears spotted his shirt.

Brandon's heart was about to beat out of his chest, but then he chose flight over fight with his son in hand. They got twenty feet down the trail before Charlie screamed again. His scream was cut short. Brandon's adrenaline kicked into overdrive, and he ran without looking back again.

A little further down the trail, Brandon and his son were passing people, and he was swinging his gun. Others started running after seeing the gun in his hand.

"Run! Run!" Brandon shouted, using the gun to direct people back.

Some rangers met them in the parking lot with their guns drawn. Frantically, Brandon explained to the rangers what had happened. By the end of the evening, there was no sign of Daniel or his son, Charlie. However, lots of blood painted the trail a crimson red. The underbrush around and near those areas had broken and snapped twigs and branches. As usual, at the end of the day, the authorities chopped the incident up as another animal attack.

CHAPTER 12
RELEASE THE BEAST

JUST OVER ONE month after someone tried to kill Jefferarri, The Order made the dreaded decision to put them in a helicopter to return home. They concluded that it was in Jefferarri's best interest to recover at home with a few guards in place. Octavia didn't complain too badly about it. It beat being locked down for sure, and with the kill switch device inside his chest, they still had a leash on him. One thing she knew about The Order was that their decisions were not always clear-cut. It easily could have been for the safety of the hospital staff. There were plenty of complaints and whispers about everyone's safety being discussed, which were understandable, but what many did not understand was that The Order never really made decisions that benefited anybody's well-being. However, that was the façade they portrayed. Octavia was one of the few who knew that.

The helicopter was a massive military chopper. Worn bench seats lined down both sides from front to back. The thin leather liner was way past its time to be replaced. Five white and three Black guards accompanied them on the flight. Two of them, one white and the other Black, sat in the two seats that guarded the cockpit door. The rest of them sat at the back, keeping a healthy distance from Jefferarri and Octavia, who sat close to the middle. Another helicopter joined the convoy, its blades slicing through the air as it approached to reinforce the security detail.

Jefferarri's head bobbed up and down in recovery mode with his mouth open. He was trying to fight sleep. He wore thin, black pajamas and slides because his clothes no longer fit him. Every time Jefferarri went through a transformation, his body mass and height increased. The last time, he grew to seven feet tall at the hospital. The problem was that he never returned to his original size. Right now, he stood at six foot seven and was 316 pounds solid. He was just under two inches taller than before and eleven pounds heavier, with an enormous appetite that followed.

At home, Jefferarri sat in his 130-gallon whirlpool filled with extra ice. His head rested against the tub's rim behind him, and his eyes were tired. After the excitement of greeting his daddy's return, Kang found comfort in resting on his cozy doggy mat. The young pup kept his eyes on Jefferarri, sensing the tense atmosphere surrounding him.

Relaxing jazz played at a low volume from the Bose speakers on the wall. Despite his quick ability to regenerate and recover, the poison severely impacted him. The ice water would help him feel better and recover quickly, removing his light-headedness and nausea.

A mysterious scent lingered in his memory, its origin eluding him. Unbeknownst to him, it was the scent of his would-be assassin. Struggling to focus, he blinked his eyes open, greeted by a hazy blur. Overwhelming waves of distress and sadness washed over him, palpable in the air, emanating from Octavia. Trapped in the tub, he lacked the strength to crawl out and offer her solace. The cold water enveloped his body, inducing a complete reboot, rendering him immobile. A thought crossed Jefferarri's mind – perhaps he should flee, believing Octavia could learn to survive without him, fearing their connection would diminish over time. Yet, he understood that abandoning her would leave her vulnerable to the sinister machinations of The Order. Reluctantly, he had to rely on Matt and Eugene to shield her from harm. But, at times, doubts consumed Jefferarri's thoughts. *What if they were forced to choose between protecting them and remaining loyal to The Order? The Order must fall*, he thought as his eyes closed. He turned his attention to the sound of the horns and drums to ease his line of thinking.

The same rhythm of music flowed through the bedroom speakers while Jefferarri recuperated. The music also flowed into Octavia's ears. She lay on the bed on her side with quiet tears soaking her pillow. The weight of her thoughts consumed her, turning her into an emotional wreck. For starters, she had seen many entities, godly and ungodly alike, but seeing the Grim Reaper as it was known to the world, was the last image anyone would want to see in this world. The fear was just as great for her as the demon that took her father's life many years ago.

As terrible as that was, multiple factors got her tears flowing. Two of them were never wavering. The first was this curse that she could only shake through death. Octavia had never known a "normal" life. She never knew how it felt to have friends and play games that normal children played. She was jealous of that growing up in a village setting. She missed the ordinary basic communication skills of a typical adolescent.

With that being said, the only true friend she has ever known was Jefferarri. Their situation redefined the true meaning of soulmates. However, after the recent events, it was clear to her that living without Jefferarri was a no-no. The thought of losing him was too much to bear.

Roseline, the sixty-one-year-old caretaker of the house, was on her way out to the store to grab some groceries when she heard Octavia sobbing, so she beelined to check on her.

She walked toward the slightly ajar door, then eased into the room. Octavia sat with her back against the suede-padded headboard. Her falling tears were caught by a soft pillow resting on top of her thighs. As she laid her arms across the pillow, she nervously crumpled a Kleenex in her hands.

"What's the matter, Octavia?" Roseline asked as she sat on the side of the bed. She grabbed her hand to comfort her. Octavia shook her head, gesturing she had nothing to say, but Roseline had other plans.

The Haitian native was handpicked many years ago, and The Order approved her. The widow was paid very handsomely to spend time at the house. She cooked and did some cleaning, which was easy since the couple was barely there, so she spent most of her time watching TV, reading, and working out in the weight room. Roseline took pride in her youthful figure. With that being said, her biggest responsibility was Kang. She had no children but found solace in this home despite the dangers of staying there. Moreover, she could move around as she wished as long as she looked after the house and Kang. They would generally let her know well in advance when she would need to be there.

So, to secure Roseline's safety, one of the two panic rooms built like Fort Knox was converted into a bedroom. Getting in the room without a code was nearly impossible. Only three people knew the code: Jefferarri, Octavia, and, of course, Roseline. The room had its own emergency power and air system. They have not used the rooms for the purposes they were made for . . . as of yet.

"Things are getting tough, I can imagine," Roseline said. "I'm here if you want to talk." She tapped Octavia's hand three times with a smile before she rose from the bed to walk out.

"I think I'm losing it," Octavia whispered.

Roseline sat back on the bed with her ears open. She had no superpowers or immortal abilities. The one thing she had of value was wisdom, and Octavia valued that. Octavia usually kept Roseline out of her business when it came to her and Jefferarri, but now, she felt like she needed a lifeline.

"I would bet there are many people in this world who would love to have your abilities," Roseline said.

"Do you?"

Roseline hesitated, then said, "Once upon a time, I would have died for it." She gave a quick chuckle before she continued. "But now, after seeing the little bit I've seen with you and what you are dealing with, honey, ain't no way."

"I never had a choice in the matter. I was born with it."

"Your gift has a purpose," Roseline replied. She cuffed Octavia's hand again. "I'm not sure what it is, but I can guess it has something to do with Jefferarri."

"This soulmate thing is for the birds," Octavia said out of annoyance.

"Sounds like you want out, sweetie," Roseline assumed.

"I don't want to live the rest of my life in fear," Octavia said in a low, aggressive tone.

Roseline had always been a woman who knew the right things to say . . . except for this moment. "You are not his soulmate. You are his guardian angel."

"I don't want it!" Octavia responded.

A siren notification from Jefferarri's cell phone in the dresser drawer made them jump. It was the notification sound for The Order. As their eyes looked toward the sound, Jefferarri had crept up to the door, dripping wet in his shorts. Only half his body was visible in the doorway, listening. His eyes locked on them with no expression. Jefferarri stood there as Kang licked his leg twice and then jumped onto the bed, where Octavia and Roseline stared at Jefferarri. The women felt the tension in the room.

Jefferarri heard their hearts beat into his ears. The one person that he trusted and loved the most on this earth, whom he would have given his life . . . did not want him. He shrugged it off and then grabbed his phone, silencing the notification.

"Hey," Octavia broke the odd silence. "How long have you been standing there?"

Water rolled down Jefferarri's tatted back. He used the eye scan security on his phone to unlock it. "Long enough," he answered. He walked out, waiting for security to clear the message. The second security feature popped up for a fingerprint scan for The Order's message. He scanned it and waited.

It read, "This message is for your eyes and your eyes only. You have thirty seconds to read this message before it terminates. Click agree if you agree and understand." Jefferarri tapped the "I Agree" button on the touch screen. With a deep sigh, Jefferarri could not understand what The Order wanted with him, knowing he was still recovering.

Roseline knew Octavia was talking outside of her neck from built-up emotions. She also felt in her heart that the two needed each other and would need each other to get past what was coming and to survive.

As Octavia stood up to follow Jefferarri to ease the situation, Roseline grabbed her with this warning, "You do what you have to do until those eyes no longer have color."

Octavia was confused, but Roseline's words passed her like a runaway train. After a fake gesture that she understood, she continued after Jefferarri.

The message on Jefferarri's phone from The Order read, "Gugwe sited just north of Ashville. Your mission is to track down the threats and find the missing. This is a highly classified solo mission. You have thirty seconds to read this message before it terminates. If you accept, tap the Accept button."

Jefferarri replaced his anger toward Octavia with a vengeful spirit. Warmth flowed down his chest.

"Burly," Jefferarri said to himself before accepting the mission.

"Jefferarri," Octavia said, walking up behind him.

Unexpected energy radiated from his presence that she could not quite grasp. His dimly lit red eyes looked back over his shoulder at her, but he did not reply. She stopped when she saw his eyes, which were like a brick wall. She realized the message on his phone was more significant than what happened with her and Roseline. Her mouth moved, but nothing came out.

The phone notification broke the silence, pulling Jefferarri's eyes to the phone's display. The message read, "A helicopter will greet you at 1500 hours at the taxi spot. This message is for your eyes only and is not to be mentioned beyond this point. Ref# 564." Then the message disappeared to a blank screen. Jefferarri had less than an hour to meet at the designated spot.

Roseline stood at the bedroom door, observing the friction between the lovebirds.

"I have to go," Jefferarri said without looking at her. "Maybe you should too. Both of you."

"What is that supposed to mean?" Octavia asked. She crossed her arms as tears ran down her face. Deep down, she knew what he meant.

"Go be happy," he replied, then leaped off the balcony to the first floor. He was so light on his feet not even a thump was heard.

"Jefferarri," she cried out to him . . . with no response back.

CHAPTER 13
IT CAME FOR THE BOY

IT HAD BEEN fourteen days since the so-called animal mauling took place at the Carter cabin. And still no explanation for Barbara's cousin, Jacob, and the snowplow accident. Only that he lost control of his Jeep and must have got dragged off by an animal, said the news. Someone discovered his arm the next day, half-eaten and folded at the elbow on a tree branch. They did not find the rest of his body or any tracks.

Chief of Police Fletcher and his deputies beefed up the community's presence with a mandatory curfew by sundown. The fears were so great that hunters sneaked into the woods in packs, looking for everything that could be the predator. Most of them got driven out, but others would get arrested or disappear. The drop in the animal population baffled the authorities in the area. They found bones, but the authorities believed someone or something drove most of the animal population away.

Since those events had unfolded, Barbara had been constantly on edge, her nerves frayed. Barbara's family consisted of her daughter, Peggy, son-in-law, Bobby, and three grandchildren, sixteen-year-old Mellie, thirteen-year-old Katie, and four-year-old Nate. They were at Barbara's house because it had more room and there was safety in numbers. Peggy lived in a two-bedroom home. Barbara was always by her side, and so was the shotgun. She constantly peeked out the window and double-checked the locks dozens of times daily. Being stuck up under her mom 24/7 was a nightmare due to the nagging that old age had brought upon her.

"That wasn't no damn bear or wolves," Barbara repeated for the umpteenth time over the past several days. "That was the boogeyman."

"And two days ago, it was the beginning of the end of days," Peggy mocked in aggravation.

"Well, it still wasn't no damn bear, Peggy! I don't care what you say," Barbara barked. "When was the last time you saw a bear around here?"

"Mama, I'm trying to muster up the mindset to go get us some food. It's been a while since I've had any good sleep."

"We got food," Barbara snapped back.

"Enough for two days, Mama, before we start eating the emergency stash!"

"Hey, Ma," Peggy's daughter, Mellie, said, walking down the stairs. "You ready to go get some groceries?"

"Yeah. Let's go and get on back before the curfew," Peggy answered.

"And before the snowstorm comes back," Barbara said.

After Peggy and her daughter left for the store, Barbara walked upstairs and checked on the other two kids. They were sleeping beside their daddy on the bed with the *Tom and Jerry Show* cartoon watching them. She closed the usually squeaky door quietly and returned to the couch to watch her evening news.

It did not take long before the news watched her as sleep draped her like a fallen curtain. Not long after her eyes dropped, the kids' feet thumped down the stairs. When Bobby arrived, he found Nate trying to open the door. His little hands had a hard time turning the knob, and even if he could, he still was too short to reach the deadbolt lock.

"What are you doing?" Bobby shouted. He looked over to his mother-in-law, still in la-la land, despite the volume of his voice. "Don't open that door! Get away from there!"

Nate looked back at his dad and said, "Mommy wants me. She's calling me . . . outside."

"Boy, get away from that door like I told you!" Bobby said in a demanding tone. He guided Nate from the door by pushing his hand against Nate's little head. With an attitude and lips poked out, Nate stomped across the living room and flopped beside his grandmother on the couch.

It did not take long before sleep attacked Bobby again, and for the life of him, he could not understand why he felt so exhausted and sleepy suddenly after the recent long nap they had taken earlier.

"Nate," a voice echoed from the outside. "It's your mother. Come outside. I have a lot of candy for you."

"Mommy," Nate replied, rising off the couch and rubbing the sadness out of his eyes. "Daddy told me I can't go."

Bobby's eyes popped open to the sound of his son's voice in time to watch his son attempt to open the door. He thought something was wrong. Nate was always a good kid who obeyed his elders.

"Come play hide-and-seek with me," Peggy's voice said in a more distorted tone to the little boy's ears. Even though Nate felt something was wrong with the sound of his mother's voice, he was compelled to comply. He ran to the kitchen and pushed the heavy oak chair past Barbara and Bobby to the front door.

"Nate, don't keep your mother waiting," the voice sounded more distorted this time.

"I'm trying," Nate said in a straining tone. Teary eyes formed at the thought of displeasing his mother as he struggled to pull the chair across the thick carpet.

Barbara's eyes followed her grandson's struggle to the door. She could not move or talk during sleep paralysis. Bobby suffered the same disability, being mentally cuffed to the chair. Unlike Nate, neither Bobby nor Barbara could hear the artificial voice.

Finally, Nate reached the door. Sniffling, with tears rolling off his cheeks, he stepped up on the chair and, with a minor struggle, he unlocked the deadbolt.

The storm picked back up outside, with the wind rattling the windows. Bobby and Barbara could only watch in fear, which visibly showed in their rapid breathing. Their hearts were trying to beat out of their chests, and dread crawled across their skins.

"Hurry!" the voice said outside in a more demonic tone than his mother's.

"Coming," Nate reassured them.

Nate cracked the door, and the wind blew the door wide open, revealing the brightness behind him. Cold air and snowflakes rushed the house with chilling intent. Paper and dust flew around the room, and curtains swayed on their rods. Nate turned and waved to his father and grandmother before turning and stumbling into the storm, wearing nothing more than a tee shirt and underwear.

Bobby watched Nate get swallowed by the storm until he disappeared. Suddenly, a squeal from the tree line vibrated throughout the house, breaking the spell over Barbara and Bobby. Bobby took off out the door, followed by Barbara. The storm quickly eased to a moderately cool breeze. Both were crying Nate's name as they bolted off the porch. Bobby nearly slipped on the snow-covered porch in his gray tee shirt, a pair of jeans, and a pair of generic white sneakers.

The grandmother had on an old sundress with only one bedroom shoe. The other one, she left on the porch, rushing down.

Bobby ran into Barbara's truck and bounced off into the snow as she eased in front of the house. Sounds of agony flowed with the vaper out of his mouth. The accident bruised his hip. Barbara frantically jumped out of the driver's seat, and Mellie jumped out of the other side. Both ran to the front of the truck to Bobby. The snow falling from the sky limited visibility.

"What's going on?" Mellie asked.

"Bobby," Peggy called out.

"Nate ran into the woods!" Barbara said as she passed them, moving as fast as her old bones would allow. "He's gone into the woods!" She did not make it far before her knee gave out, forcing her to the ground.

"Oh my God!" Bobby managed to stand up and stop Peggy in her tracks before she could run any further. "My baby," she exclaimed.

"Peggy! Peggy!" he said, grabbing her by her arms. "You, Mellie and Barbara, go to Katie in the house! Call the police!"

Bobby cut her off before she could argue.

"*Now*, Peggy!" he ordered, taking off to the tree line. "Katie needs you," he said to get her to obey.

"Nate," Peggy called out toward the woods.

A piercing scream erupted from the depths of the dense woods, causing an abrupt halt in everyone's movements. Its dreadful tone resonated, resembling a haunting, demonic rendition of Nate's voice. All heads swiveled in unison towards the source, captivated by the deafening noise that reverberated through their very cores. The sheer intensity of the sound was overwhelming, causing their bodies to tremble as if a powerful force was vibrating through them. Overwhelmed by the cacophony, Barbara instinctively clasped her hands over her ears, desperately seeking refuge from the piercing noise. "No! No, no, no," Peggy cried out. She attempted to move toward the woods when Mellie grabbed her.

"Mommy," Katie called out from the front door. "Mommy." She caressed the sleepiness from her eyes. "What's going on?"

"Katie," Peggy said, her voice filled with urgency. It was enough to make her sprint towards her daughter, heart pounding. With her daughters in her arms, Peggy stood outside the front door, her eyes filled with worry as she scanned the surroundings. She directed the girls back to the porch before rushing to help her mother. Peggy helped her mom off the snowy ground, then watched Bobby disappear into the trees before they reached the porch.

"Mommy, where is Daddy going?" Katie asked.

"Come," Mellie said as she guided Katie into the house.

This was not a fight-or-flight situation for Bobby. He had to protect his son despite feeling scared. With limited visibility under the snow-filled treetops and the fact that the sun was hiding above the cloudy skies, he ran on.

"Nate!" he called out into the trees. "Nate!" he called again.

He tried to decipher whether this was a nightmare or real. The numbing cold that crept up his legs through his feet told him it was real.

"Nate!"

"Daddy," Nate's voice called calmly.

"Nate!"

"Daddy, I'm over here."

The voice sounded more like a recording and echoed everywhere, so Bobby could not pinpoint it. He pushed deeper, but the pain slowed him down. His body shivered from the elements, and his feet burned with every step.

"Where are you, son?" he cried out. His fear turned into tears. "Nate?" He walked deeper into the woods.

"Daddy . . . Daddy, I'm over here," the voice said again.

A large hand suddenly appeared and moved from around a tree to his left, about twenty yards away, cutting short his cry of "Son—" The long, bony fingers had dark-colored nails at least two inches long. Deep scratch marks followed the razor-sharp nails as they moved around the tree. The fingers were dripping blood that ran down from the scratches on the tree.

The thumping of the bass drum echoed in Bobby's ears, causing his chest to vibrate with each beat and his breath to quicken even more. The icy tendrils creeping up his legs seemed to sear his flesh even more fiercely. Fear tightened its grip on his soul, constricting his thoughts and filling him with doubt. The overwhelming urge to chase after his son was now overshadowed by a nagging sense of cowardice. For so long, he had boldly declared his willingness to sacrifice his life for his family, but this harrowing situation now tested the authenticity of his words and the very essence of his manhood. "Daddy, I'm over here," the voice sounded even more distorted than last time. It dragged to a slower, evil pitch.

Something at the bottom of the tree caught Bobby's attention. It looked like his son's clothes as he ran out of the house.

"No," he begged. "Oh God, please, no." The tears ran down his face against his cold, bluish flesh.

Snow cascaded down from the same tree, creating a mesmerizing flurry of white. Bobby's eyes were captivated by movement in the treetop, as something vigorously shook the branches. The gnarled limbs blended seamlessly with the surroundings, creating a hazy blur. Suddenly, a booming snarl pierced the air, causing Bobby to instinctively shield his ears from the jarring sound. In that harrowing moment, fear took hold, coursing through his veins as he spun around, his numbed legs propelling him forward with all their might. The falling snow from the trees closed in on him, a chilling embrace, as the relentless pursuit of the Flesh Eater grew nearer. Bobby's heart raced as he glimpsed the approaching tree line, its edges looming closer. He hesitated, uncertain if he could reach it in time. Refusing to glance back, he feared it would hinder his speed. As he hurried forward, the thudding sound of the creature's heavy footsteps echoed menacingly behind him. The ground shook beneath the thunderous pounding, the sound echoing through the air. Suddenly, its colossal claws swiped across his back, propelling Bobby forward, crashing into the cold embrace of the snow. The monstrous creature emitted a blood-curdling shriek, its mouth watering in anticipation, as it loomed above him. Bobby's heart raced, knowing that the short-awaited reunion with his son was imminent. Out of nowhere, the deafening sound of gunshots echoed through the air from the tree line. The Flesh Eater quickly grabbed Bobby's leg and dragged him deeper into the woods. Bobby felt a sharp pain as the claws pierced his leg, causing him to let out a squeal. A dark, crimson trail of blood followed in its wake. It dragged him a few yards, but it let go after being hit and overwhelmed by bullets. The creature released a yelp before blending back into the trees.

As the thick smoke slowly dissipated, Peggy stood at the edge of the dense tree line, gripping a rifle tightly in her hands. Fletcher and four other deputies anxiously flanked her, their guns trained on the mysterious woods. From within the shadows, pained groans pierced the air, echoing through the silence. Some of the chilling sounds seemed distorted, resembling haunting howls. In that moment, a sense of foreboding washed over them, as they realized the unsettling possibility of multiple unseen threats lurking in the darkness. As the thick smoke cleared, Bobby's life had been taken away as a bullet found its unintended target, piercing his skull. Amidst the grim aftermath, a grotesque discovery awaited them – Nate's severed leg lay pathetically at the foot of a towering tree. The ground was littered with shreds of his blood-soaked attire, while fragments of torn fabric dangled from the branches above. Yet, amidst the haunting scene, no other remnants of human remains were found.

CHAPTER 14
THE HUNT

MATT SAT AT his desk, finishing his final report on the Gibson farm. He rubbed his eyes, trying to keep his concentration on the screen in front of him just before he pressed "submit" on the keyboard, then took a long stretch and looked at his watch. He was ready to go. *Just a few more minutes*, he thought.

He relaxed momentarily before taking one last browse through his emails. At the top was an email with an exclamation point marked *urgent*! He sighed, knowing that urgent meant more work on his plate. *It's time to retire. It's time.*

He clicked the email, and a thumbnail of a video of a young white male with the play icon popped up on the screen. He sighed, knowing somebody would get a visit from him eventually. The email read, "Norman Williams, twenty-nine years old . . ." His Social Security Number and address followed. The email continued, "Subject is a National Security Risk and needs to be shut down at all costs by any means necessary."

Another kid out here trying to save the world, he thought. *You are in so much trouble, young man.*

He clicked on the video. He watched Norman talk about the road closing and his government conspiracy theories. Matt chuckled with a headshake and thought, *He doesn't sound believable.*

Suddenly, the office door swung open, grabbing his attention.

"Anna," he greeted, rubbing his forehead.

"Were you aware Jefferarri is on a hunt in North Carolina for the Gugwe clan?" Anna asked in a concerned voice.

"What?"

"Right now, without Octavia," Anna said.

Usually, Octavia would stay in the transport until the job ended, and she eased him out of his rage.

"Are you sure?" Matt asked, giving Anna his full attention. "How do you know this?" An adrenaline rush overcame sleepiness.

"I'm Anna," she replied. "I know *everything*."

"Does the Councilmen know?"

She pressed her lips. "That I do not know, Matt."

Matt grabbed his black coat from the back of his chair and put it on as he walked toward the office door. "Meet me down at the Command Station ASAP!"

"Take us to the Gugwes," Jason Reed instructed Jefferarri, determination in his voice. He continued, competing with the whirring of the helicopter blades. "You return to the rendezvous point, and we will do what we do. Got it?" he said with a commanding voice, but Jefferarri smelled the fear on him and the rest of his team. "Then we'll come back for you."

The side door opened, and cool air rushed the tension inside of the helicopter.

Without saying a word, Jefferarri stood up, towering over the men in the helicopter, then fell backward out of the opened side door as the helicopter hovered a few yards above the dense trees below. He disappeared as he fell through the top of the trees. The sun was on point to set in thirty-five minutes.

Jefferarri landed on all fours as he touched down on the ground. All rules went out the window on this mission from this point forward. The one monster had slayed everyone who cared and loved him unconditionally except Octavia. He closed his eyes and sniffed the air.

Not far away, Jefferarri's nose led him to a clue. He squatted and touched the footprint of a Gugwe on the ground. He wore only cotton shorts with no shoes, and light rain tapped him on his bare back. It was just hours ago since the Gugwes had attacked the Gibson farm. A light breeze ran from the west. He closed his eyes and smelled the mud on the tip of his fingers. The scent confirmed what he already knew. The powerful stench was enough to survive the thunderstorm before. A quick grin plastered his face before he stood up and surveyed the empty scene. He noticed more footprints. Some small and some big ones, all headed in one direction. A shot of adrenaline hit his body as revenge made his soul tingle.

Closing his eyes, he raised his nose toward the rain and sniffed the air for another moment. He opened his eyes, and before he could bring his head down, he huffed at the drone hovering high above him in the sky. Then he remembered the mission—a mission they must have known was not going to go as planned.

"Burly," he muttered to himself, studying the deep imprints as they vanished into the thick woods. "I'm coming for you."

He jumped up and started jogging toward the tree line, picking up speed with each step until he was in a full-blown sprint as the trees engulfed him. The drone above tailed him through thermal technology when he was not visible. The helicopter followed the drone from a distance to remain undetected.

Jefferarri bobbed and weaved through the trees and underbrush of the forest. He swung from tree to tree when necessary to stay on the scent. Although the path had already been disturbed, Jefferarri found it easy to follow. He uprooted dirt and disturbed branches during his rampage. Revenge was his fuel, and killing was his destination. With his teeth bared, it was clear that his emotions were getting the better of him. His transformation slowly took shape the deeper he tore through the thicket. His nails on his hands and feet had turned dark, and his facial features and body also started mutating.

He suddenly slowed down and eventually came to a halt. His eyes surveyed ahead into the zigzagging tree patterns. Then his eyes crawled up a tree not twenty yards ahead.

"Blood," he said to himself.

From above, the drone followed the swaying of the trees through the camera, but thermal cameras on the split-screen watched the beast move with incredible agility and speed. The Command Station received all the feeds from the drones and the information from the team.

The Command Station was a low-lit room with a large TV monitor covering the entire north wall, showing four split screens facing the workstations. Agents of all races and genders worked on three rows of desks filled with computers and phones.

Moody nervously stood on edge at the back dark left corner of the Command Station, biting his nails and giving commands through radio frequencies. There was no way Moody would be in the same facility this early, if ever, with the friction between him and Jefferarri. He fixed his eyes on the split-screen upon him. Usually, he would be on the helicopter with his subordinates, leading the charge on missions. He would never admit that after the hospital scare a month ago, he had turned into a cowardly lion.

After all that mayhem, this mission had the potential to go sideways in so many ways and on so many levels. They had sent a world-class slayer to scout another killer. A killer who took everything away from Jefferarri that made him human. Moody and other members of The Order knew they must put down the rabid dog if it crossed the threshold.

Standing to the left of Moody with a slight smirk on his face was Bill. He was keen to learn what all the fuss was about. This highly praised and feared anomaly had been so protected by his organization, and the only nonhuman tracker left made him more treasured.

"Impressive," Bill said, noticing the pantherlike movements and agility as he rubbed his scruffy beard.

Moody's eyes glanced at Bill and then quickly returned to the screen before him. "You ain't seen nothing yet," Moody followed.

"This guy should be demolishing our enemies," Bill said before a quick chuckle. "If he is as good as on paper."

"Wars make money," Moody replied. "It would never happen."

Bill looked at Matt with the "we will see" expression on his face but did not reply.

Everyone turned their heads as the double doors burst open, making way for Matt and Anna. Concerned was plastered across Matt's face with a pep in his old bones. His long trench coat flapped behind him like in the comics. Anna walked behind Matt as if she were all business.

"What the hell is going on?" Matt said, looking around the room for someone to step up with the answer. Then he looked up at the screen.

"Didn't you get the memo?" Moody said in a confused tone as he walked toward Matt and Anna.

"Memo?" Matt responded. "Hell no, I did *not* get any memo!"

"Excuse me," Bill said as he slipped from behind Moody. "What are your concerns about this animal? Aren't you a field agent?"

Silence covered the room like a heavy blanket. Almost everyone in the room listened or looked back at the confrontation.

"The man just had an assassination attempt on his life! And you put him out in the field without even an evaluation?"

"Not to mention sending him out after the Smoky Mountain Gugwe clan," Anna interjected. "We all know the history there. Where's the official paperwork?"

"You just left the Gibson farm. It didn't make you angry seeing the evil done there?" Moody asked.

"He stopped!" one staffer exclaimed.

Everyone turned their attention to the big screen.

CHAPTER 15
REVENGE

THE FOREST WAS wet and quiet, meaning a predator was nearby. Jefferarri was not sure if it was him or something else. Perhaps the Gugwes brought the sounds to a halt, but a peculiar second scent made him stop in his tracks. He lifted his nose and sniffed the air. The second scent was blood—human blood. The scent was a combination of freshness and age, with some hints of decay.

His head snapped to his one o'clock. Then he started climbing the large tree to his right. His eyes searched for the dreaded unknown.

The drone descended below the tree top to get a better look at what stopped him. Aggravating as the drone was to Jefferarri, he remained focused on the matter. His claws dug into the bark as pieces of tree skin flaked to the ground.

Jefferarri climbed to a thick branch and, after making sure it could handle his weight, hung on it upside down, looking to get a better view. That was when he saw it. After a quick look around, Jefferarri swung through twelve trees until he reached the one overlooking a horrific sight. He carefully landed on the tree to not shake the gruesome human skeletal remains and some animal remains that littered the tree. Hats, coins, eyeglasses, and clothes were just some things he witnessed below. The smell was so strong that Jefferarri shook his head to get the stench out of his nose. They intentionally wrapped old vines around the victims' remains to keep them up high. Looking down, he could see where some bones had fallen to the ground due to Father Time.

"Old feeding ground?" he asked himself.

Jefferarri stood up on a branch. His eyes widened to the horror of many trees filled with bones that seemed to go on for miles and miles in a tunnel visionlike state. He started moving through the trees with the drone trying to keep up. He leaped from one to the other with speed and power.

The arrival of darkness brought with it another familiar scent, prompting him to halt and carefully sniff the air. This one made his chest burn from the possibility of what it could be. Slowly, he turned his head to his right. It did not take his keen eyesight long to see what he knew was there. With a brief hesitation, he leaped over to the infant's body tied to the tree branch by a vine. A Gugwe had bitten off the child's face. It was fresh. Teeth marks dug into her small head where the monster had taken a bite. There was enough blood running down the limb of that tree that made Jefferarri think it ate her face while she was still alive.

He flashed back to the Gugwe's ambush when he was a child. When Burly held the decapitated head of his beloved Margaret by her hair like a trophy with her face missing and blood oozing down its chin, it exploded emotion from the depth of his soul. This thought caused a few gruffs to leave his gut and travel a short distance amongst the surrounding trees. Jefferarri crashed down to the ground seconds later, causing a resounding thud to echo through the air. He closed his eyes and lay still on his back, bracing himself for the pain that accompanied the transformation.

"All units stand back and stand by." Moody talked to his crew on the helicopter through the microphone in the workstation before him. His narrowed eyes never left the screen in the Command Room.

"Standing by . . . over," Jason replied over the speaker.

"Drop the drone down," Moody commanded the pilot controller in the room. "Let's see what's going on with him."

"Yes, sir," the young, chocolate female replied, sitting dead center of the screen with her joystick-style controller. She also had three monitors in front of her. Her white female assistant sat to her left.

The drone had three cameras, one of which was fixed on its underbelly and used by the driver for guidance. One of the assistant's jobs was to control the other two camera functions and what they showed on the screen. These cameras were also adjustable from the assistant's control panel.

"Wow!" Bill said in amazement, watching Jefferarri move through the woods on the screen. "This dude moves like a cat."

Matt rolled his eyes at Bill's comment. "How much do you know about him or what he's capable of?"

"I know what's on paper, but to see it live is a whole different thing," Bill said with a smile.

"This is no play toy, sir," Anna said, pointing at the screen.

"A life," Matt said. "He has feelings and a life."

"Yet expendable," Bill came back. "He is the future of The Order's franchise. Physically . . . or in spirit."

"What does that mean exactly?" Anna asked with a creased brow as calmly as she could, but Bill gave her no response as he kept his eyes peeled on the monitor.

The pilot guided the drone flawlessly through the thick of the trees, dodging limbs in infrared mode. Skeletal bones littered the tree branches like Christmas ornaments. Old vines wrapped around weathered skeletons. Most of the skulls' faces had deep bite marks or holes. The drone dropped just enough to see Jefferarri crawling up the tree toward it. She had to move the drone quickly out of Jefferarri's path up the tree.

"A graveyard," Moody said somberly.

"In trees," Bill cracked.

"This is definitely a Gugwe trademark," Anna said as she looked at Matt.

"How can you tell?" Bill asked. "Because of the bodies are in the trees?"

"No, the Gugwe loves to eat the faces of humans for some reason," Moody answered. Moody wondered how Bill got his job. In his eyes, Bill was an idiot.

Jefferarri leaped from the tree to another tree, landing on one of its branches, and the drone followed him. What they saw next made some in the room gasp and paused the bickering in the back of the room. An deadly silence haunted the room.

"You think that's the baby from the Gibson farm?" Anna asked Matt.

Matt was at a loss for words. Just that quick he had forgotten all about the missing baby at the farm he had left not long ago. He bit his bottom lip and knew the Smoky Mountain Gugwes had to be eradicated. They had gotten out of hand, and finally, there was a trail.

Jefferarri flipped off the tree, hitting the ground hard. There was not much underbrush to break his fall.

"What's happening?" Bill said in a confused voice.

"Hell," Moody replied. "Hell is coming."

His eye shine pierced through the darkness, and the crackling sounds of skin and bone structure transformations groaned from a painful pit. Rapid breathing and wheezing whispered through the cool, dark air. As he emerged, his body transformed, becoming completely covered in a short coat of fur. His once human-like head now resembled that of a wolf. His shirt, torn into shreds, hung loosely from his body, leaving him completely exposed.

The drone used night vision and hovered closer to the ground to see the beast better. Suddenly, Jefferarri sprang from the ground and swiped at the drone, missing it by only a few inches. The drone quickly elevated out of harm's way. Turbulence from the swipe wobbled the drone.

A thunderous rumble bellowed from the predator before it scrambled up the tree and lashed out at the drone. Again, its claws missed it by mere inches. Jefferarri landed on a different tree and launched at the drone once more before the drone sped up high above the trees.

Giving up on the drone, Jefferarri took off through the trees twice as fast as before. He tore through the valley to make his ascent up the mountain. Now, a thunderstorm dropped heavy rain upon the region, which did not prevent his nose from guiding him to his target.

The drone followed right above the trees around the side of the mountain to the shoulder area that overlooked the saddle of the mountain. Jefferarri's sharp, keen eyes pierced through the dark across to the opposite side of the saddle. He sniffed the night air, then looked back over the area. His eyes locked on a ledge right between the saddle and the mesa of the mountain. There was a cave entrance that was camouflaged by old trees and shrubbery. Even with his keen eyesight, the shallow light that escaped the cave was difficult to see. He was not hunting for food. This was war, a desire to kill, and with that, Jefferarri let out a bloodcurdling scream. The scream sounded like a mix between a lion's roar and a wolf's howl . . . A warning to Burly that he had found him and death was coming.

The howl rang across the land and echoed through the cave of eight families of Gugwes. Around a small fire, Burly was playing with some children of his clan. That stopped as the howl rumbled through the cave's network.

Burly was beloved by his clan and once led a rebellion against the original clan's framework in the late 1970s. The up-and-coming young buck was not a fan of the old leader, who always ran from danger instead of taking it head-on. That leader was his father. The young Burly taught four adolescents how to hunt when some human hunters mistakenly ran up on the Gugwes. The scared humans opened fire, killing three of them as they fled for their lives. But by the time the humans began loading their trucks with the bodies of the dead for proof, Burly had returned with reinforcements unknown to his father and had slaughtered the men and retrieved the dead adolescents.

This enraged his father, who feared a hunting party would search for whatever was responsible. His father's worst nightmare came to pass. Armed men had tracked the Gugwes' location in the woods, and a massacre followed. A few had gotten away before an intentional fire destroyed all the evidence to cover up the mess. The men reported the fire to the public as random due to a dry spell and the summer heat.

Burly directed his clan to evacuate, just as they had planned. He stood guard at the ledge, scanning over the darkness as all the families frantically climbed the secret path to the mesa of the mountain. With a large handmade tactical hammer in his right hand, Burly looked for the red eyes shining through the darkness, but he heard helicopters closing in from a distance instead. Multiple helicopters were closing in quickly. Burly followed the last family of Gugwes up the path. After a quick look back over the ledge down into the saddle, he finally saw what he had been looking for earlier. The red eyes cut through the dark and were closing in quickly from about two hundred yards away.

Burly directed his lieutenant to continue the plan and that he would catch up with them later. After a very brief dispute, his lieutenant understood the situation. They embraced forearms before he left his childhood friend Burly to defend himself.

After watching his clan move out of sight into the darkness, Burly turned his attention back to the ledge. Despite the helicopters closing in, he knew they could not escape if Jefferarri were onto their scent.

Finally, the last of the Hellams's bloodline. It must end here tonight. The future of Burly's clan all came down to this moment. One of them will not walk off this mountain alive.

It didn't take long before the glowing red eyes popped up over the ledge with the lightning crackling in the background. Jefferarri made his way onto the mesa of **the mountain**, crawling on all fours at first. He shook the water off his coat like a wet dog before he stood on his two hind legs.

Burly observed the transformation of Jefferarri compared to Jefferarri's father when he killed him many decades ago, as well as his grandfather. How Jefferarri's leg bent back like a dog's with a stifle and hock but still with a little human element in them. The torso area had a tapered waistline up to his large shoulders. His arms were built like a bodybuilder's, with huge, large hands and five long-fingered claws at the end of each. Short, brownish hair or fur covered his entire body except for the front of the torso area. A shaggy mane covered his short ears and flowed down his face to the middle of his back, forming a V-shape. Long, sharp canines were in his short muzzle, and white vaper flowed with each breath. The Hellams's eyes were still there, giving away his identity if there was ever a doubt.

"I'll end your bloodline . . . this night, Hellams!" Burly professed, raising his hammer for the fight of his life. He wielded a giant roofing-like hammer as big as a man.

Jefferarri tilted his head to the side like a dog listening but not comprehending. Drool dripped with the rain. The rage that grew inside of him, Jefferarri did not understand, but it motivated him to attack and slaughter what stood before him. He let out a guttural growl.

The helicopter flew up from behind Jefferarri, shining its high beams through the heavy rain at the two beasts. Emitting a shrill, Burly charged Jefferarri. Jefferarri dropped to all fours with a sinister grin to meet Burly halfway.

Burly swung his hammer, cutting through the falling rain, just missing Jefferarri's face as Jefferarri ducked under it. Jefferarri's claws cut deep into Burly's side as he slid by in the mud, causing Burly to yelp and clench his side. Blood oozed from the four gashes and ran down his leg.

Lightning continued to light up the stormy night. Jefferarri swiped his claws at Burly, backing him up. Burly tried to get a little distance to reset, but Jefferarri was much faster than Burly remembered, not to mention the size difference that came with it. In this form, Jefferarri was nearly as tall as Burly when standing on his hind legs. A smile formed on Jefferarri's face again as he walked a half circle around Burly before Burly leaped at him. Jefferarri was not expecting to be stabbed deep into his shoulder with the pick end of the hammer. Blood splashed through the falling rain that covered Burly's face and chest. Jefferarri threw his head into the falling rain, letting out a cry that was heard across several mountains. Burly's brute strength tossed Jefferarri across the wet, grassy mesa, slinging him off the hammer. A blood trail followed Jefferarri as he slid across the wet mud and weeds. He squirmed in pain, favoring the wound on his shoulder. Burly rushed Jefferarri, slamming the pick of the hammer where Jefferarri's head was. However, Jefferarri heard him coming and sprang out of the way.

Two more helicopters pulled up on the opposite side of the mesa as their beaming spotlights lit up the flat top like a circus. Burly wasted no time rushing Jefferarri with the hammer, swinging away, backing Jefferarri up, who was still yelping in pain. Jefferarri ducked under the hammer, then jumped on Burly's shoulder, biting and gnawing at Burly's neck. Knowing this was Jefferarri's favorite target, Burly used his hands and arms to protect his neck, but the canines were ripping off chunks of flesh and fingers. Deep, painful lacerations caused Burly to yell out in pain before tossing Jefferarri off to the ground. Loose flesh hung from Burly's arms and hands. Blood ran with the rain down to the ground as he winced in pain. The exposed bones in his right arm were so painful that he had to switch hands with his hammer.

Jefferarri shook the torn flesh out of his mouth, not enjoying the taste. Seeing Burly injured, he pounded the ground, rushing in for the kill. However, not as skilled with the hammer with the other hand, Burly was too slow swinging the hammer at Jefferarri. Jefferarri pounced on him, knocking Burly on his back, and the hammer slid away from him. They wrestled in the mud. Jefferarri's jaws snapped at Burly's face, but Burly couldn't hold him off with his bloody forearm. Burly fell into deep survival mode. Jefferarri's claws dug into Burly's flesh from every angle, cutting his skin like a hot knife through butter.

Burly got weaker by the second as more blood continued to spill out of his body into the mud and rain. The two locked eyes for a quick moment. Both were breathing heavily. The rain poured off Jefferarri's face into Burly's. Burly's wide-open eyes signaled the end, while Jefferarri's bared teeth and lowered eyebrows told a different story. Jefferarri let out a deep gruff.

Quickly, Jefferarri rose up and slit Burly's throat before biting a chunk of flesh from it. Blood painted Jefferarri's face faster than the rain could rinse it away.

Burly, the mighty leader of the Gugwe, took one last look at the beast that had been a thorn in his clan's side for decades. The two locked eyes again as Burly took his final slow breaths that flowed from the ripped windpipe of his throat, splattering blood upon his very own face. Fog blew from Jefferarri's gaping mouth from exhaustion as he looked down at his conquered foe.

Then Jefferarri stood up and looked down at Burly, whose dead eyes stared into the abyss. He let out a victory howl that rang out for miles. He focused on savoring the revenge so much that he did not see the six mercenaries sneaking up quietly from his left wearing night vision goggles. They opened fire on Jefferarri, hitting him in the shoulder and his leg. Jefferarri grunted before he took off faster than expected, zigzagging among the bushes. Bullets flew everywhere from the men. Suddenly, two more helicopters appeared and opened fire on The Order's helicopter that had been tracking Jefferarri across the mesa, causing it to crash to the ground, lighting up the mesa in a hot red flash. Luckily, four of the men jumped out before the crash.

Jefferarri rushed to the opposite edge of the mesa. Down below, a river flowed between the mesa and the butte of the mountain. The mercenaries opened fire on Jefferarri again, with some bullets opening up his torso. Jefferarri fell to the ground and whimpered in pain. Blood poured out of the enormous bullet holes that riddled his body.

The task force shot at the mercenaries, killing two of them before they returned fire, wounding one of them. The wounded soldier fell to the ground, screaming in pain as his calf muscle flapped out of his pant leg. One of his comrades stopped to assist him.

"We gotta slow him down to get close!" the head of the mercenaries shouted.

As soon as the head mercenary said that, his comrade beside him got snatched away. His gun flew into the air as Jefferarri dragged him away before any of them could react. The man screamed in pain . . . until it halted.

Suddenly, Jefferarri tossed the lifeless body back into the pack of men, knocking one of them down to the ground.

The task force posted up behind a large boulder, shooting back at the mercenaries.

"Keep an eye out for that beast!" Jason informed his comrades. Another mercenary got cut down as a bullet from one of the task force's men passed through his neck.

"Mayday! Mayday!" Jason yelled into his headset radio. "Need immediate reinforcements and evac ASAP! Under heavy fire, over!" But all he got in return was static. "The radio is down," he blasted to his men.

The white noise continued over the radios as the task force awaited a response. From a safe distance, Jason observed Jefferarri taking out the mercenaries, one by one, through his night vision goggles and the flashing gunfire. The spotlights from the helicopters could not keep up with the beast, even with the bullet holes in his body. He listened as the mercenaries yelped in turmoil and confusion. Through his night vision goggles, he saw body parts tossed around. The more body pieces littered the ground, the less screaming they heard.

Suddenly, all the screaming stopped. The only sounds were the rain and the helicopter propellers. The moving spotlights pierced through the night revealing the heavy gun smoke from the carnage. .

Bullets abruptly ripped through the landscape again. Jefferarri chased down the mercenary who was shooting back at him and ripped open his neck from behind. Blood flew from his neck like a geyser into the air. The last mercenary ran behind Jefferarri until he reached about fifteen feet away. He held something in the air as Jefferarri launched into the air at him, then . . . *boom!*

The left side of Jefferarri's chest exploded and knocked him back to the edge. Jefferarri stumbled to his feet. Smoke rose out of his chest as he staggered closer and closer to the edge. His head flopped backward, and his arm hung down his side like the walking dead. Smoke flowed from his opened mouth.

"Bye, mutherfucka," the lead mercenary said as he opened up the assault rifle upon Jefferarri, sending him over the edge down the long drop to the river.

Jason opened fire on the last mercenary, who fled behind large rocks. The helicopter opened its big guns on the task force, making the last two take cover. Trees were chopped down, and bullets around the men ripped up the shrubbery. The mercenary escaped on a rope from the helicopter before it disappeared into the darkness. Then the radio stopped singing static.

"Bravo, copy." Jason came through the radio. "The chopper's down! The chopper crashed! Jefferarri is down!" he said in a weak voice. "He's gone. I repeat . . . Jefferarri is gone. Come get us out of here."

CHAPTER 16
JEFFERARRI IS GONE

"**H**OW LONG BEFORE the crew gets there?" Moody asked as the view of the drone followed Jefferarri, climbing up the mountain.

"ETA 140 seconds," the monitor responded.

"Jefferarri is no longer in tracking mode," Anna informed. "He's hunting to kill."

Matt's words put a smirk across Bill's face. He was eager to see the beast at work and learn what the talk was about. He had plans for the beast if things went his way.

The drone rose from the side above the ledge as the monsters had their standoff. Jefferarri had some size on him. He was easily seven feet tall, but compared to the massive humanoid across from him, it seemed like an unfair fight. The Gugwe was nearly twice as wide as Jefferarri, with a significant height advantage. Matt had seen the aftermath of Jefferarri's fallen foes, but like Bill, he'd never seen him in action. Even though that was about to change, Matt was very nervous about what was about to go down on the mountain.

"What's the history behind these two?" Bill asked.

"Ugh, this guy," Anna said in response to Bill's question.

"Read up on your history of The Order," Matt said in disgust. He had grown aggravated by Bill. Something in his spirit just did not sit right with Matt about Bill.

Continuing with the same smile, Bill raised his eyebrows and directed his attention back to the fight.

The two titans clashed in the rain. The amazing speed of Jefferarri and the brute power of Burly were on full display. Not long after the clash started, the helicopter arrived.

"Sir, the helicopter has arrived and is awaiting your orders," the staff person said.

Moody had a moment of hesitation. It was no surprise Jefferarri was going to war with this clan of Gugwe. The target was the entire clan, not just Burly, even though erasing Burly would be a plus.

"Drop 'em!" Moody commanded. "See what they can find. And tell them to be aware that Jefferarri is a wild card!"

"Mobile Command, you are clear to land," the staff person said. "Eliminate any Gugwes. Be cautious of Jefferarri."

"10-4," came over the speaker.

The nervous Command Center watched the task force undock the helicopter. Each one of the task force had a camera on his helmet.

Some of the staff gasped when Burly stabbed Jefferarri with the pick of his hammer. As scared as people were of Jefferarri, remembering the events back at the Gibson farm, everyone in the room cheered for the antihero.

"Sir, I'm picking up incoming on the radar. Two more helicopters coming from the south," a second staff person said. "They just appeared from out of nowhere."

"They were flying under the radar," Moody said.

"Ours?" Bill asked Moody.

"Negative," Moody answered. "Can we get an ID?"

"No ID showing on the radar, sir," the second staff member said.

Moody quickly walked over to the second staff station and pushed the button to speak. "Bravo, be advised—"

Static flowed from the speakers, and some of the staff members put the palms of their hands over their ears. Even Moody squinted his eyes during the noise. Someone turned the volume of the speakers down. The monitor also showed no video, just a black display.

"Communications are down, sir," the staff person said. "They are using some type of communication block."

"A jammer!" Moody slammed the palm of his hand on the second staff person's workspace in frustration, causing a clamorous thud, "Gotdammit!"

"Sir," the second person said to Moody as she pointed at the fuzzy monitor.

Silence filled the room. The unknown and confusion ramped up many of their heartbeats. The staff people worked diligently to fix the problems.

"What's going on?" Matt asked Moody.

"Can't you see that I don't know!" Moody snapped, then caught himself. "Get me something!"

Matt waited patiently for any news to pop up as he paced back and forth. Anna sat in the corner of an unused chair she removed from the workstation. She hoped Jefferarri was okay, but something deep in her gut suggested otherwise.

"You need to send backup!" Anna yelled at Moody. "Send more helicopters!"

"Let me do my fucking job!" Moody returned the same energy before asking a staff member to send another team. "It will be at least an hour and a half or two. This was unexpected."

The static over the speaker stopped, breaking the friction in the room. The staff person turned the volume back up.

"Bravo, copy?" the staff person spoke.

"The chopper is down!" Jason said, his voice coming through choppy.

You could hear a pin drop in the room. The drone screen had remained dark, letting everyone know the drone was also down. Five of the six helmet cameras had returned to the bottom of the screen. One camera view showed dead eyes locked into the camera as if they were looking at the people in the room. Only two of them had any movement. Another camera view showed the bloody, injured partner next to the other body.

Moody got ready to speak but was interrupted by Jason.

"We need evac and medical. Only two of us are left. Jefferarri is down," Jason said in a weak tone. "He's gone. He is gone," his voice tapered off.

A dark cloud of energy filled the room. Anna stormed out of the Command Station. Matt stared at Moody with the look of death, then followed behind Anna.

In the hallway, Matt caught up with Anna as she walked in a circle with her hand on her forehead. She tried to fight off her feelings, but it was obvious to Matt how much pain she was in. Matt was bombarded with his own emotions and confusion. He followed her down the hall, trying to keep up with her younger legs moving toward the elevator. She pressed the up button on the panel, then turned away, keeping her back toward Matt.

They remained silent until they got to Matt's office. Matt opened and locked the door behind him after Anna walked in. Anna could no longer hide her emotions as a tear dropped from her left eye and then the right.

"Something stinks," Matt ranted. He flopped down in his chair at his desk before taking off his jacket, letting it fall behind him in the chair.

Anna tried to wipe her face, knowing there was no longer a need to hide her feelings anymore. It was apparent Matt could see. She took a second before responding, "This was clearly intentionally done. And right after what happened a mere month ago at the hospital."

"Clearly," he quickly responded. "I'm going to get to the bottom of it."

"This rabbit hole may run deeper than you can imagine," Anna said. "The outcome could be bad." She leaned over on Matt's desk next to him, locking eyes with him. "I'm in. The bigger question is, now, who can we trust?"

"It could get messy," Matt warned.

"I'm a messing bitch," she replied.

Matt took a deep breath and leaned forward, propping his elbows on the desk. His hands cupped his scruffy chin. "I have to tell Eugene and Octavia."

Octavia's prolonged ear-piercing wail filled the room, prompting Roseline to rush into the bedroom. The vision she just received moments ago brought uncontrollable tears streaming down her face as she crumpled to the floor in pain. Her chest burned like being poked by a hot branding iron. *She knew, she just knew.*

Octavia wore a white tee and pajama pants. Her body was held up by the side of the bed, and her cell phone was facedown on the floor a few feet away.

"Octavia." Roseline bent down beside her to comfort her. She knew it had to be some bad news about Jefferarri. Maybe it was something he said on the phone or a message he had sent. In her mind, it was surely nothing that could not be fixed. The two were inseparable. She pulled Octavia into her chest, squeezing her tightly in a warm, welcoming embrace. Roseline's blouse became wet from the tears that flowed uncontrollably, mingling with the snot from Octavia's runny nose.

After letting Octavia express her emotions, Roseline placed her hands on each side of Octavia's face. "What's the matter, dear?" Roseline asked in a soft tone. She watched the purple veins travel and pulsate on Octavia's face. "Calm down, calm down," Roseline begged. "Talk to me."

"Jefferarri is dead!" she wailed, followed by another uncontrollable cry.

Speechless, Roseline stood frozen in place, her eyes wide with disbelief. The weight of Octavia's words settled in her mind, sinking deep like a sponge absorbing water. The air held a hint of uncertainty. Roseline's thoughts swirled in a whirlwind of confusion and curiosity. She resisted the urge to question Octavia's words and instead allowed them to replay in her mind, hoping for clarity to emerge from the fog of uncertainty. *This can't be real.*

Roseline was in the kitchen, putting the finishing touches on Octavia's hot tea, the warmth of the cup seeping through her fingers. All kinds of thoughts floated in her mind. Even though this outcome was not that farfetched or uncommon, the fact that it happened to Jefferarri was so surreal. *What now for Octavia?* Roseline thought as she poured the steaming tea into the cup from the pot. *Octavia would be all alone in a dangerous and corrupt organization.* Now, the last of the hunters, her love and protector, was gone. Things could get rather interesting and *not* in a good way.

Roseline brought the tea into the bedroom and set it under the lit lamp on the nightstand beside Octavia. Octavia rested her back against the headboard. Her knees were pulled up to her chest with her arms wrapped around them. She was just staring off into the distance. Roseline sat down in front of her feet.

"Did Matt tell you what happened?" Roseline asked.

Octavia lifted her head and shook it. "No," she said. "As soon as he told me, everything went kinda blank. I don't remember much."

Roseline reached over and grabbed the tea. "Drink some tea. It will help you rest."

Octavia put her knees down and took the tea. She blew across the top of the cup and then took a small, quick sip.

"Thank you," Octavia said as she glanced into the cup. She paused a moment before she continued. "This whole day just didn't feel right. Now that I look back on it, when they sent him home, security left him alone just hours after his arrival, knowing someone tried to kill him." She took another sip of tea. This time, the sip was a lot more aggressive. "The only thing that was mind-boggling to me at the time was them sending him out right after that shit."

"What are you thinking?" Roseline asked but already knew the answer based on her own speculation.

"I'm not sure. I need to talk to Matt," Octavia enunciated.

"Are we safe?" Roseline asked in a concerned tone.

All Octavia could do was look at her because she did not have the answer and had not thought about it. It was a legit question now that Jefferarri was gone.

CHAPTER 17
WHO TO BLAME

MATT STOOD AT the see-through glass door to Eugene's room at the hospital. Matt usually checked on his friend once or twice a day, so when he walked into the room and saw his friend flirting with the nurse, he smirked before quickly realizing why he was there and took a deep breath. *Give the women hell* was the saying Matt had for his old friend when it came to the ladies.

"My man," Eugene said in a more upbeat tone. "You're here early, I see."

"And you're up and at it early this morning giving them hell, I see," Matt joked, trying to hide the dismay in his voice.

"Not yet," Eugene replied as he looked at the nurse.

The shapely blonde blushed at the freaky words of the old man. "I'm sure you two were something else back in the day."

"I'm still something else today," Eugene cracked. "Wait until I get out of this bed, girl. You can run, but you *cannot* hide."

Matt dapped up his buddy. It was a good look to see Eugene in better spirits.

"Could you give us a minute, please?" Matt asked the nurse with a fake smile on his face. "Just a few minutes."

Eugene knew his partner, and he knew that fake smile better than he knew himself. Eugene's chipper face turned into a more serious expression in the blink of an eye. He knew his friend had some bad news.

"Sure, take all the time you need," she said, grabbing the trash, her chart, the used medicine cup, and the syringe before leaving.

Eugene continued to look at Matt in anticipation of whatever blow he was about to deliver. Deep down, he prayed it had nothing to do with Jefferarri, Octavia, or both. Once the nurse closed the door behind her, Eugene wasted no time rushing it out of Matt.

"Give it to me straight, no chaser," Eugene said with his eyes still locked on Matt.

Matt unbuttoned his black jacket before he sat in the recliner across from the bed. Eugene noticed Matt swallowing and biting down on his teeth. Eugene abided by his wishes to cut through the chase.

"What did Jefferarri do?" Eugene asked, and then he continued. "Or what happened to him?"

Matt went through the whole story about what happened in that very room when Jefferarri attempted to kill Moody up to the assassination attempt on Jefferarri's life in the hospital. Eugene's anger rose, and his blood pressure spiked, causing the vital sign machine to alarm the staff. The nurse rushed in and silenced the machine.

"Come back in a minute," Eugene demanded of the nurse.

He had no smile, so she decided she would do as she was told. She could sense the contention in the room and figured it was best to leave it be. It had to be important and was not for her ears, so she nodded and left the room.

"I take it they never found the son of a bitch?" Eugene asked in disgust, but he had already known the answer before asking.

Matt answered his question with a headshake. He went on to explain to Eugene about that he'd only found out about the mission several hours after Jefferarri had left.

"That's bullshit," Eugene fussed, slightly raising the numbers on the vital sign machine even more. "Jefferarri is expendable to those motherfuckers," Eugene continued with even more heated emotion.

"Was," Matt said.

"Come again?"

"Was," Matt responded, followed by a brief pause. "*Was* expendable," he continued.

Eugene's eyes widened for a few seconds before the shock set in. Matt glanced over to the vital sign machine to check out the numbers, then exhaled and continued to tell Eugene everything he observed in the Command Center.

"I don't have any other details yet. What's left of the task force will be debriefed. Hopefully, in the next hour or two after they receive medical attention," Matt explained.

There was a moment of silence in the room; the only audible sound was the strong current from the A/C vent. Eugene held his emotions better than Matt had expected. Still, the hurt in his heart was visible on his face. He woke up one day, and the man that he looked after as a child was now dead before he had a chance to say goodbye.

"I tried so hard to protect him," Eugene said in a low voice. "I was so scared that he would reach level five . . . that someone would push the button to terminate him, and I'd be the one to die trying to prevent it."

Matt thought back to the moment in this very room where he almost pushed the button before the trigger tumbled to the floor.

"Octavia knows?" Eugene asked.

Matt nodded.

"Who ordered the tracking?" Eugene asked.

"I don't know," Matt answered. "I'm going to find out. As you know, normally, someone from The Order makes the call. It's possible that Moody had a role in it. He hates Jefferarri."

"And last but not least," the investigator reported, "there was evidence in corroboration with the surviving members of the task force that a trigger was used to detonate the bomb attached to Jefferarri's heart."

Back in the corner of the room hidden from view, Matt and Anna sat side by side, observing everything. Anna's body posture changed once the investigator took his seat and opened his notes. Their facial expressions were of shock and misunderstanding. Unsurprisingly, it was an inside job, but only two people outside of The Order knew about the triggers, where to find them, and had the necessary codes.

Whispers filled the chamber from the men of The Order who sat around the table of the dimly lit room. The lights bouncing off the table from the bottom of the balcony did little to illuminate the surrounding space. At the head of the table sat the old man, Mr. Haskins, who looked like his health was in question. His body was trembling, and Matt wondered if it was from health issues, nervousness from guilt, or alcoholism.

"How do you know it was a trigger, not a bullet?" Mr. Anderson asked.

"Our investigation uncovered that a trigger is unaccounted for and missing from the vault. Video footage has either been altered or tampered with. And the code used to enter the vault could not be retrieved," the investigator said. "And samples of his chest cavity, including heart muscle fragments collected from the scene, showed traces of the explosive that was found on those tissues that are not found in bullets or gunpowder."

Matt sat up in his seat. The news about the inside job did not surprise him either. So many possibilities were at play that pinpointing the wrong person would be too easy. This would be a game of "catch me if you can." He paid close attention to the faces and mannerisms to see if he could pick up anything, but nothing stood out except how quiet Bill was compared to how he was usually. But it still was not proof he was in on it. Matt turned and glanced at Anna, who met his gaze. He could see that Anna's eyes were watery before she attempted to wipe them dry. The description was a lot for her to hear let alone hide.

In the opposite corner, not far behind Bill, was Moody. Matt could see the alcohol course through his veins. *Guilty or not, he has got to feel the heat, but I seriously doubt he would put his brave men's lives on the line, even if he hated the sight of Jefferarri*, Matt contemplated.

"Where is the body?" Bill asked. "We need to get it before the buzzards." He had another agenda. He did not want to lose the body for personal purposes.

There was a long silence that seemed like minutes, but in reality, it was only a few seconds as the investigator adjusted his body in his seat and leaned into the microphone.

"Due to the rising levels of the water and the blood trail down to the river, it is believed his dead body was carried downstream, and we have yet to recover it." Whispers echoed through The Chamber again. The investigator continued. "With teams working around the clock and with the best equipment on the planet, I expect his remains will be found at any moment, provided the alligators or large snapping turtles do not get to him first."

Matt observed Bill drumming his pen on his pad before he made a quick note on it. Matt had no special abilities, but he felt a negative aura flowing from Bill. Anna felt the same way, but it was much deeper in her gut. She automatically felt Bill's wicked vibe. In her mind, all she had to do was to prove his guilt.

Both Matt and Anna knew they brought in Bill to take over the highly classified research department, and rumor had it that they were using old cryptid cells to create their own monster. They were creating a monster that could be controlled.

"How is it possible for someone to get a trigger?" Mr. Anderson asked. "Things like that are locked tight. We have military-grade security, do we not?"

"Even though the technology and security here have been maintained, upgraded, and updated on a regular basis to the highest of standards, it's a constant battle to fight off some security threats. I said that to say this . . . It's harder to maintain when there is help from the inside. All it takes is a little knowledge of how the system works."

"So, is it safe to say it was an inside job?" Mr. Strickland asked in a blunt voice. He pushed his glasses further up on his nose with his pointer finger.

"No, sir, I cannot say it's safe to say," the investigator replied. "But—"

"I'm sorry," Mr. Strickland cut him off. "You mentioned that one of our triggers was stolen, correct?"

"Yes," the investigator answered.

"You need a code to get in where the triggers were located, right?"

"Yes, sir. From what I was told, that is correct," the investigator answered.

"And everybody has their own code. There is no sharing of codes, nor was your investigation able to retrieve this . . . this 'ghost code,' I guess we can call it. Do I understand correctly?" Mr. Strickland said. His tone got more aggressive with every question.

"That is correct, sir," the investigator's tone was one of submission.

"We stored the triggers in an undisclosed location that only The Order members and two others knew about. And with all the video cameras posted up around here . . . We have nothing. Even if it was hacked from the outside, someone had to take it physically. I'm sorry. I know you deal with facts of evidence, but my gut feeling is telling me someone or some people in this room, or the gentleman who is recovering at the medical building, had a hand in this. Tell me about your findings from the assassination attempt on our once-beloved prized hunter. And does this have any relevance to this case, sir?" Mr. Strickland said, dropping his glasses on top of his notes. He sat back in his chair, giving the investigator his full attention.

"This case interrupted that investigation," the investigator responded.

"You're short of staff?" Mr. Strickland cut in with the question. "Are you a one-man show? I'm confused."

"We are a three-man team," the investigator replied. "And that's based on a budget given by The Order." The investigator slid in the smart comment. He continued, "But that's probably because there are never any major injustices happening within the organization until now."

"What is the status of what happened in the medical building with Jefferarri?" Mr. Haskins interrupted.

"Last night, the staff person that was to be on duty that day was found murdered in his apartment. He was found on his kitchen floor with his throat cut. Several fingers and his badge ID were missing. That's all we have for now. Other than that, we still don't understand how the intruder could get into the room with the ghost codes."

"Thank you. I know you are doing your best," Mr. Haskins praised. "Please continue to apprise us as things develop."

"Thank you, sir," the investigator said.

"One more thing," Mr. Strickland added. "How were our communication capabilities rendered useless during the . . . the ambush, I guess you could call it?"

"At this time, I have no clue, Mr. Strickland. We expect it was on board one of the helicopters that arrived on the scene," the investigator said.

"How did they know where our boys were going to be?" Mr. Stickland asked.

"I don't know, sir."

"Again, is it not safe to say it had to be from someone of knowledge?"

"That is correct, Mr. Strickland."

"Well, from my understanding, the only people who knew the mission were insiders," Mr. Strickland pressed.

"Sir, I don't have any info on how the information was leaked."

"That is all," Mr. Haskins said, dismissing him.

The investigator nodded before getting up and leaving. Matt watched him pass before his eyes squinted over to Mr. Haskins. *Why did he cut Strickland off from asking the tough questions?* he thought.

"Everybody's guilty," Matt joked in Anna's ear.

Anna gave a quick smirk and a headshake as she watched the investigator leave, then strolled her eyes at the table of misfits. A dark cloud filled her gut. Getting her hands on the culprit would be her priority, no matter their rank or title.

Bill broke the silence. "We have another issue that has brewed up north."

"The Flesh Eater," Mr. Anderson added.

"Out of all my years in this organization, this Flesh Eater is a thorn in our side," Mr. Haskins said.

"We lost two of our best hunters to this monster, and now we don't have any," Mr. Anderson said, pressing the palms of his hands down on the table. His skin turned purple.

With a deep breath, Mr. Haskins looked at Matt. "What's the latest on Hopkinton?" he asked.

Matt met Mr. Haskins's gaze as he paused for a moment. He tugged to shift his mindset from Jefferarri's death to a different beat that was just as important but had lesser meaning to him at this moment. He cleared his throat and found the energy to stand up. His knees popped, and a stiff back showed through his face. *They could have done this at another time. This is bullshit.*

"So far, we have installed a curfew on the residence."

"A curfew?" Bill interrupted. "We have an alpha predictor feasting like it's Thanksgiving, and the best you can do is a *curfew?*" Bill took a moment to give Matt a hard time out of spite.

"If you don't mind, shut the hell up," Mr. Strickland said. "He has more time out in the field than you have on earth. Respect this man."

Bill nearly choked on the lump in his throat. "My apologies, sir. With all that's going on, I have to do better. I will get it together," Bill said, putting on his best acting job, but the slight smirk told a different story of his thoughts. "I'm just as distraught about the events and what happened to Jefferarri as most of you."

With another deep breath and a slight headshake, Matt continued. "We have boots on the ground, and they are working with the local authorities. As Mr. Haskins mentioned, this is nothing like we have ever dealt with before. We believe this thing took down not one but two elite hunters. The Twins, I'm talking about. They haven't been seen since."

"Why wasn't Jefferarri sent in after the Twins disappeared?" Mr. Strickland asked. "Or why wasn't he sent instead? I mean, it was no secret what he could accomplish."

"Well, sir, there were two reasons. One was he had just come off a hunt just a week before. Under rule four, section two, the hunter is mandatorily suspended for two months if the hunter was physically engaged with a hunted subject."

"And the second?" Mr. Strickland said.

"He was closing in on the red zone. Level five." He paused for a quick second, then continued. "He was also struggling with mental health issues."

"Mental health?" Mr. Anderson blasted.

"Yes, sir. The doctors thought it was due to the changes in his anatomy."

"He had a girl for that," Mr. Anderson said. "She had just one job."

"Yes, probably why it didn't get any worse than it did."

"I understand," Mr. Haskins said. "Thank you."

Matt took a seat. His eyes met Anna's eyes as his back touched the back of the chair. *All these old, fat-ass buzzards no longer care to know about what goes on in the field. It's apparent those old fools don't read the reports anymore.*

CHAPTER 18
THE FLESH EATER

As THE DYING overcast light filtered down past the naked treetops, two rednecks jumped out of an old white beat-up F-150. The youngest, Jimmy Blue, a young Caucasian male, slammed the door hard.

"Quiet down before we get caught," Bert Busbin whispered in a low tone to his nephew as he lowered the hunting rifle that touched the four inches of snow below him. With the curfew in full effect, Bert felt the urge to go against the grain. He wanted to be a hero.

Jimmy's wide eyes scanned his surroundings as his heart nearly beat out of his chest. He had a million questions about hunting the mystical creatures. If he had it his way, the chubby teen would be back home playing his favorite video game online from the safety of his room under the tutelage of his mother. Unfortunately, his uncle bullied him to *become a man* and *do something meaningful for once*. Jimmy struggled with the gray, oversized, Russian-style fur hat that dangled over his eyebrows.

Just thirty feet away from them, the FBI agents, along with the local authorities on duty, kept people out of the streets during the curfew. Three agents huddled around a heater next to the black camper-style RV. Automatic weapons hung from straps off their shoulders. Laughter came from them as one became the comedic one. They let their guard down just enough for Bert and Jimmy to sneak past.

Bert had a lot of hunting experience. His first kill came at the age of twelve. On the other hand, Jimmy only shot tin cans in the backyard with a BB gun. Bert led the way, eating jerky and sipping on rum. Jimmy had no appetite for the first time in a long time. The snow was shallower under the cover of the trees than outside the woods, but it was still high enough that they had to lift their feet higher than usual to walk. A cracking sound flowed from the woods like someone heavy had stepped on a twig.

The sound halted Jimmy in place. He asked, "What was that?"

Bert rolled his eyes and twisted his lips. He took a deep breath before turning to Jimmy and jacked him up by the collar. An owl flew past and landed on a branch a few feet ahead of them.

"I'm sick of you acting like a pussy," Bert said, backing Jimmy up. The stench from Bert's mouth nearly choked Jimmy. "My sister ain't raised no sissy!" He tossed Jimmy to the ground. The snow fluffed around him. "Get your mind together, boy! This is no time to be a fucking pussy!"

Jimmy was a momma's boy and not the brightest star in the sky. He was kind of slow compared to others in his age group.

Bert took a sip from the flask, then extended his hand to his nephew. Jimmy didn't want his help but took his hand to keep the peace. *As much as I hate leaving my mother, I will leave this place. I will join the military if I don't get accepted into college.*

"Here," Bert said. He shoved the flask into Jimmy's chest. "Have some of this."

"I'm good." Jimmy rejected the offer.

Bert looked at him with an icy stare and said, "I'm not asking."

With a brief hesitation, Jimmy firmly took the flask, took a small sip, and immediately squished his face before letting out a long grunt. Bert laughed at the rookie, then took another big swig from the flask.

"Whew! Here . . ." He shoved the flask back into Jimmy's chest. ". . . have another. This time, get a good swallow."

In fear of what would happen if he rebelled, Jimmy took another drink. He let out a longer grunt, this time with a squinted face. The queasiness in his stomach overwhelmed him.

"There you go, Nephew." Bert aggressively patted Jimmy's chest in approval. "Put some hair on your chest. I'ma make a man out of you yet. One that your mama would be proud of."

Bert broke off a piece of jerky and handed it to him. "Here, chew on this to put something on your stomach."

Suddenly, they heard a similar grunt in the distance, but it had a more demonic undertone, like a low-quality recording on a cassette tape. The sound paralyzed their bodies. No sound followed as if the forest had gone dead. Bert raised his rifle as his eyes scanned their surroundings. An adrenaline rush mixed with the rum had Bert on ready.

"What was that?" Jimmy asked. His eyes opened wide, and his heartbeat slammed against his rib cage. In the cold, chilling air, quick bursts of misty clouds escaped his breath.

"It's time to earn those stripes, young man. Get yourself together. It's showtime."

Next, they heard footsteps running in the distance. Whatever it was, it wasn't trying to hide from them.

"You hear that?" Bert asked.

"Yeah!"

Both men aimed their rifles from a ready stance into the surrounding woods. More footsteps crunched in the snow, obviously circling the pair. A horrible smell of roadkill and wet dogs cut through the silent, frigid air.

"Jimmy," his mother's voice called out to him. The pair could not tell where the voice was coming from.

Bert turned in a complete 360, trying to pinpoint where the voice originated and ensure it did not sneak up behind them. A gust of wind nearly pushed Jimmy's hat off, but he grabbed it before it took sail.

"Mom," Jimmy said in a surprised tone.

"Hush, boy," Bert said. "I don't think that's your mom, Jimmy."

"Jimmy, what are you doing out here?"

"I'm with Uncle Be—"

"Boy, hush up, I said!" Bert hollered. "That's *not* my gotdamn sister. It's trying to separate us or draw you in somewhere. Don't fall for it."

"Jimmy, you're in so much trouble if I have to come and get you!" the voice warned.

Snow flurries came in behind the wind and picked up steam by the second that shook from the trees above. The footsteps increased in speed, circling them again. Jimmy's eyes watered from the frigid wind.

"Ready your rifle!" Bert said. "Get it up! Shoot anything that moves—except me." He spoke in a forceful tone against the wind.

Sniffling, Jimmy readied his rifle as he was told. Chills ran through his body. *Coming here was a big mistake*, Jimmy thought. The wind howled past them, and the swirling snow made seeing twenty feet around them hard.

"Jimmyyyyyyyyy!" the voice said as it tapered off into a darker tone.

Jimmy's breathing became more rapid and sporadic. *I want to go home*, he said to himself, something he dared not tell Bert.

"C'mon out, you son of a bitch!" Bert squawked.

"Bert, come here and rape me over and over again like you did the day after my husband's funeral," the voice said. Now, the voice sounded like a recording being played backward.

"Shut the fuck up!" Bert barked through the howling winds. "Fuck you! I ain't do nothing."

Jimmy always noticed that his mother's demeanor changed for the worse when his uncle came by the house. Now, he knew why. *I should shoot him right now.* Jimmy pointed the rifle at his uncle's back, but a sense of danger overcame him, and something made him look up into the branches of the trees surrounding them. That is when he saw the face peeking from the shadows of the trees. Through the swirling snow and the wind pounding against his eyes, he saw deadly, dark eyes pierce through his soul and darkly stained teeth lining an agape mouth. Without saying a word, Jimmy dropped the rifle and took off running. He was unsure if he was going in the right direction, but he just needed to escape the boogeyman.

"Jimmy, come back here. Don't believe what it says. It's messing with your mind."

A heavy crunch in the snow sounded directly behind Bert. His heart fell into his stomach as his eyes widened and chest tightened. The potent odor choked him. Pride created a fake smirk across his face before he turned around with the gun. Nothing was there. His eyes stirred across the dark woods. *I need to get out of here.* Without hesitation, he scurried through the snow in the same direction as his nephew ran.

"Jimmy!"

The temperature dropped 20 degrees below what it was ten minutes ago, and now Bert's clothes were not working as they did earlier. The freezing wind was too much to bear. He heard clicking and popping sounds following behind him. Crunching footsteps accompanied the sounds that kept pace with him.

"Hunnngryyyyyy," something whispered in his ear. Warm breath breezed across his frozen ears. The smell choked him again.

He turned around with his rifle, ready to pull the trigger, but he saw only a blur of footsteps right behind him. The wind did not mask the lingering stench that filled his nose. *You better stop playing with me.*

"Fuck you, muthafucka!" he blasted. His emotions got the best of him. "I'm Bert Busbin, bitch!" He flopped his arms out to the side.

He turned around and saw it about twenty feet away Its pale skin blended with the snow, making it even more challenging to see through the snowstorm growing by the second.

His face turned blue, and his body shivered from the cold as he lifted his rifle in its direction. The creature crawled a few feet toward Bert before it stopped and slowly rose on its two legs. Bert could not see much more than a vague outline. He raised his head as the figure towered over him. Now, he was hyperventilating, knowing he had made a grave mistake coming there. *If this is the end of me, that's fine, but I ain't going out like no bitch.*

"Come on, you son of a bitch!" he belted while stumbling forward but kept his balance.

Then without hesitation, Bert squeezed the trigger.

After several minutes of running, the pudgy teen stopped and bent over with his hands on his knees to catch his breath. Jimmy gasped in the cold air. The weather had lost its strength the further away he ran. A rifle boomed and echoed from a distance. Jimmy stood up and looked back in the direction he had just come from. *I hope you die, you fucker.* He took off in the opposite direction toward the agents. He figured he had to get to the agents if he wanted to live another day. *Please, God, let me be going in the right direction!*

He heard the ghastly sound again. This time, much closer than before. He huffed and puffed with each step. The cold air beat against his stinging, dry eyes as the storm picked back up in strength very quickly. The sound of snapping branches closed in on him. Another screech rang out not far behind him to the left.

"Help meeee!" he cried to anyone who could hear him.

The next one hurt his ears. It was so close. He zigzagged through the trees, hoping it would buy him some time. The wind bombarded him, and the snow diminished his visibility.

"Helpppp meee!" Unfortunately, his screams were drowned out by the howling wind.

"Where are you?" a voice from a distance asked.

"Help me! Help me! Please! Oh God!"

Suddenly, a sharp pain burned his back, causing him to yell in pain. It was enough to force him into the snow face-first. The creature grabbed Jimmy by the leg, sinking his sharp fangs into the flesh, and cold crawled deep into the bone. A gunshot rang from the left, and the creature released him. The Flesh Eater's screech relayed its anger.

Jimmy looked to his left and witnessed the dark figure violently toss the agent into a tree, breaking his back. The smoking Ruger pistol flew in a different direction.

More gunshots blasted nearby. Four agents closed in on the creature. Muzzle fire brightly lit up the trees and snow. The AR-556's bullets dug into the creature's flesh, spilling black goo across the snow and on Jimmy. This only pissed it off more. The beast moved through the heavy snow and trees like a blur. Screams of a dying agent ripped through Jimmy's ears, then quickly was followed by another. Now, Jimmy only saw three muzzle flashes. He tried to get up and run, but the pain in his leg dropped him back into the snow. Something grabbed Jimmy's arm, and he let out a scream.

"C'mon!" the Black female agent commanded. She tossed his arm around her shoulder. She grunted, trying to help the heavy guy up from the snow. "We got to get to the RV *now!*" she yelled, moving as quickly as possible since Jimmy favored his bloody leg.

They heard another agent scream. His scream was short-lived, and now only two AR-556s were shooting.

"Help me," an agent called from a distance, followed by a horrific scream that also ended abruptly. Only one AR was shooting now.

"If you don't get a little more hump in your step, I'm going to leave your ass. C'mon!"

The RV was within reach, about thirty yards away. Jimmy toughened it out through the unbearable pain and the swirling wind and snow. A blood trail followed behind him. Now, the gunshots stopped. Jimmy looked back as they ran to the RV. Even with the howling wind, they heard thunderous steps rapidly approaching. A mangled body flew past them, just brushing against Jimmy's shoulder. The bloody body slammed into the RV, leaving a large bloodstain next to the door.

"Shit!" the female agent shouted.

They made it to the side door of the RV, and she swiped her ID badge, but it did not open.

"What the fuck!" Jimmy said in a frightened tone.

She swiped it again, and it cleared this time. She opened the door, pushed him inside, and she quickly followed, slamming the door behind her. He flopped into one of the desk chairs, grimacing in pain.

The inside of the dark-lit RV smelled like black leather that covered the three office chairs on the right of the door and the booth bench and table by the left wall. Three computer monitors were set above the extended desktop that faced the door. They sealed the front of the RV like a cockpit.

Boom! The RV shook. The creature ran into it, causing the RV to rock. Jimmy nearly fell out of the chair from the impact.

The agent tried the radio, but it did not work. So, she dropped the radio and stood guard, facing the door with her handgun out. Her eyes were wide open. She was shaking so badly that she jumped and hissed each time the creature pounded against the RV. The creature continued its attack on the door and the side in rage as it shrieked . . . and then it just stopped. Both Jimmy and the agent were panting by now.

After a moment of silence, the agent relaxed a little, then grabbed the first aid kit to treat Jimmy's wound.

"What the fuck were you doing out there?" she asked.

Confusion and exhaustion settled upon his face. He could not get the words out of his mouth from shivering.

A desperate pounding came at the door. "Let me in, please," the muffled voice said through the door from the outside that imitated one of the dead agents lying on the snow. The agent's eyes got big, and she put her finger to her lips to warn Jimmy to be silent. She gripped her gun and stood guard once again. Jimmy noticed that her gun shook in her hand that aimed at the door.

"Let me in before it comes back, *please!*"

The pounding and begging continued, but she knew better than to open the door with the storm still at full strength, making the RV creak.

"Open the door, bitch!" Now, the voice turned demonic. The RV rocked side to side like a baby cradle close to tipping over. The foul odor filled the tightly sealed RV. It continued, "I'm going to rip your skin off and eat your guts—both of you as I feed the hunger!" Then it stopped. A silence lingered in the air that left them uneasily quiet.

Finally, the creature let out a yelp before retreating into the woods on all fours.

CHAPTER 19
THE COMPOUND

THE SUN PEEPED through the noon clouds after many days of rain. It'd been six days since the botched raid on the Gugwe and Jefferarri's demise. Mr. Haskins stood at the top of the six-story building overlooking the Vista Apex Compound, known simply as the "Compound." His eyes swept across the forty-five-foot, barbed-wired electrical fence that separated the mini-city from the surrounding woodland. The cool breeze moved his blue and white scarf and the thin strains of hair that fell from under his black skullcap. *So much has changed since I started. We've come a long way.* He admired the work that had taken place since he started with The Order as he looked down at the guards that patrolled the perimeters. The elevator chime caught his attention.

"I've never been up here," Bill said after he stepped off the elevator. "It's cold here." He gripped his jacket around the collar to shield the wind.

Mr. Haskins checked his watch. "You are early," he said. He strolled over to Bill with his hands in his wool black trench coat.

"I was already up," he said.

"No cane today?"

"Nah. My mind is so forgetful these days. Call it old age."

Bill held the elevator doors open until Mr. Haskins finally entered. *How the fuck did you forget your cane?* Bill rolled his eyes as the door closed. Noticing the camera in the top right corner, they kept quiet from the sixth floor to the first. Once the elevator door opened,

Bill followed Mr. Haskins into the lobby. A few people hurried about their day in passing. Mr. Haskins kept the conversation light.

"How's that project of yours coming along?"

"Good," Bill replied. "We're so close."

"Good. I want to see it before I croak."

"You mean before you use it?"

Mr. Haskins stopped and turned to him with a serious gaze. "That too, my boy." A smile popped on his face.

Bill opened the silver Rivian R1T electric truck parked in the no-parking zone for Mr. Haskins. After shutting the door, he walked over to the driver's side, got in, and clicked his seat belt. Then he glanced over at Mr. Haskins, who was not wearing his.

"No seat belt, sir?"

"Oh, hell no. Fuck that rule!"

"Now, now, Mr. Haskins. Seat belts save lives, right?" Bill cracked.

"It should be *my* decision."

"It's the law," Bill egged on, getting a kick out of Mr. Haskins spazzing out. A slight snicker escaped his mouth.

"Didn't I tell you, the hell with that law?"

Bill chuckled at Mr. Haskins's old ways. "You're a piece of work, sir."

"That I am, young man. That . . . I am."

They drove off the sloped curve onto the light brown brick road. People headed to work, walked on the sidewalk, and drove golf carts on the road, including the Military Police and guards. A sign came up quickly, reading the fifteen miles per hour speed limit. The Vista Apex Compound ran a good three-mile radius.

The living quarters housed everyone essential to The Order, from some maids to the heads themselves. There were some exceptions where some individuals and families lived off the Compound as Jefferarri did, but the rules made it nearly impossible to enjoy. Also, retired people moved out to make room for the new replacements.

The round buildings were to the left of the road, and the tallest stood eight stories high. Modern living arrangements had ivory-colored balconies surrounding each floor of the same-colored building. Plants hung off the balconies, giving the buildings a more vibrant appeal even in the cool season. Four other tenant buildings surrounded the Compound, each with its own design and style.

"The breakfast food smells good over there," Bill said, referring to one of the two food courts on the left after the left turn. "It makes my stomach hungry after my little oatmeal this morning."

"Hmm."

The food court had a sandwich spot, a buffet, and a pizza and hamburger restaurant. The courtyard provided ample outdoor seating with tables and chairs and the choice of indoor dining.

"What did you have this morning?" Bill asked, making small talk until they reached their destination.

"Buttered toast and coffee."

Bill glanced at him, waiting for him to add more, but it never came.

"Just buttered toast and coffee? That's it?"

"Uh-huh."

"Okay, then," he said, raising his eyebrows.

The Hoffa Building, at only ten stories high, towered over the other buildings. It stood in the center of the Compound, heavily guarded on all sides. Those wishing to enter had better not have forgotten their badge. The Medical Annex was located opposite it and was much smaller, only five stories high, with a landing pad on top. Armed guards patrolled the perimeter of the all-white building. This was where Jefferarri and Eugene had been. They drove between the two buildings on a road with major traffic. Some people were on foot, and others were in carts.

"I see we haven't found Jefferarri's body yet," Mr. Haskins said as Bill turned into a parking space labeled for the executives. "By now, I don't expect us to."

"Are you sure he's dead?" Bill said, killing the power to the cart.

The surgeon implanted the device between Jefferarri's left and right ventricles. Even Jason's statement said there was a hole big enough to stick your head in.

"I was told you had to sever the spine from the head to kill him. Not even a bullet to the head could kill him."

Mr. Haskins let out a quick giggle. "Well, that would just about kill anything, you think?" He opened his door to ease out.

Bill jumped out to rush over to give the old man a hand, but Mr. Haskins was already out by then. They weaved through the passersby to the revolving door, where they scanned their badges to get in. Security awaited them on the other side as they walked through the metal detector and X-ray machine.

"Mr. Haskins," the security guard greeted with a nod.

He nodded back with a titter and continued through. Bill followed and then caught up with him. Everyone moved around in a hurry. Some carried papers or briefcases, and some nothing at all, but all with the same goal.

The duo jumped in the middle of the three elevators, the only one that went down. Two service elevators on the hall around the corner ran to the top and the lower levels. Everyone called the lower level "The Down Below."

"How long has it been since you have been Down Below?" Bill asked.

"Oh God, years."

"Why so long?"

There was a moment of silence before Mr. Haskins exhaled. "The smell of the evil we do down here for the betterment of man stinks." He paused for a moment as his eyes lifted to the ceiling of the elevator. "Sometimes, I had to question my own values. People need people like me. Like us. People who disapprove of what we do, but they can't live without it."

Bill raised his eyebrows and pressed his lips together with a slight nod. *The old buzzard is on to something.* "I understand."

"People want medications to cure illnesses and diseases to feel better. They want the best military, but yet, many of them don't appreciate using animals, or even humans, to research those cures."

"It's a cold game, Mr. Haskins."

"Indeed, it is." Mr. Haskins followed him off the elevator. With a smirk, he rolled his eyes at him.

The elevator opened up to a thirty-by-thirty-foot room with a desk and four heavily armed security guards. The duo continued to the eye scan on the left. Mr. Haskins went first, trailed by Bill. A guard read the results of the scan on her tablet. The results gave their names and the status of whether they were cleared to enter.

"Enjoy," the young guard said, then directed them through the door.

They entered another area constructed of brick walls except the glass wall in front of them. A well-lit lab faced them from the other side at a lower level. While upstairs, people in casual clothes and suits roamed. Most of the people Down Below wore shrubs and lab coats. Armed guards stood in random spots with high-powered assault weapons. Their clothing was entirely black. Computer stations and monitors aligned the tall, white walls in various areas. Stairs surrounded the middle floor from the elevated platform for easy access, excluding the floor-level hallway that ran to double doors at the end of the room.

"My God," Bill said, staring through the glass.

Mr. Haskins stood beside him, speechless, and focused on the same thing.

The two took themselves right to the shrub room to put on the personal protective equipment, consisting of a nonwoven Tyvek coverall suit, gloves, hairnet, and shoe covers. Once suited up, they walked through the air shower and onto the floor.

With his protective equipment on, Moody met them halfway at the bottom of the steps. "Good morning," he said, without any emotion.

"Moody," Mr. Haskins replied.

"Good morning," Bill said.

They tread on the heels of Moody to the table. Chills ran down Bill's spine as he followed Mr. Haskins. Moody looked back at Bill, then back at the steel gurney. *Punk!*

"Burly?" Mr. Haskins said.

"Yup," Moody acknowledged.

"Burly?" Bill said, standing back from the gurney. "Of the Gugwe?"

Moody nodded and pinched the top of his nose. "In the flesh."

"Our boy did a number on him," Mr. Haskins said.

"Yup," Moody replied.

"Why is it still chained down if it's dead?" Bill asked. He pointed at Burly.

The gargantuan creature's enormous feet dangled over the edge of the stretcher, its weight causing the gurney to creak under the strain. The lifeless form was securely fastened with sturdy steel cables, tightly binding the carcass in position. Two laboratory technicians meticulously scrutinized the remains, their gloved hands delicately tracing the jagged wounds and shredded flesh that disfigured the robust physique.

"Because sometimes when we think they're dead," Moody said, then turned to Bill, a grin crossed his face, "they are not."

"You got to be fucking shitting me right now!" Bill spat.

Mr. Haskins smirked at Bill's reply, then continued. "I almost forgot how bad they stink."

"Mr. Bill," a voice called from behind them.

They all turned in that direction. The pretty, petite, chocolate assistant in her protective gear stood at the top of the stairs. Her protective equipment fit a little too long for her short stature.

"Yes," Bill responded.

"It's time," she said.

"Okay," Bill said. He smiled at his constituents and waved them forward.

After leaving the lab, they disposed of their gear and traveled down the long, dim hallway to the end. An armed guard accompanied them to the elevator. All five of them went down the elevator to a lower level nicknamed "The Abyss."

"Creepy," Bill said. "And we haven't even gotten to the real shit yet."

The woman scanned her badge on a monitor next to the elevator at the end of the hall. The doors quickly parted to allow them entry. She tapped the D3 button, and the elevator descended.

The doors opened up to another hallway that curved back on both ends. The hall had little air movement and less light than the hallway above. They entered a door directly across from the elevator where Dr. Vera, a short, pecan-tan woman, greeted them with a smile from ear to ear.

Moody's heart melted as her alluring scent hit his nose before he saw her.

"Good morning, everybody. Come on in," she said. "Have a seat."

"Giorgio Armani Si," Moody said, naming the smell-good she was wearing as he walked by her. She smiled at his words. It made his legs weak, so he quickly grabbed a chair.

The room had luxury, stadium-style seating with rows of five seats each. A large window opened to a view of a large floor the size of a basketball court with twenty-five-foot-tall white walls. Two large-sized garage doors faced the window, each with its own number and color.

"I'm hoping everyone is having a great start this morning. I'm not going to hold you people up. Surely, you have more important things to take care of. However, I hope to, at least, have you leave here with a positive outlook for the C-9 file of the Cryptid Project."

She stepped aside, and Moody observed the ten-inch spider web-shaped crack at the bottom of the window. *Something hit that window pretty hard.* He quickly got back on point.

"What type of glass is that?" Moody asked, pointing at the large nine-foot-tall window that stretched across the wall before him.

"Polycarbonate glass," the escort said.

The lights dimmed in the room.

"Open door number one, please," Vera said into an intercom on the wall.

The lights in the observation room went dark. Only the lights from the window gave some light. The blue garage door labeled number one slowly rose open. A white male peeped out of the door. His head and eyes roamed side to side.

"Hello!" the man called out before looking up at the dark windows up high.

"Mr. Roger Hedell, Caucasian male, born July 6, 1987," Vera said. "Tried and convicted May 7, 2019, on sixteen counts of rape and sodomy, sixteen counts of kidnapping, and fifteen counts of first-degree murder on September 10, 2022."

"The Mississippi Snatcher?" Moody asked.

"Excellent, Mr. Moody," Vera said, impressed.

"But he was executed by lethal injection," Moody said, leaning forward in his chair and making eye contact with Mr. Haskins.

"That's what the public thought," Mr. Haskins said. "But he was only given something to put him out temporarily. He was immediately transported here. For this moment."

"You know how the saying goes. Play stupid games," Bill said, "win stupid prizes."

Moody wanted to ask more questions but figured that *the less I know, the better.* He played it safe and shrugged his shoulders. "It is what it is," he said, flopping back into his seat.

Roger crept out in the open, wearing only a hospital gown. The black garage door closed behind him. He looked at the window in front of him and realized this was an awful place to be.

"Open door number two," Vera spoke again into the intercom. The red door slowly crept up, revealing the darkness behind it. A chill ran across Roger's skin, and he backed away from the rising door.

His heart pounded fiercely in his chest, weakening his knees. He continued slowly, taking a step back from the door. Finally, the door reached the top, displaying darkness. An aggressive, snarling reverberated from the darkness that shook Roger's body. Heavy bipedal footsteps echoed from the dark.

An enormous figure stepped out of the darkness. The sight of the creature caused Roger to fall back on his butt. He back-crawled up against the wall with nowhere to go. His arms were spread out in mercy toward the glass. "Help me, please!" he sobbed. "Help!" He curled up like a kid in the corner, about to get an ass whipping.

Everyone in The Chamber stood up except Mr. Haskins, who smiled in delight. You could have heard a pin drop in there.

They watched the beast stalk Roger. Its shoulders and chest rose with every breath. The creature looked down at the much-smaller being in front of it. It had a short snout around the jawline but with other facial features, like Jefferarri in werewolf form. It had Jefferarri's eyes with a slight glow of red, broader shoulders, and larger arms than when they last saw Jefferarri. Immense muscles twitched under the skin. The beast did not have any hair. It had more pointed ears but a smaller lower body than Jefferarri. It had sharp, three-inch claws that could cause some serious damage to any flesh. Although powerful, the skinny legs and hocks did not match its bulky upper body, unlike Jefferarri.

"Clone?" Moody queried after noticing the distinct features.

Vera smiled at her accomplishment. "Yes, but bigger and faster than the original." She paused for a moment to relish the expressions on their faces. "And controllable."

"Impossible," Moody replied.

"J-C149, stand down," Vera said into the intercom.

The beast grunted, then stepped back as it glanced up at the window. The look on his face said he did not like the command. It turned its attention back to Roger and squatted in place for the next command.

"Wow!" Bill shouted, followed by a standing handclap. "Marvelous!"

Vera smiled at Moody, observing the wide-eyed look on his face. He glimpsed at her stare, then sat down. He placed his forefinger under his nose and continued to watch through the window.

Mr. Haskins stood up finally and shook Vera's hand and then Bill's. The smile on his face stretched for miles.

"So, what other tricks can your dog do?" Moody said, with a slight tilt of his head and interlocking his fingers resting on his lap.

"C'mon, man," Bill said, not liking Moody interrupting the moment. "Lighten up, will you?"

"I'm impressed," Moody said, then sat back up. "I just want to see more."

"Even if that's the only command it knows, it's a start," Bill snapped. "You fuck—"

Vera touched Bill on the arm, interrupting him. She returned to the intercom. "J-C149 . . ."

The beast's ears twitched as thick saliva hung from his lower jaw. An evil grin blossomed on his face as he continued to keep his eyes on Roger.

"Sic'em."

Roger did not know what hit him. A short wail filled the large room. Within a heartbeat, the beast's canines ripped Roger's throat to pieces in just a matter of seconds. His claws ripped off his head from what remained of his neck and slung it across the room, leaving a trail of blood and gore that escorted it. Blood covered its face as the beast continued to tear into the headless body, feasting on Roger's warm flesh.

"Anything else, Mr. Moody?" Vera asked. She smiled, but her sinister eyes gazed into his own.

A thump from the window redirected everyone's attention to it. A lot of blood dropped down the window as the mutilated body fell to the floor. J-C149 focused on the window above him. It waited for his next command.

"Good job, boy. Return to the kennel," Vera commanded.

J-C149 bared his teeth and shook its head. It turned and dropped to all fours and ran back through the red door. The garage door closed behind it.

"He did not like that," Moody said.

"What is your problem, Moody?" Bill replied.

"My problem is you get that killing machine outside these walls, and it decides it doesn't want to come back or follow the damn commands! You'll have a huge, bloody problem on your hands. And you talking about an *army* of these things?"

"All right, all right," Mr. Haskins said, losing patience with the bickering. "It's a work in progress, and we've got time. Now, if you will excuse us, Vera and I have other pressing issues to discuss."

Moody did not turn Vera's way as he walked out with the rest of the spectators. A small lump formed in her throat. She made a mental note to catch up with him later.

CHAPTER 20
JIMMY RETURNED HOME

JIMMY SAT AT the dinner table for twenty minutes, using his spoon to play with the grits and eggs he loved so much. The skin around his eyes was slightly darker than the rest of his face, and he had not combed his hair in days. A chair propped his freshly bandaged leg up beside the table. The chubby kid usually had a problem just tossing food down his throat without chewing it properly. That used to drive his mom crazy. The morning sun's rays from the window separated them at the dinette table in the kitchen. His mom, Ashlee, had only taken a couple of bites from her grits, which now lay in a cold, solid state on her plate.

"Son, you haven't eaten in a few days. You need to eat something before you get sick."

Her son had been eating less and less by the day since the events in the woods. She had noticed a change in his demeanor as well.

The usually kind-mannered teen rolled his eyes at his mother without lifting his head. The hairs on the back of her neck stood up. She waved it off as the stressful situation from the past few days.

His eyes locked on her for a long time, and silence filled the kitchen before his eyes blinked. He shook his head, then turned to her with a smile. "Yeah, I know, Ma." He forced a small portion of eggs into his mouth.

"Your clothes are getting too big for you already," she said. The neck part of his AC/DC tee hung slightly off the front of his neck. His shoulders and chest, which once filled out the top of the shirt, no longer did so. She also saw it in his cheeks. Ashlee had always been on her son about being overweight, especially since his father passed away from complications of diabetes.

Ashlee was tall and skinny but ate just as much as Jimmy did. However, she never gained any weight. She blamed herself for her son's obesity, never forcing him to put the fork or the game controller down to go outside to get some fresh air and exercise. She never paid as much attention to Jimmy as she needed to because of her very own demons.

"I'm hungry," Jimmy said. "Just hard to eat for some reason." He forced another spoon of grits into his mouth, trying to keep his facial expressions from showing his displeasure. The eggs did not feel the same in his mouth as they used to. He just could not put a finger on what it was. *Maybe the grits will taste better.* His spoon sliced through the cold, gelled grits, and he forced them into his mouth and down his throat. They tasted horrible.

Ashlee remembered getting the call from the hospital. After rushing to the hospital, the men in the black suits held her up from seeing her son. As she waited, the authorities told her a bear attacked them, killing Bert and injuring Jimmy. Once the men in the black suits came out of Jimmy's room, one man handed her a business card and told her to call this number if she saw a change in his appearance or he started saying weird things.

When Ashlee entered the hospital room, she could see tears streaming down Jimmy's face. She rushed to the side of the bed and hugged him. That evening, Jimmy was unusually quiet and responded with terse, one-word answers. She chalked it up as part of the shocking experience and decided not to pry him for details.

Suddenly, Jimmy started vomiting up the grits and eggs back onto his plate. Ashlee tore off some paper towels from the roll on the table and hurried over to him. She put her hand on his back, and he suddenly hopped up on one leg.

"Get your fucking hands off me, bitch!" He looked at her with twisted rage in his eyes.

She jumped and fell back against the sink. The paper towels *and* her heart sank to the floor. She placed her hand over her heart, trying to catch her breath.

Jimmy's piercing gaze penetrated her soul, causing a shiver to run down her arms and the hairs on the back of her neck to stand on end. In that instant, her heart raced, a surge of adrenaline coursing through her veins. Without warning, Jimmy collapsed to the floor, his body convulsing uncontrollably. The sight of foam frothing at his mouth filled the air with a pungent smell of fear. Shell-shocked, she struggled to regain her composure, her senses momentarily overwhelmed. With uncertainty weighing on her, she knelt beside him, feeling a mix of confusion and helplessness, unsure of how to intervene.

"Jimmy," she called.

Hesitantly, she put her hands on him. The air felt heavy and suffocating, causing her to struggle to catch her breath and tense up.

"Oh my God," she said. She reached for her cell phone off the table to dial 911, but the weak signal prevented her from completing the call. She shook her head, but not surprised. The signal strength in her area worked when it wanted to.

Jimmy's shaking and foaming at the mouth stopped abruptly, and she scrambled to find a way to help him. There was no way she could tote the big teen to his bed.

Several hours later, a cold draft slowly woke Ashlee up from her sleep. The cold air brushed against her eyes, making them blink. A flattened blanket lay next to her. She lifted her head and realized Jimmy had disappeared. Dandruff and flaky skin covered the pillow. She looked around and saw the back door in the kitchen wide open, then looked up to see both doors on the refrigerator were also wide open. She sprang up as fast as her middle-aged bones would allow. Then she saw him through the back door. His white tee stood out in the night with the help of the kitchen light passing through the doorway. They were a tad smaller than the last time she saw Jimmy, but the clothes stood out. His shorts had fallen to his knees.

"Jimmy?"

He stood there without responding. The chill in the air made her body shiver, and she hugged herself tightly to keep warm. Her breath misted in front of her face as she inched closer and closer to the door.

"Jimmy?"

Still no reply. She crept forward. The strong, chilly winds ripped waves through his shirt. She saw something in his hands but couldn't quite make it out at first, but the closer she got, she saw and recognized the pack of pork chops she bought from the market the day before.

"Jimmy, are you okay?"

"Jimmy, are you okay?" he repeated. "Jimmy, are you okay?"

She grabbed the knife off the counter and then stepped out the door. Her muscles trembled, and her breath misted white from her mouth. The cold, howling winds made her shiver more, and the porch floor reminded her that she wore no shoes.

"Jimmy, are you okay?" he repeated.

She noticed frozen meat with a bite mark while looking down at his hands. His nails had darkened since she last remembered them. She eased her way to his side and saw his pale face. Blood had smeared and frozen across his cheeks, lips, and chin. His dark eyes did not move even as the freezing wind brushed against them. They stared motionless out into the abyss, piercing through the darkness before him.

He quickly took another bite into the frozen pack of meat. The sudden movement made her hiss, and startled, she stepped back. His teeth crunched through the frozen pack of meat.

The cold air cut through her shivering bones and caused some tingling in her fingers and toes. Her mind begged her to go back inside. Hesitantly, she swallowed the lump in her throat and reached for his arm. He turned his head to her in a blur. His dark eyes quickly faded back to normal.

"Mom," he said.

Ashlee nearly fell on the slippery, cold porch but maintained her balance.

"I'm cold," he said, dropping the pork chops by his feet.

She extended her arms out, keeping as much distance between the two as possible, placing her hand on his back and slowly guiding him inside again. His dingy, tighty-whities and shorts cuffed his ankles, causing him to take baby steps. She closed the door behind them.

"Let's get you in the bed," she said.

"I'm hungry, Ma."

The foul odor from his mouth made her breath stall for a moment. *It smells like something crawled up in you and died*, she thought. "Okay. I'll get you something to eat, but first, let's get you into the bed."

"I'm so hungry," he repeated.

She laid him on his back in his bed and removed his underwear and shorts. After placing his dirty clothes in the basket, she got a wet rag and wiped the blood off his face and hands. More than just blood clung to the rag. Her eyebrows furrowed, and a dazed look of bewilderment crossed her face when she saw the number of dead skin flakes on the rag. *This is not normal. I got to get you to the hospital. The odor now seems to come from more than just your mouth. It's filling the room.*

"You'll need a shower later on, son." She covered him with the comforter and then left the room.

Still shivering, she grabbed her cell phone and stood beside the living room heater. "Dammit," she said, with no bars on the phone shown.

Something caught the corner of her eye. Just outside the kitchen window, an owl sat on the windowsill giving Ashlee its full attention before it flew out into the dark. Paying the owl no mind, she unsuccessfully attempted to use the cell phone again. With her battery on 9 percent, she took it to her bed and lay down. She plugged the charger into the phone and made a few more unsuccessful attempts to place a call. Before she knew it, drowsiness had overcome her.

She felt her eyes close and her mouth open as she rested on her back. Nature took its course without a fight. After an eventful day, exhaustion took over her body.

The creaking from the bedroom door made her open her eyes. She realized she could not move or speak. Clomping noises slowly inched their way closer to the bed. Her breathing became more rapid the nearer sounds came. As she listened, the incomprehensible whispers in her ears grew louder. Now, she detected the smell of rotting meat. The same smell she had last remembered from her son. Her eyes looked over at the door, still unable to see what she heard, but she felt the presence as tears ran from the corners of her eyes. She felt her heart beating a hundred miles an hour.

What she saw next made her wet the bed. The light of the lamp on the nightstand displayed something large and hunched over on the opposite wall. A shadow of a creature with large antlers, like a deer, looked over from the foot of the bed. A static sensation crawled on her skin. She felt the impact of something climbing onto the bed. The weight of it made the bed squeak. A muffled hiss hummed from her mouth. Her chest rose and fell more rapidly by the second as she fought to move. She heard and felt something cold and wet dripping on her T-shirt.

It did not take long for the monstrosity to reveal itself. It had the head of a deer skull with an enlarged snout and dark, empty eye sockets. Its gaping mouth held five-inch canines surrounded by razor-sharp teeth. Unable to see the creature in its entirety, she knew it could not fit through the door. The repugnant odor choked her. The teeth had flesh snuck between them. It let out a screech that caused dark brown drool to land on her face and in her eyes. The creature's jaws stretched unnaturally wide before it bit down on her face.

Ashlee jumped up in a sweat, breathing uncontrollably. She frantically rubbed her face for drool, then scanned the room. Nothing out of the ordinary stood out. Finally, believing she experienced a horrible dream, she focused on calming her breathing. She sat on the side of the bed, took deep breaths, and grabbed her phone before she got up to check on Jimmy.

A cold draft in the hallway gripped her body as she reached Jimmy's room. The cracked door revealed an empty bed and a rotten odor made her scrunch up her nose, even with the window opened. Snow formed on the window and floor from the outside. She did not see Jimmy but saw greenish-brown matter tainting the bed sheet. Vomit filled her throat. Hand and footprints of the same substance plastered the wall and ceiling and led out through the opened window, causing her eyes to widen.

"Jimmy," she said, clutching her phone to call the police. Then she remembered the men in the black suits who had told her to call if anything unusual happened with Jimmy. *Yeah, this shit is definitely out of the norm.*

She grabbed the card the men gave her and called the number. "Yes, this is Ashlee Busbin. Men in black suits asked me to call this number if my son's behavior changed. Yes, I'll hold." She held for a moment while she peered out the kitchen window. She hoped to get some answers.

CHAPTER 21
PLANS FOR HOPKINTON, NEW HAMPSHIRE

COMING OUT FROM the surrounding tree line, twelve guards, including Jason, closed in on Jimmy's house in the quiet, still, cold air. Heavily armed men with automatic weapons crept through the shallow snow and the low, thick, foggy yard in all-black fatigue with black baseball caps to match.

Moody followed behind his soldiers. Most of them were new to The Order, as he had to replace those who died in the North Carolina fiasco against the Gugwe. Being ex-military with impressive résumés and interviews made it easy to fit them right in, and they came right on time.

Moody casually walked up to the door with his gun dangling by his side in his hand. Six of his soldiers trailed behind him. He stopped a few feet in front of the door before gesturing the men to go forward.

Matt stepped out of the RV to watch from the distance. Like many times before, he got into character, as he had done for so many decades. Anna stepped out and stood beside him. Usually, she would have had something to say, but today, she had been unusually quiet.

"You okay?" Matt asked as he turned his head in her direction.
"Yes."

An agonizing scream flowed through the door, followed by heavy footsteps moving quickly, the men felt the pounding vibrations from the wooden porch. Another scream just a couple of seconds later, more high-pitched sound pierced through the heavy wood door.

Moody discreetly flashed a quick hand signal, signaling to the men to crash the party. *Bam!* One of the men kicked open the door, and then all of them rushed into the house, one behind the other, with guns drawn. Immediately, the smell of iron and death pierced through the cold air and hit Jason in the face. He looked left to right, checking the position of two other men in his sight, then over to the black paddy wagon, followed by the RV roaring up the path.

Matt hurriedly descended the RV's cold steps, his boots crunching through the freshly fallen snow. He plowed forward, determination etched on his face as he made his way towards the house. "Be ready!" he shouted over his shoulder to Anna, his voice filled with urgency.

Moody walked into the home in time to see Ashlee's naked body hung by the cord that had once fed to the ceiling fan, swinging and twisting in place. Her dead eyes stared back at him as her body turned. Blood dripped into a puddle on the floor. The room was in disarray, with the oak table and chairs scattered and damaged. The beast had ripped her clothes to threads and spread the tattered pieces across the floor with broken parts of the ceiling fan, everything covered in blood. Her chest, buttocks, and stomach bore the marks of a violent attack, with huge chunks of her flesh missing. Her left arm had been violently torn from its socket, and her right thigh was gnawed down to the bone. The sight and putrid smell made him gag and cover his face with his hand. At that moment, he knew it was not Ashlee who screamed.

An ear-splitting scream from down the hall, alerted the men to that direction. However, a crash made the men hesitate and slow down. Finally, the men rushed into the open third bedroom. A large hole in the ceiling dripped blood into the bed below where the ceiling plaster had fallen. The automatic weapon lay under the bloody rubble on and around the bed. Heavy footsteps pounded the attic. Jason rushed with his weapon drawn as he weaved through the men. The sight startled him, and sounds filled the air, causing his eyes to widen.

"He's dead already. Kill it!" he yelped, talking about his comrade. They shot up in the ceiling, causing dust and debris to fill the room. Another screech sounded before the ceiling collapsed over the bed and onto the floor. With a thud, Jimmy landed on the bed, collapsing the bed to the floor. His elongated claws clutched Ashlee's heart tightly. He turned to face the men, his dusty jawline streaked with blood, and met their stares. One of their comrades' body dropped out of the ceiling behind him as it flopped and bounced over the debris on the bed.

Stopping at the door, Matt could feel the rapid, rhythmic thumping of his heart against his ribcage. Jimmy grew about four inches taller than when Matt last saw him. Jimmy's discolored bloody and naked skin had tightened around his bone structure from head to toe. Clumps of hair were missing from his head. His eyes sank back into his head, and his arms and fingers were longer than normal. Even his legs, feet, and toes were unusually long. The nails on his bloodstained fingers and toes had turned black and overgrown.

Jimmy shrieked through the dusty mist at the men. His jaw dropped a little wider than a standard jaw. His teeth got longer from the back to the front.

Jason quickly raised his gun and put two bullets into Jimmy's chest. Jimmy scratched at the wounds Jason gave him, then took a few steps toward Jason before Jason shot him with a single shot in the forehead. The other men followed suit and riddled him with bullets. Smoke flowed out of the bullet holes. Jimmy tossed the heart into his mouth before he sprang out of the window behind the headboard, shattering the glass.

Outside, behind the house, Anna swung her ancient daggers at Jimmy, missing her mark. Ducking under the knives, Jimmy swiped at her with his claws, but she sidestepped and stabbed him in his side. Jimmy released a gut-wrenching scream as he dropped to one knee on the snow. Dark reddish blood, almost black, stained the snow below him from the bullet holes and dripped from the handles of the daggers.

Anna positioned her other dagger to decapitate Jimmy.

"Anna," Moody said, rushing from around the corner of the house. "Step back! Now!"

Pointing her daggers at Jimmy, she obeyed and took a few steps back.

"Follow the plan," Moody said to her.

Jimmy lunged at Anna but did not get very far as one man shot a stainless-steel mesh net around him. Jimmy tangled up in the net and then fell into the snow. The paddy wagon truck rushed in reverse to within a few feet of Jimmy. The back door flipped down, forming a ramp, and then two men ran up the ramp into the truck.

One man stood beside Anna with his gun aimed at Jimmy, who was still struggling in the net. "Knives?" The Caucasian man with the gun said. "Why not just use the guns you have on your hip?" He displayed a crooked smile, looking over at her.

She felt a bad vibe from him. Her eyebrows and forehead wrinkled as she sized him up. "What's your name?"

"They call me Ego."

The two men brought out a chain and quickly hooked it to the net before running out of the way. Another man hit the side of the truck twice, signaling the driver to roll the chain. They watched the chain drag Jimmy up into the truck.

"Well, Ego, how did those bullets work out for y'all in the house?"

Ego smiled. "You have a point."

Jimmy let out a long cry as he left the snow and was dragged on the ramp. The men double-tapped the side of the truck again, and the ramp started to close up.

"Jason," Moody said, walking up to him. "Burn it down—quickly."

"Yes, sir." Jason ran off into the house.

Matt walked up beside Anna, biting his bottom lip. He felt responsible for what had taken place here. "I should have never let her bring it home."

"You weren't sure."

"That's the problem. I didn't know. That's the reason why I should not have let him go."

Once the ramp closed, Moody commanded everyone to move out. Within moments, smoke came from within the house as Jason ran out the back door.

"Let's go!" Moody yelled to his crew.

Everyone double-timed it to their respective vehicles and sped out of dodge. The fire in the old house spread quickly and burned in the background of the fleeing vehicles.

"I'm not feeling the new henchmen, Moody," Anna said. "I got a bad vibe from one of them."

"Me too," he replied.

CHAPTER 22
DIXON X THE FLESH EATER

DETECTIVE DIXON PULLED up at what little remained of the Blue House. Smoke swirled with the wind and snowflakes. Three other deputies' vehicles aligned in front of the house. Tiny snowflakes began to land on their windshields as the snow drizzled down.

Fletcher greeted Dixon as he stepped out of his black 2019 Ford Explorer with a cup of store-bought coffee.

"Cream and sugar, as usual," Fletcher said, handing him the coffee.

"Appreciate you kindly, sir. So, what do we got?"

"Welp, we have not seen or gotten in contact with Ashlee or her son, Jimmy, yet. The family and friends are in the same boat and haven't heard from them either. Once the fire is completely extinguished, a more detailed search will be carried out, although no bodies have been discovered yet."

"We just gonna let it burn?" Dixon asked, then took a sip of his coffee. "God, this is hot."

"Yes. The place was already a total loss by the time we got here. Adding water will only weaken any evidence at this point. I'll leave the investigation to the expert," he said, referring to Dixon. "I plan on searching the woods once more deputies show up."

That makes sense, Dixon thought. He took another sip of his coffee and turned toward the tree line. It felt like someone—or something—was watching them. So that he would not sound paranoid, he kept that feeling to himself.

"There are also several faded tires and boot tracks all around the place."

Dixon scanned the snowed landscape. Gusts of wind moved snowflakes across the area, which would surely cover any imprints in the snow.

"Most of the footprints appeared to come from the woods in unison. And then there are these weird sets of deep footprints coming and going to the woods."

"I need to see it."

"Okay, if the wind ain't worn them out yet. Follow me." Fletcher started walking out into the opening. Fletcher studied the ground overlooking the wide tire tracks.

"There are more than one pair of tire tracks out here," Dixon said. "These look like RV tracks. The other set could be truck tracks. Hard to say in the worn imprints."

"Here," Fletcher said, looking down at the ground. "Not much left, but you'll see what I'm talking about."

Dixon walked over beside him. From what he noted in the faded, odd imprint, the footprint had five long toes, long, jagged toenails, and whatever it was, possibly walked on the balls of its feet.

"I have never seen anything like it before, but with what little I have to go on, I can't tell," Dixon said.

"It . . . Whatever it was seemed to stop here, then made its way back to the woods," Fletcher said.

Two more deputies' SUVs drove up to the scene. A large owl flew over the two authority figures. Dixon watched the large, black owl land on his Explorer.

"You have no idea what it could be?"

"No," Dixon said as he stared at the wood line fifty yards away.

"Well, that makes two of us. Let me go rally the troops to do a quick search. I really don't like those woods. Never did."

That makes two of us, he thought. His eyes followed the faded footsteps into the tree line.

Moments later, Fletcher and five other officers fanned out and searched the woods in pairs of twos. Despite the ample daylight filtering through the treetops, the forest was shrouded in an ominous darkness. The high-beam flashlights gave the search party very little help piercing the dusk.

Two deputies stayed back and guarded the smoking house while Dixon searched through the rubble.

"We got about four hours of sunlight left to search," Fletcher said to the deputy beside him.

The twenty-year-old deputy, Diana Young, was an ebony beauty following in her father's footsteps to be a part of law enforcement. She swallowed a lump that formed in her throat after hearing those words. She did *not* want to be there. The stories that her grandmother used to tell her and her siblings about the evils of these woods used to give them nightmares.

"Okay, Chief," she said, as her wide eyes scanned between the surrounding trees.

"You okay over there?"

"I'm good, sir," she lied.

Crackling from a distance made her hiss and frantically wave her flashlight. Wind gusts howled between the trees.

"You sure?"

She faked a chuckle. "Yes, I'm fine." She pointed her light behind her to confirm nothing would sneak up from there.

Ensuring that she was protected, he commanded her to stay close.

She kissed the cross that hung down from her neck. It was a gift given by her beloved grandmother many years ago. She clenched it in her hand for a few seconds before letting it fall back to her chest.

Another weird sound rose from a distance. This time, it came from high above. A tree creaked, catching Fletcher's attention.

He could not deny it bothered him and found himself using the flashlight to search up high. The creaking got louder when he saw a tree falling in their direction.

"Move!" Fletcher lunged at the young deputy and shoved her out of the way. The tree crashed, barely missing him. They heard a piercing scream from a deputy not far from them.

Dixon rose from the rubble and strained his ears to locate the source of the crashing sound, followed by a chilling scream reverberating throughout the woods. Both deputies sitting in their vehicles to stay warm jumped out and looked toward the tree line. Dixon ran toward them, looking in the same direction.

"What the hell was that?" Dixon asked.

"Coyote?" a deputy answered.

Gunshots soon followed the screams. The three men ran toward where they thought the noise came from. More screaming made the men redirect their route toward the wood line. A squeal from an unknown creature halted the men in their tracks just fifteen yards outside the woods. The snow started falling heavier now, and the men could feel the cold air change instantly.

"What the fuck was that?" one deputy asked, nearly out of breath.

"I don't know," Dixon said. He looked into the shadowy forestand nearly ran back to his Explorer.

To the left, two of the deputies tore out of the woods, running for their lives toward the vehicles with guns in one hand and flashlights in the other.

"Hey," Dixon called out to them, running toward them.

"James," one deputy called out. "Coe!"

The deputies tailed Dixon as he ran toward the frantic men. The men glanced over toward them but did not break their stride escaping the woods. Dixon caught up with the men at the vehicles. The swirling snow flurries had gotten heavier, making it more difficult to see into the distance like before.

"What … the fuck … is going on?" Dixon asked between breaths.

Coe, a forty-two-year-old Black deputy, ex-marine straight out of high school, with twelve years of experience, pointed toward the woods, still trying to catch his wind. Before he could speak, a woman's scream erupted from the woods. As the men turned to the woods, another scream pierced from the wood line.

"That's Diana," James said, a twenty-six-year-old Caucasian male.

Diana burst out of the woods, shrieking at the top of her lungs. She dropped the flashlight a few steps out. Dixon ran to meet her … and that's when he saw it.

About thirty yards away, standing in the path where Diana just came from, stood a tall figure that blended in with the surroundings and the unnatural gloom of the woods. Its eyes reflected enough light through the heavy snowfall and the wind to give it away, whether it wanted to be seen or didn't care.

Dixon froze for a moment. His feet stayed in place no matter how much he tried to move. Diana ran up to him, breaking him out of his trance. Blood covered some of her outfit from head to toe.

"Go! Run!" he said, guiding her past him. He turned back to the woods, but the figure was gone. He stepped back and scanned the tree line, but nothing caught his eye. Then he turned and ran back behind Diana. Coe met Diana and ran her back to the vehicles.

"Get out of here," Dixon said.

"What about the others?" James asked, touching Dixon on the shoulder.

More screeches followed by a distorted howl pushed a gust of wind behind them, or so it seemed.

Dixon grabbed Diana, pointing at her shirt. "Do you want to fuck around and find out?" he asked, looking him dead in the eyes for a moment.

"Helpppp meee," someone whimpered. "Helpppp meee." The voice sounded like Fletcher but with a distorted pitch from an old tape recorder. "Helpppp meee," the voice pleaded again.

"That's not the Chief," Diana said. "He's dead. We need to get the fuck out of here."

"Helpppp meee!" The voice sounded much closer this time and much deeper in tone.

The weather had changed into a full-blown blizzard, and seeing past ten yards in the distance was difficult.

"Let's go!" Coe snapped.

"Let's get the fuck out of here," James said.

They wasted no time jumping into their vehicles. Diana got in the passenger seat of the Explorer parked behind Coe's vehicle, and he wasted no time starting it up. He used the windshield wipers to clear the snow. However, without warning, a decapitated head slammed into his windshield, leaving a bloody, gory trail on the windshield, causing Diana to scream.

"The fuck!" Dixon whisper-screamed.

The wipers spread the blood across the windshield, mixing it with the snow, which impeded his vision even more. Then something smashed against the windshield, leaving a deep bull's-eye crack on the right side of the glass. Diana hissed while covering her face by crossing her arms. Dixon locked the doors, then threw the gear into drive. Something tried to get in the passenger door. It tugged so hard on the door that it rocked the whole vehicle.

Gunshots close by sent a thick, black liquid substance across Diana's window and her windshield, followed by a deafening shriek. Even with the doors closed, the two had to muffle their ears with their hands. The repulsive smell of death crept into the Explorer, making it difficult to breathe and making them want to vomit.

Dixon punched the gas pedal and moved the steering wheel to avoid Coe's vehicle, but the tires just spun on the slushy ground.

Out of nowhere, James's vehicle side-swiped the Explorer, then slid into Coe's patrol vehicle.

Dixon and Diana saw James get out of the vehicle through the windshield, firing his sidearm. To the left, the creature moved like a flash to get a good look at it, and James's bullets just pissed the thing off, so it turned its attention to him, quickly leaping into the air on top of James. Dixon tried to see as his eyes widened, watching the blood mix with the thick snow from above. Diana cowered in a ball with her head in her hands.

Bam! Bam! Bam! The two jumped before realizing it was Coe.

"Let me in," Coe demanded frantically, beating on the window. "Open the fucking door."

After a split second to catch himself, Dixon finally unlocked the door, and Coe jumped into the backseat.

"Go! Go! Get the fuck out of here," Coe woofed.

"I'm trying!"

"Fuck, try harder!" Coe beat the back of Dixon's seat with the hammer fist.

The spinning of the tires in reverse splashed mud on the back of the Flesh Eater, grabbing its attention. Not appreciating the mud shower, it slammed James's lifeless body onto the hood of the Explorer. Diana let out another yelp. More blood splashed across the windshield, being spread by the wipers.

"What the fuck is that?" Coe barked. *"What . . . the fuck . . . is that?"*

"I don't know and ain't trying to find out right now!"

The creature jumped on top of the Explorer as it swung backward, tossing the creature off to the side, along with James's body. Coe reloaded his gun, then searched out the windows. Dixon put the vehicle in drive and drove as fast as possible with limited visibility.

"Where is it?" Coe asked.

Just then, the Flesh Eater's claws crashed through the back window, gripping the seat. It pulled its head into the cabin. Blood and guts hung from its hideous face and teeth. The smell of rotten meat filled the vehicle. The creature roared into the cabin part of the SUV, forcing the men to cover their ears.

"Fuck you!" Coe said as he unloaded the clip into the creature's face and shoulders, barely fazing it, but it was enough to make it let go. He reloaded a new clip, his last one.

"Can you drive this motherfucker any faster?" Coe asked, still looking out the back with his gun ready. The wind nearly drowned out his voice.

"If I run into a tree, we're fucked," Dixon answered. "I can barely see."

Coe clenched his teeth and then replied, "True that. Do your thing, man. I got it back here."

A short moment later, the Flesh Eater rammed the driver's side of the Explorer, nearly causing it to run off the road. Less snow lay on the ground the further they drove away from the smoking house, giving Dixon better traction for driving. Realizing this, he put more pedal to the metal.

"Hang on," Dixon said, making a quick right turn.

"That's how you fucking do that shit," Coe encouraged.

Up ahead, they saw the parked RV and two Black SUVs in an open area to the right of the road.

"I don't know what's going on, but I bet these people know exactly what that was," Dixon said.

Coe rose to take a peek. "The Feds?" He thought about it for a second. "Makes sense. They have been hanging around for a while now. Ever since crazy shit has been happening."

"We'll play it cool at first," Dixon proposed.

"Roger that," Coe replied.

Dixon steered the battered vehicle beside the RV and blew the horn. Three agents came out of the RV with their hands on their holstered firearms.

CHAPTER 23
DIXON & MATT

DIXON SAT AT his desk in his office at the police building, waiting for reinforcements to arrive. He thought of every excuse for what he and his people had just faced. *Was it a mutated bear? An alien? Or has some creation gone wrong from a government lab?* The palms of his hand rubbed his face up and down as his elbows rested on the old, steel desk. Then he sat back in his chair to gaze out the small window.

The deaths of the five individuals left in the woods near the Busbins' former home were the subject of his pondering. He waited for more Feds' backup despite lacking trust in them. He realized that the cabin, the Busbin house, Barbara's place, and her rental property were linked and required serious attention. Officer Coe walked in after tapping on his office door.

"Those people are here," he said, referring to the Feds. "Three SUVs deep."

"That's the bully government for you," he replied with a grin. He got up and walked with Coe out to the lobby.

Typically, at least one deputy would be on duty, but half the force was left back in the woods where the Busbin home had been—dead.

Matt and another agent in a black suit, hat, and dark shades entered the main entrance, leaving four agents standing by their vehicles. Dixon remembered seeing Matt at the hospital a few days ago with Jimmy. *Something stinks, and I'm going to sniff it out.*

"Dixon?" Matt said.

"You have your people ready to go search for my people?" Dixon asked.

Matt and his agent kept serious faces behind their shades, showing no emotion. Dixon sized Matt and the other agent up, noticing the straight-up posture with their arms straight down their sides. He knew this would intimidate most people, but Dixon was far from impressed.

"We're taking care of it," Matt said. "I want to talk to you about what you saw."

"I saw something that looked like it wasn't from this world— *or* from hell."

"Just one?" Matt asked.

"There's supposed to be more than one?" Coe butted in.

The two agents glanced over at Coe.

"What? I asked a damn question." Coe doubled-down.

Dixon held his hand out to tone down Coe.

"You have to forgive my man over here. But he just lost his boss and about five or six colleagues. All we want is some transparency and help to resolve what is happening in my little town."

They turned their attention back to Dixon. "We are here to help. Please tell us what happened."

"I think you already know what happened," Coe said.

"Tell us what's out there," Dixon said, placing the palms of his hands on the counter that separated them from the agents.

Matt remained silent, keeping his deadpan expression intact. He reminded himself not to fall victim to people's feelings. His eyes scanned through his dark shades, and he noticed the high-powered rifle leaning against the wall beside Coe. Playing Coe's background in his head, he knew he had to be careful with the unstable ex-marine. "It was a mutated bear."

Coe chuckled at the blatant lie. "You got us fucked up if you expect us to believe that bullshit."

"You can't be serious," Dixon said in a less aggressive tone than Coe's. "I know what a bear looks like, and that wasn't no freaking bear."

"Did you actually see the animal?" Matt asked, still keeping a calm demeanor.

Dixon remembered how the silhouette moved through the heavy snow. The speed at which it moved and how tall the figure stood. *I didn't get a good look at the creature, but no way was that a bear*, he thought. He knew the tactic the man in the black suit would use. Before he could respond, Coe spoke up.

"I saw it. I put two full clips into that motherfucker, and all that did was piss it the fuck off. I watched it tear my partner from limb to limb. I watched it eat his flesh as bullets ripped through its gotdamn body! A bear is a bad motherfucker, but that was something evil. And I think you know that. So, don't lie to us about a damned bear"

Diana broke the tension with a cough as she came out of the locker room area. She walked past the two agents without acknowledging them and stood between Coe and Dixon.

"How you feeling?" Dixon asked.

She looked at him through the dark circles that surrounded her eyes. "I'm okay. I've been better."

Noticing the baggy eyes and exhausted demeanor, Matt focused on her. He needed to avoid another Jimmy situation at all costs. "Have you had contact with the bear, Diana?"

All three law enforcement officers looked at Matt, realizing he knew her name without asking.

"I see you have been doing your homework," Dixon said.

"Bear?" she said, looking confused.

"Yup, a bear," Coe replied in a facetious tone.

"It's called 'Coverup 101,'" Dixon said, looking at Matt dead in his shades.

"Have you had contact with the bear, ma'am? That is a question," Matt asked in a more direct tone.

"No, but I saw what it did to Fletcher. Well, what I did see before I took off. He got trapped by a limb from a falling tree. And no, that *wasn't* a bear," she said as tears developed in her eyes. "In fact, I think it was dead."

Matt took a deep breath. Regardless of hearing the truth, he had to protect the truth at all costs. Back in his youth, this would have ended in a whole different way. *At my age, I'm not sure I'm cut out for this job anymore.*

"I need you to listen and listen to me good," Matt spoke. "What happened out there will never leave this place. You will *not* tell a soul what happened out there."

"Or what?" Dixon asked.

"Dixon, you have a wife and a little girl, if I remember correctly. You have a nice little savings account and a pension waiting for you on the other side of retirement. A cozy house that's almost paid for. You're living the American dream. My advice to you is do not whisper the things that you saw to anyone. Not even to God."

"Are you threatening me?"

"I think he is," Coe said.

Through his years of service, Matt knew that getting to the ringleader always worked out. They were usually the ones who had much more to lose than the rest in most cases. "I don't make threats," Matt said. "I tell you how it's going to be. It's up to you whether you take heed to what I said. Whether what I tell you is worth the trouble—or not. And that goes for all of you."

Dixon felt a lump forming in his throat as he listened to Matt's threatening words, rendering him speechless. As he reminisced, memories of the happy moments spent with his family flooded his mind. Above all else, he prioritized his little girl's future. He was well aware of the government's ability to resort to nefarious tactics to achieve their goals. But he had to push the issue. It wouldn't be like him if he didn't.

"Fuck that," Coe spat. "Fuck you and your threats! You don't scare me."

"Officer Coe, you were given an 'other than honorable' discharge. But we both know why you left the military. Or should I say, were 'forced out of it'? Sometimes, the past has a way of coming back to haunt you. Then *click*, the doors behind you close—for good."

"I don't give a fuck about that shit," Coe said, not thinking clearly.

"Well, how about the lives of the people who helped you? Who falsified evidence and lied on your behalf? They have families. Happy lives, kids in college. It would be a shame if all that came tumbling down because of a mistake made many years ago. So, tell me, Coe, are you that selfish, Mr. War Hero? Call my bluff if you think I'm full of shit." Matt matched Coe's last tone.

Coe quickly digressed, feeling the weight of the man in the black suit's presence. The dimly lit room seemed to close in around him, suffocating his thoughts. He couldn't risk jeopardizing the safety of those who had protected him, so he bit his tongue and kept his silence as anxiety tightened its grip on him. "You should date Diana," Matt said to Coe. "She could use you in her life. Being a struggling young mom and all."

A look of surprise developed on Diana's face, but she dared not to speak. She didn't need any other issues in her life other than what she already had going on. She too tucked her tail and remained silent.

"You all are some cold sons of bitches," Dixon said.

"And I'm that same son of a bitch that's going to fuck you in the ass if you try me." Matt's words rolled off his tongue as if he meant every word.

With a deep breath, Dixon lifted his chin and asked, "Okay, so what do you want us to do?" He surrendered to Matt's demands.

"You are going to tell everyone there was some kind of unknown animal attack that killed everyone. You will state that the Feds are taking over the investigation, and you will end it there. We will have people to handle the press and your community. And if everything goes smooth and you do as I say, then everyone can have some type of closure." Matt nodded his head and walked toward the door. "See you around."

Both agents walked out of the lobby, leaving the three officers helpless and speechless.

CHAPTER 24
THE RETURN OF THE BEAST

"SO GLAD YOU are feeling better and able to join us to go check on Jefferarri's grandparents' home, Mr. Eugene," Octavia said. The short ride from the airport felt like an eternity through the rolling hills and mountains of North Carolina. She watched the beautiful mountain range scenery from the third row. Water trickled down the side of the carved-out mountainside, and the brown and green valley intrigued her. The rented, gray Chrysler Pacifica Touring L Plus managed the bumper-to-bumper highway traffic between the narrow, wet lanes. However, these conditions did not distract the other drivers from murdering the speed limit on the side of the steep mountain ranges.

She had inherited Jefferarri's estate by the order of his will. She had never been to the property, and, to her knowledge, Jefferarri had not been there since Eugene took him away as a child. Jefferarri never wanted to return to those memories, and The Order preferred he did not for their benefit. They wanted to keep Jefferarri on a leash for as long as possible. Too many emotions threatened that.

"Uh-huh. I appreciate you having me," Eugene lied, tilting his head back to her from the second row of seats. "I needed the fresh air anyway. I couldn't wait to get away from that place. Yesterday, I got tired of being cooped up at home too."

Despite their chuckles, Eugene remained fixated on the moving rocks on the side of the mountain, taking a deep breath as he turned his head out the passenger window.

"I definitely understand."

The assistant, Roseline, sat in the driver's seat. Her body nearly hugged the steering wheel with both hands on the wheel. Octavia focused on Roseline's well-being since the absence of her beloved Jefferarri. Roseline knew all too well the grieving side of love. Her soulmate died many years ago due to a heart attack. The loner had no desire for love since then. As much as she hated to think about it and wished it could have been different, she knew in her heart Octavia and Jefferarri would not make it. The life support on Jefferarri's life ticked down the day he took his first breath—not in the hands of The Order.

"OG," Octavia said to Eugene, "can you tell me about Jefferarri's father? Jefferarri never wanted to talk about it. And how did all this come to be?"

He made intentional eye contact with Roseline through the rearview mirror. She gave him a slight nod. Eugene sighed silently as he looked out at the passing rock of the mountain. His hand ran down his salt-and-pepper jawline, displaying a frown. He dreaded the memories to come once he saw the house.

"In short, he came from a unique bloodline of werewolves. Somehow, over three thousand years ago, his clan became immune to the moon. Instead of changing on a full moon, anger triggered their transformation. All of this, of course, starts as early as seven years old. The transformation progressed, but the younger they are, the slower the progression. They were bigger, faster, and stronger than the other clans and very hard to control and kill. During the rebellion against the bloodsucker—"

"Vampires?" Octavia asked.

"Yes, it is said that Jefferarri's direct ancestor defeated the head bloodsucker, which ended the war. Jefferarri's father was the same age when Matt brought him to the Compound. Kinda like when I brought you there, Octavia."

"Wait—Matt brought Jefferarri's *father* to the Compound?" Octavia asked. "How did he get him?"

Eugene hesitated, then explained, "I have no idea, and Matt always shied away from the subject. Matt and I did not hook up as partners until later that same year. But Jefferarri's ancestors had been a part of The Order for many years before they separated. I never knew why the relationship ended, though, and couldn't find much of anything on it. The Order doesn't like people sneaking around into their horrible past. I believe they want to erase it."

Silence filled the van before Octavia's sniffles got everyone's attention. Roseline grabbed a box of Kleenex from the glove box and handed it to Eugene. He pulled out some tissues and gave them to her.

"Thanks," Octavia said.

"You're welcome."

"Why are you with such a company if they are so corrupt?" Roseline asked.

"Roz," Octavia called to her.

Roseline's eyes met Eugene's through the rearview mirror.

"I'm sorry," Roseline said, not wanting to disappoint or embarrass Octavia. "You seem like a good person. I was just curious. I'll stay in my lane."

Eugene took a moment of silence, then cleared his throat. "Ahh, it's all good. I don't mind answering, but I'll give y'all the quick version."

"You owe us no explanation, Eugene," Octavia said. "It's not our business. I'm grateful for the things you did for us."

"My daddy was thirty-seven. I was a twenty-one-year-old troublemaker," Eugene said with a chuckle. "Ended up going to jail for defending a sister being bullied on the street by some white punks. I beat their asses. Then the police came and beat mine. They beat me really well too. I forgot the number of stitches I received. I think I was in the hospital for almost a week."

"Wow," Octavia said.

"They trumped up my charges, and the old white judge gave me the option . . . life or military. The Vietnam War became my next stop. The Order sent the men in black suits to me before my time was up . . . and gave me an offer I couldn't refuse. So, I took it. They released my daddy from prison, and my mom got a good job, a nice house, and a bank account to match."

"So, why do you have to be mean to people y'all encounter on the job? Why threaten them with all kinds of harm?"

"Bully tactics are part of my job. It was what they had inbred in us. It's the government. Either people obey or suffer the consequences. Scared people are more likely to do as told. The government didn't want the population to know about the cryptics, aliens, or anything out of the norm."

"So much for the government working *for* the people," Roseline said.

"It's what they want you to think," Octavia replied.

The GPS turned Roseline off the interstate and onto the winding roads that cut through the mountains. Now, on an easier drive, she relaxed her tight knuckles on the steering wheel. The new path offered stunning views of the deep and colorful valley below, just like the interstate.

"It won't be much longer, and we'll be there," Roseline said. A relieved look came over her face.

"Ohhh, shit!" Octavia uttered, grabbing her head.

"Octavia?" Roseline called with a glance back and then through the rearview mirror.

"What's wrong?" Eugene asked, rising over the back of the seat to get a better look at her.

She reached for her handbag and pulled out a small brown bag. She unwrapped the matching colored strings from around the bag, then dumped a small set of bones onto one hand. Turning her hand, she released the bones onto the seat next to her.

"Octavia, what is it?" Eugene asked.

She could not get a reading because the van was moving and the seat was uneven.

"Pull over!" Octavia said. She grabbed the bones and dropped them again. Her tears started to flow freely, and her face twisted with the weight of her concerns. Beads of sweat developed on her forehead, and she started hyperventilating.

"What's wrong?" Roseline asked.

"Pull the fuck over!"

"All right, all right!" Roseline replied. She found a lookout parking point to the left of the road and turned into the empty lot.

The lookout point overlooked the valley across to the mountain ridge on the other side. A few cabins and homes with smoking chimneys were visible amongst the sea of trees in the valley and on the side of the mountain across from them. The wind pushed the cold air underneath the gray skies.

Octavia rounded up the bones into her bone bag and exited the van before it stopped. Her knees fell upon the paved parking lot. Then she used the palm of her hand to clear some debris from in front of her.

Eugene slowly eased out of the van. His old back reacted to the long ride sitting on the firm seats. Roseline stood beside him as they huddled over Octavia with concern. Both folded their arms in front to block what they could of the cold air cutting to their bones.

Octavia shivered as mucus ran out of her nose to her lips. This time, she dropped the bones out of the bag onto the pavement. Then she shook her head and tried again.

"C'mon, gotdammit!"

Her two companions remained silent and confused. The overwhelming anxiety about the moment took their minds off the cold. Eugene's eyes scrolled between Octavia and the passing cars, and he reminded himself of his Glock on the seat in the van. *Octavia acting like this . . . There is no telling what's going on*, he thought.

"No!" Octavia dropped her face into her hands in disappointment. "No," she continued. "I can't read it."

Eugene bent down on one knee. "C'mon, grab your bones so we can get out of this cold air."

"Get her in the van," Roseline said. She flipped Octavia's bone bag inside out and scooped up the bones the way a dog walker scoops up dog shit.

After Eugene closed Octavia's door behind her, Roseline sighed, standing next to him. "Something is wrong where we are going, and it ain't good," she said.

"I agree. She can't even read what it is."

"So it seems," she said, twisting her lips.

His eyes met hers, and he started thinking.

"You think she *can* read it?" Eugene said as he turned to her.

She cut her eyes to the van, then cautiously back to him so she could not be heard. "All I'm saying is she's the most powerful voodoo priestess today. It's just hard to believe if she can't. I know her, and that heffa don't miss."

"But why? Why would she pull that on us? I'm not saying you're lying, by no means, but I can't see her putting us in danger."

He sighed, then glanced down into the valley, "All right, let's get a room, then go to the house in the morning. Cool?"

"Fine by me."

They got back into the van and immediately turned to Octavia.

"Go straight to the house," she said before anyone else could speak.

"I think it's been—"

"— we need to go to the house," Octavia said, cutting him off. "Please," she asked with a fake smile.

"To the house, we go," Roseline said before turning around and heading back to the road.

Half an hour later, the van pulled up to the gate. The sun began to creep behind the western mountain range. Roseline diverted her attention into the rearview, and Eugene turned to Octavia. She dangled an old, large key ring containing many keys.

Octavia's face cast a different person than they had ever seen before. Her eyes were colder than outside. Eugene grabbed the keys and his Glock. He got out and looked around. It was a far cry from what he remembered the ranch in its heyday.

Tall grass and weeds filled the landscape. Some had some grown on the driveway. A few fences had collapsed. The hole in the front of the old stable was still there from when Clifton and Burly fought many decades ago. Most of the paint had fallen off, revealing some areas of rot. The house had the same run-down issues as the stable.

Eugene quietly hummed as he alternated between checking each key and his surroundings. After many unsuccessful tries with some potential-looking keys, he wondered if the old rusty lock needed oiling. Finally, the lock popped open, relieving his sore fingers from trying to turn keys that did not work. *Thank goodness.*

He pushed the large, galvanized gate open that rolled on a wheel. The gate took a little muscle from the old man, and hinges roared in protest from years of not being moved. Roseline had stepped out of the van to chat with him privately. She gave him a hand, pushing the gate, making it open much faster. The smell of decaying flesh permeated the air. Once the gate had been completely opened, the old man stood up for a breath. As his eyes panned across the tall grass and broken-down outdoor equipment, he noticed something in the grass further up the path.

"Hey," he tapped Roseline on the arm. "What's that? My glasses are in the van."

Her eyes squinched into the distance to see what caught his attention in the tall grass. A large, black mass with some white, which appeared to be dried bones, caught her attention in the tall grass. Specs of dried blood spots masked the bones. "I'm not sure," she said.

"Let's go," he said, not liking the chill that just slithered down his back.

They scrambled back into the van and slowly drove down the long path. Roseline kept her eyes on the mass on the right ahead of them. Coming up on the left, a patch of shorter grass revealed a mutilated deer lying with its bones exposed through ripped and torn skin. Over a hundred flies buzzed around the carcass that was crawling with maggots.

"That was done recently," Eugene said. He turned his attention back to Octavia. Octavia's eyes bounced from window to window as if she were looking for something.

He turned back into his seat to catch Roseline's eyes on the rearview mirror as he bit into his top lip. The van passed the horse stable on the right. The roof had started to cave in due to the lack of care. A door hung on one hinge. A strong gust of wind would easily blow the large door off. Similar structures appeared in the same condition over the tall grass and weeds in the background.

The van came to a slow halt in front of the house. Some boards from the porch's ceiling littered the porch floor. *I've had some good times here many years ago.* A moment of sadness overcame Eugene as he was momentarily sucked back into a time of playing cards, drinking, and good music. Roseline's question snapped him back into reality.

"What the fuck are those?"

The hair on the back of everyone's necks stood up. The front door had deep gouging scratches all over it and around the door frame.

"Scratches," Eugene tensed. "We don't need to—"

Octavia immediately rushed out of the van and up onto the porch.

"—in," he blurted, interrupted by Octavia's erratic action.

"Octavia!" Roseline shrieked as she scampered behind her.

"Octavia! Gotdammit!" Eugene grabbed his gun and followed.

Octavia slid past the cracked open door and disappeared behind it. Eugene caught up with Roseline, who stood at the door, hesitant to go in. He covered his nose with the back of his free hand as the putrid odor assaulted his nostrils at the door.

"I guess there's no asking you to get back into the van, huh?" he queried, stepping in front of her with his gun ready.

"She is my responsibility."

Using the barrel of his gun, he pushed open the door as it loudly squeaked in protest. *I'm too old for this shit.* His legs felt heavy. He scanned the dusty, dark living room. The place had been tossed, for the most part. Everything had been thrown out of place. Roseline held onto the back of his sweater as they moved cautiously through the room.

Roseline was startled at seeing a half-eaten wild hog tossed into the corner beside a pile of broken furniture to the left. Eugene's breathing got heavier with each step, with a matching heartbeat. The sounds of sudden movement upstairs made them both look at the balcony next to the stairs. With a deep breath, Eugene marched toward the stairs. Scuffling knocked dust down from the ceiling.

"Octavia!" Roseline called in a low, hesitant voice.

The whiff of the wet dog came from out of nowhere and mixed with the rot of the hog. Then they heard heavy panting right behind them. Now, Roseline felt some hot breath on the back of her neck. She closed her eyes and tightly clutched Eugene's sweater.

Eugene slowly turned around, pushing Roseline behind him. His head tilted back to glimpse the towering beast hunched over just a few feet before them.

"Fuck . . ." he murmured.

The seven-and-a-half-foot creature rose from his hunched position, exposing its ripped, slender, muscular body. It was covered in gray fur except for its humanlike chest and abdominal area, which had a mix of black and whitish spots. Its oversized head did not match its body, and it curled its lips back, showing its massive canines and incisors. A short mohawk mane flowed from the top of its head to the middle of its back. Its eyes gave off a dull, faint hue of red with massive legs that ended with bare hocks similar to that of a dog but much more muscular. Its ripped muscles flexed through the skin as it moved. A low moaning flowed from its throat. Long, ripped arms hung out to the side with large human hands and long claws for fingers. Its chest and shoulders rose with every intake of breath. A large keloid scar was in the middle of its chest.

"We are in his territory," Eugene thought out loud.

Roseline whimpered behind Eugene. She held onto him tightly. Her eyes squeezed shut as tears flowed down her cheeks and soaked into his sweater.

The beast's claws unfurled, emitting a low growl from its throat, intensifying Eugene's fear of being shredded by a single

FALL OF THE ORDER 201

swipe. It bared its teeth even more. Eugene nearly pissed his pants in fear and knew his gun would only make it angrier if he fired into the beast.

Something must be done.

"Jefferarri?" he quaked at the beast.

The beast quickly relaxed its hand, closed its mouth, and twisted its head to the side as if it recognized the voice. Then it bent its head to the opposite side. The red glow in its eyes remained.

"Where is Octavia?" Roseline said. "She's the only chance we have."

"Jefferarri?" Eugene said. *Please, recognize my voice.* "It's me, Eugene." He raised one hand and then placed the gun on the floor.

"What color are his eyes?" Roseline asked, refusing to look.

"What?" Eugene said as calmly as he could.

"What *color* are his eyes?"

"Red."

The beast shook the trance from his head, causing its mane to wave down his back.

Roseline opened her eyes and yelped at that point, causing the beast to break out of the trance. The beast leaned forward, sniffing their scents, then stepped back with thudding steps creaking the floor. The familiar scents and familiar memories rattled his predator senses. Like a malfunctioning fluorescent lightbulb, the red eye glow flickered. Its forehead furrowed before its back slammed into the wall behind him, causing the walls in the house to shake and old dust to fall from the rafters.

"Let's go," Eugene whispered. He grabbed her hand to sneak by the big fella through the door next to it.

It shook its head before falling to all fours, blocking the entrance. Eugene and Roseline abruptly stopped. The beast rolled its eyes over to them before baring its teeth again. The eyes lit up brightly as it stood, looking down at its next kill.

"Jefferarri!" Octavia called from the balcony next to the stairs.

The beast lifted its head to see where the familiar voice came from. It sniffed the air in her direction. A whine flowed from his throat before he leaped over Eugene and Roseline, leaving a saliva trail in the air behind him. The floor ripped to pieces from the power of its jump. When it landed at the top of the stairs, the staircase cracked. Pieces of wood scattered across the room from the power of its claws.

"Octavia!" Roseline shouted.

Eugene started up the stairs with his gun, but Octavia held her hand out to him to lower the weapon. "I've got this," she said between accelerated breaths. Her muscles tightened as she felt her heartbeat knock in her chest.

Eugene stopped on the third step. Sweat beaded up on his forehead.

The beast wagged its tail, then cautiously leaned toward her on all fours, sniffing her from toe to head.

Octavia stood motionless, her body trembling as she swallowed her spit. Its eyes flickered again and then quickly stopped.

"Jefferarri," she said.

The beast licked her, then placed its head under her hand and rubbed its face across her body, unintentionally moving her backward. Unable to keep her balance, she fell to the floor, and the beast pounced and continued to rub its head against her body as it purred like a cat but much deeper. She wrapped her arms around its neck as much as she could. Her tears went from nervousness to joy.

"Jefferarri," she beamed.

Eugene slid down with his back against the wall, using the side rail on the staircase. He took a deep breath, then dropped his head, relieved to be alive. Then he released a quick chuckle—my God.

Roseline caught her breath with her eyes drawn up to the beast on the balcony. Her heartbeat started to slow down. She was grateful to be alive as well. *Next time, we may not be so lucky.*

Darkness covered the windows. Octavia jumped up out of her nap on the kitchen floor with her back against the cabinet under the sink. She frantically scanned the area. Hair scattered across the floor that led out into the living room. Her stiff bones from sitting on the hard floor caused her to wince as she stood up and used the countertop as leverage. "Jefferarri," she said.

The commotion from Octavia jolted Roseline out of her nap. Her drooping eyelids turned to Octavia, then to the floor where she last remembered Jefferarri curled up next to Octavia.

"What's the matter?" Roseline asked as she stood up.

Eugene's eyes opened wide, taking a deep breath. Adjusting his glasses, he nervously scanned the room to see what had got the two ladies looking around.

"What happened?" he asked.

"Where's Jefferarri?" Octavia said. "Jefferarri!" She took off into the decimated living room.

Roseline and Eugene trailed behind her, trying their best to keep up. One lamp on its side in the corner next to the broken end table lit up the living room.

"Jefferarri!" Octavia called. She followed the hair on the floor, ending abruptly a few feet before the door.

Adjusting his glasses, Eugene walked in front of her and looked out the partially opened door. He looked beyond the porch, out into the dark field. He paused momentarily, letting his eyes adjust to the shape in the moonlight before opening the door fully. "Here he is."

Octavia walked from behind Eugene with unknown anticipation. Twenty yards from the edge of the porch, Jefferarri stood naked in the cold air with his head tilted up to the full moon. Tall weeds surrounded and brushed against his long legs. The silhouette of his shoulders rose and fell with each breath he took.

The trio walked out the door. Octavia, then Eugene, followed by Roseline.

"Jefferarri," Octavia called in a low voice.

"Wait," Eugene said, grabbing her firmly by the arm before she stepped off the porch.

She looked at Eugene as she brought her foot back on the porch.

Roseline stood beside Eugene. "Oh my God," she uttered.

"Look," Eugene pointed out into the darkness beyond Jefferarri. "You see that?"

"Eyes," Roseline said with concern in her voice. "Glowing eyes."

Octavia looked out into the darkness, and then she saw them. Six pairs of yellow eyes that could easily be mistaken for fireflies. Some appeared to be in trees, while the rest of them shined from ground level.

"What are those?" Octavia said as the eyes sent chills down her back. She wrapped her arms around herself.

Roseline began to rub her neck and shoulders. "Maybe . . . We need to go back inside," she suggested.

The eyes began to fade away, one at a time.

"They're leaving," Eugene said.

When the last pair of eyes faded into the darkness, Octavia built up the courage to step off the porch.

"Octavia?" Eugene called.

"I've got this," she said, looking back at him before slowly walking up behind Jefferarri, still gazing at the moon.

Eugene tailed her until she stood in front of Jefferarri. She had to tilt her head back now to look up at him. *God, he has grown.*

Roseline hesitantly tiptoed behind them, keeping her head on a swivel.

A musky smell from Jefferarri filled the air. In the moonlight, flaky skin covered most of his body. *Nothing that a good bath can't fix*, Octavia thought to herself.

"Jefferarri," she said, inching closer.

He stood in a trancelike state. A salt-and-pepper scruffy beard lined his face. Only his chest and shoulders moved with every rapid breath. As she reached her hands up to his face, he let out an ear-splitting howl that made her cringe. It was a bone-chilling sound, a mix between a wolf's howl and a man's scream, sending shivers racing down her spine.

The sound vibrated right through everyone.

"Gotdammit!" Eugene yelped.

After a long-winded cry, Jefferarri stopped and sniffed the air, then slowly looked down at Octavia, who held her hands tightly against her ears. A smile crossed his lips. He slowly tilted his head to the side, then sniffed the air. He quickly caught Eugene's and Roseline's scents before turning to them.

Jefferarri ambled over to Eugene and looked down at him. Flight mode took over Eugene's thought process, but he held his ground firmly, not looking him in the eyes. Jefferarri sniffed the air over Eugene. "Do not be afraid of me in this form," Jefferarri said in a much-deeper voice than ever before.

He turned to Roseline and sniffed her. Not liking what he smelled, his eyes rolled to the ground in front of her. "You are hiding secrets," he told her, "and even though your intentions are good, I can't trust you for this cause. Continue your loyalty to Octavia. She'll need you even more than ever now."

Surprised, Roseline met eyes with Octavia, who had a baffled look. Roseline's eyes rolled to the ground, displaying the guilt of the moment.

"Roz?" Octavia said.

Roseline looked up at Jefferarri. Her lips sucked in, and her eyes watered. She turned and hurried back to the house.

He turned his attention back to Eugene, then squatted down right in front of him. "I need you to get me up north . . . to the Flesh Eater."

"What?" Octavia said, directing her attention from Roseline to him.

"You are the only one I can trust to it," Jefferarri continued, addressing Eugene.

"No, no, Jefferarri, we need to stay off the grid to figure out what's next, baby."

"Octavia!" he snapped, then quickly caught himself. He walked over to her on all fours and stood before her. "I must do this . . . to heal from the rage. I won't be right until it's done." Deep down, Jefferarri knew he would not return to her, but he would dare not tell her that to her face. It would break him down even more to feel her sadness.

"Fine, but you are not going without me."

"Your stubbornness is why I can't trust you either." His voice got a little louder.

"We can do that," Eugene interrupted. "But The Order has foot soldiers in the area too."

Jefferarri cracked his shoulders, and a crooked smile crossed his face. He walked up to Eugene and said in a demonic tone, "Good. The Order was next on my list."

CHAPTER 25
PLANNING FOR HOPKINTON

"HOPKINTON IS GETTING out of control," Bill told Mr. Haskins. They sat at the dinette table in Mr. Haskins's place. "Please reconsider sending Subject J-C149 to eradicate the threat."

A bell from a distance chimed.

"Oh, it's my teatime," Mr. Haskins said. "I hope you like tea, son."

"What ... tea?" Bill asked, blindsided by Mr. Haskins's demeanor.

The maid entered the room. Both men remained silent. She placed a tray on the table with a pitcher of hot tea, two cups with a spoon in each, a saucer of sliced lemons, and another with sugar. She poured each cup. Aggravated by the interruption, Bill mumbled under his breath as he looked off into the distance. Mr. Haskins rolled his eyes at him, not liking the disrespect shown by his young protégé. She bowed, and Mr. Haskins returned the gesture before she walked out of the area, leaving them to their privacy.

The opened curtains displayed a large, open view of the sun setting in partly cloudy skies above a garden of bushes and flowers on the other side of the window. A brick walkway cut a path down the middle of the garden.

"Did you read the report for Hopkinton?" Bill asked.

Mr. Haskins added lemon to his tea, followed by a teaspoon of sugar. He stirred this with his spoon and enjoyed the annoyance and frustration he caused Bill.

Bill tilted his head to the ceiling and let out a heavy sigh. His face had turned red, and his patience strained to his limits.

"You don't like tea, Bill?" Mr. Haskins smiled.

"I prefer iced tea, sir," Bill said brashly.

"Preposterous." Mr. Haskins smiled before sipping his tea. "Hmm, that's good. So good. You don't know what you are missing. Anyway, yes, I've seen the report. Remember, I see them before anyone else does."

"There are a lot of dead people now, including the captain and almost their entire police force. And people in that area are starting to talk. I'm sure our people running around there are adding to the conversations. It won't be long before what's going on there gets out. It's our job to make sure that doesn't happen."

"Are you telling me what my job is, Bill?" His tone became a little aggressive.

Mr. Haskins knew deep down Bill couldn't care less about the people of Hopkinton. Bill only wanted to see the prototype in action.

"Not at all, sir." Bill toned down his approach. He dropped two teaspoons of sugar and a lemon in his cup. "Just let me take the lead on this one. If things go wrong, I'll be the fall guy." He sipped on his tea, hoping to gain some affection and trust.

"I have complete confidence in Moody's ability to handle the threat and Matt's ability to control the masses. You should too. They have been doing it for years." He placed his cup on the table and then used the white napkin to dry his lips. "More tests need to be done on J-C14 ..."

"9," Bill reminded the older gentlemen.

"Yes ... 9. What we can't have are two monsters running around out there wreaking havoc on those poor people. Do you understand?"

Bill wanted to be careful about how he proceeded with the conversation without overstepping his boundaries. "Yes, sir." He sipped on the tea. "It tastes pretty good, actually. What happens,

Mr. Haskins, if they don't get it under control? Do we have a backup plan?"

"It won't get to that point."

"I hope not as well," Bill said, breaking eye contact as he squirmed somewhat in his seat. "At least, if we had to do it, we have the kill safe at hand for J-C149," Bill added to see if it moved Mr. Haskins into thinking more in his direction.

"I know," he said before sipping his tea, playing off that he forgot all about the kill safe. *Old age is getting the best of me*, he thought to himself.

"You know she needs to be there," Roseline said, walking out to Jefferarri standing on the porch, breaking his trance as his eyes rolled across the grass and woodland.

He took a deep breath but remained silent, looking up at the sky as the sun fought to peep through the clouds. If he would have had a better way to get to Hopkinton, he would have been there by now. But his body needed more time to recover from yesterday's transformation. Now, with his new transformation level, it took longer for his body to recoup, especially with no ice-cold water or certain conditions to aid in his recovery. It would have taken much longer and required too much energy to navigate on foot. He thought about taking the car keys and leaving, but he could easily pass out on the long trip, which would have done him no good.

"Jefferarri."

"You and I both know the dangers there," he said, turning to Roseline. His voice was a little less demonic than before. He walked over to the steps and sat on the porch. His elbows rested on his thighs with his thumbs twiddling.

Roseline sat in the wooden rocking chair but faced Jefferarri. "I could never understand what it feels like to deal with what you're going through. It's a hard curse for anyone to bear, knowing the ending is out of your control, no matter how hard you try to control or change it . . . Knowing all you can do is slow it down, and that's a task within itself. But you and Octavia are connected in more ways than you could ever imagine. With a little love on top, of course," she smiled at her last line.

"You're right. You have no idea. I'm not completely human. So, the way you see love, I don't view it the same. It is different. I can't explain why or how; it just is. The more I change, the more I feel like her pet. You know how a pet loves its master. But I can still turn on her at the drop of a dime . . . like a pet lion. The more this thing grows inside me, the more things change within. Not just my body, but my mind."

"But you still love her. You still feel for her, right?"

Eugene stepped on the porch for some fresh air with his pipe in his hand. He sensed he had walked out on a profound conversation. However, instead of returning to the house, he continued to the edge of the porch.

Jefferarri glanced in Roseline's direction, not making eye contact. "More than I love myself or anyone would ever know, including her. But I must go to the north and take revenge for what this thing has done to my friends. I'm drawn to it. Even if it means my death. It's like destiny. And trying to talk me out of it will only piss me off."

"The Wendigo thing, known to us as the Flesh Eater?" Eugene interrupted.

"Even if you kill the Flesh Eater, its spirit will live on to snatch another soul."

Jefferarri stood up and stepped in front of Roseline. "I want the evil that took my friends' lives." His voice deepened, and the red hue developed lightly in his eyes.

She felt his demeanor change in an instant, as if a switch had been flipped. The air around her grew heavy with fear, causing goosebumps to rise on her skin. The sound of her own racing heartbeat echoed in her ears, drowning out any other noise. As he stood towering over her, her throat constricted, making it difficult to breathe.

"If you all want to come . . . come. Either way, I'm going up north," his voice seethed menacingly. The scent of tension hung in the air, intensifying the palpable sense of danger. "You want to put her in danger? Be my fucking guest."

Eugene heard Jefferarri's unstable attitude and saw his demeanor. "Yo, Jefferarri," Eugene said, placing his hands out in front. "Take it easy. You're going to get your wish. I already have something in the works."

"How soon?" Jefferarri asked.

"Hopefully, by morning. No later than noon," Eugene answered.

Jefferarri's eyebrows furrowed, creating deep creases on his forehead. His lips pressed together firmly, causing his face to tense up. He shifted his gaze from Roseline to Eugene, his eyes filled with intensity. Inhaling deeply, he took a step back. As he exhaled, the red glow in his eyes gradually faded away. A sense of calm washed over him, and his breathing became slow and steady. He sprang off the porch and dashed through the ranch into the tree line without warning.

"Damn, he's moving," Eugene gawked at Jefferarri's speed.

Roseline sighed in relief, placing her hand over her chest. She watched Jefferarri disappear into the tree line. *I don't know how much longer my heart can take this.*

"You all right?" Eugene asked, walking over to her.

She let out another sigh of relief and looked up at him. "This doesn't get any easier to deal with."

"What happened? What made him get like that?"

"His lust for revenge. I think he is losing more and more of himself by the second now. It's accelerating. He's doing an outstanding job of keeping it together . . . partly due to her." She glanced toward the front door. "Soon, he will not know any of us anymore."

Several miles from the ranch, Jefferarri stopped at a small creek running through the mountain range, still in his human form. He sipped from the creek on all fours as any four-legged animal would. He recognized his reflection between the small waves from his tongue but still looked like a stranger. He paused to continue to study his reflection. Suddenly, that ended when a four-foot-long water moccasin swam right underneath his face. He quickly snatched the snake from the water by the neck and held it up to observe. After a moment, he tossed it back into the water.

He squatted next to the creek, and his ears caught the sounds of nature: birds, insects, and the steady stream of the water. Then a noise grabbed his attention from the distance through the trees. He sniffed the air, targeting the scent. His stomach rumbled from hunger pains as he found the direction of the sound. He took off in that direction. From land to trees, he bounced around like a squirrel on a mission.

He jumped halfway up a tree about a quarter mile away to scan for his target. It didn't take long to spot the five-point buck grazing near a log about fifty yards away. The buck looked around, twitching his ears, sensing something.

Once the buck returned to grazing, Jefferarri climbed down the tree and quietly stalked toward the creature on all fours. About twenty yards away, the buck raised his head again. He moved his ears from left to right before taking off in the opposite direction.

Jefferarri sprang up out of his crouched position and beelined toward his target. His faint red eyes locked in on his prey.

The two creatures dashed between trees and underbrush. Jefferarri gained on the speedy animal. It didn't take long for him to track down and pounce on the buck's back, bringing it down to the ground with a thunderous crash. Then Jefferarri's teeth tore into the buck's neck, eating away at it. Blood flowed freely to the ground and all over Jefferarri's face as the buck kicked and yelped . . . until it lay lifeless. Swallowing a clump of flesh, Jefferarri raised his head and let out a sonorous, humanlike howl that could be heard for miles.

Back at the ranch, Octavia rushed out the front door of the house upon hearing the distant howl. She met Eugene and Roseline on the porch, looking out into the tree line. She didn't see Jefferarri anywhere.

"Is that Jefferarri?" she asked.

Neither one of them responded to her. Birds quickly flew from over the trees and the ranch and headed south. *We don't have long*, Eugene thought.

Next, they heard a helicopter moving in from the west of the ranch. Finally, the aircraft came into view just above the treetops.

"There's our ride," Eugene said.

The helicopter landed in an open space on the ranch and powered down. The pilot door opened, and a middle-aged, bearded, Black man stepped out, examining his surroundings. He toted a duffle bag strapped across his chest and shoulders.

Eugene eased off the porch to greet his longtime friend who once worked with him. A smile crossed the pilot's face as they closed in on each other.

"My main man, Eugene," the pilot said.

"Calvin Beltron. What's up, my man?"

Calvin, fifty-one years old, worked as a pilot for The Order a decade ago. He had since left and started his own helicopter services company.

"How you been, old man? I'm glad to see you're alive and well. They wouldn't let me on the Compound to see you."

They chuckled and embraced with a handshake and a tight hug.

"I saw the card, my friend. Thank you. And I appreciate you doing this for me on such short notice."

"As much as you have done for me, it's an honor."

Octavia and Roseline strode up to them, catching the men's attention.

"Hey," Eugene said. "This is—"

Jefferarri sprang out of nowhere with lightning-fast speed, surprising everyone as he slid fifteen yards before stopping. Blood stained his face and body. His body rose and fell to the rhythm of his breathing. Everyone froze in place for a moment.

"Baby," Octavia said to Jefferarri.

Jefferarri didn't recognize her for a split second, and then his eyes blinked. Everyone saw his reaction.

"You all right?" Jefferarri asked Octavia, moving closer to her and keeping his eyes on Calvin.

"Yes. What happened to you?" she asked about the blood on his face.

Jefferarri glanced over at the helicopter. "I got hungry."

CHAPTER 26
PREPARING FOR THE QUEST

AT 46 DEGREES Fahrenheit, Jefferarri enjoyed the cool Carolina breeze from the wind thrust of the helicopter's propellers brushing against his face as he stood between the house and the aircraft while his black hoodie flapped against his ears. The sun peeped upon the mushy wetland as the clouds broke apart. He opened his eyes and took one last look at the place where half of his childhood memories came into play. Vivid images of him playing with the pigs and chasing chickens put a smile on his face that he had not had in some time. His eyes followed the trail his granddad used to ride the horses around the ranch. At that point, a tear formed in his eye. Then flashes of the night his granddad met his death at the hands of the Gugwe caused his eyes to glow. Thinking of his grandmother's death at the hands of the same bastard, he dropped a second tear from his other eye. Although he savagely avenged their deaths, it did not make him feel any better. Jefferarri was not over what happened to them and felt responsible because he could not stop it.

"Jefferarri." A voice broke him out of his memory stupor.

As Octavia's hand touched him, he looked down at her bundled up in her large, tan, hooded parka coat. A calmness overcame him. He admired her beauty for a moment, causing a slight grin to cross his face. He looked back and saw the rest of the crew making their way up behind him.

Octavia noticed the tear trails on his cheeks that ran into his beard. The same beard that was way more peppery now than salty just before he ran off into the mountains to fight the Gugwe. "Are you okay?"

He glanced back out to the ranch for a moment, took a deep breath, and then nodded.

"Ready?" Eugene asked, stopping next to the big fella in his duffle coat and a gray shoulder-strapped bag that hung down his side. "Are all the bags loaded on the helicopter?"

Jefferarri nodded at Eugene. "I want to give everyone another chance to stay," Jefferarri said seriously. "I appreciate your help, but it's not necessary." Jefferarri looked back at Roseline standing about eight yards away between them and the house with her parka coat buttoned to the top.

Now, everyone looked back at Roseline. Her face held a look of uncertainty coupled with shame. Her lowered eyebrows and tight lips told everyone she would not make the trip.

Jefferarri walked over to her and sniffed the air around her. The smell of fear was overwhelming. He looked down at her. She evaded looking at him. He dropped to one knee and grabbed her hand. "I want to thank you for being there for Octavia and looking out for me over the years." He cuffed both his hands, wrapping them around hers. "You take care of yourself if I don't see you again."

She looked into his eyes, feeling she would never see this soul again. She struggled to hold back the tears in her eyes, but her feelings overwhelmed her. Slowly, she reached out her freed hand and touched his face. He closed his eyes and rubbed his beard against her hand like a cat does when a hand touches it. Then he turned and walked away.

Jefferarri walked past his two comrades and beelined straight to the helicopter. The others went and gave Roseline a long group hug.

"Here," Eugene said, giving Roseline the keys to the Chrysler. "Take care of her until we get back." He had to speak up over the wind tunnel the propellers made around them.

She took the keys with a small smile. "I will."

Octavia reached into her pockets and handed her some cash. "Don't use a credit card until you absolutely have no choice. Go gas up and grab a room somewhere."

"We'll call you on the way back or when we return," Eugene added. "Hopefully, within a day or two. If not, then you can rest assured we will not be coming back."

Roseline swallowed hard from the last part of his statement. "Okay," she replied.

"See you soon," Octavia said, grabbing Roseline's free hand with both of her hands.

As Octavia stepped away, Roseline clutched her hand a little firmer. "Octavia, listen to me, and listen to me good. Whatever happens, you two don't want to be around Jefferarri if his eyes turn white."

"Turn white? How will they turn white?" Octavia asked. This was the first time she heard Roseline mention the white eyes. "What happens?"

Roseline stepped closer to her. "Once his eyes turn white, Jefferarri is long gone. Dead. His soul will have moved on, and he will no longer know you—any of you. You don't want to be anywhere around him if that happens. The only way to kill him is to completely sever the head from the body which would be nearly impossible."

"Roseline, we have to go," Eugene gently reminded the women.

Octavia glanced across at Jefferarri as he stepped up into the helicopter. She turned back to Roseline and nodded before she caught up with Eugene, and they strolled toward the aircraft together. Before she could enter curiosity got the better of her, and she jogged back to Roseline. "How do you know that?"

With a half smile, Rosaline touched Octavia's cheek. "I was once in your shoes." A tear flowed from her eyes, landing on her sweater.

Octavia's eyes grew large, and her mouth dropped open.

"We gotta go . . . now!" Calvin bellowed from the side of the helicopter.

"Octavia." Eugene grabbed her arm. "We got to go if we're going to make the deadline."

Octavia glanced at him and then back to Roseline before turning and heading to their ride.

Finally, Eugene and Octavia boarded the helicopter. Eugene showed Octavia how to strap in, and he did so as well.

"Everything's going to be all right," Eugene said, seeing the apprehension and concern on her face. "We will get through this and figure it out."

Octavia watched Roseline stand in the cool, windy place beside the vehicle. *Now it all makes sense*, she thought. *Does Jefferarri know? Was that why she was there, under the guise of a helper?* As the helicopter turned away from Roseline, she turned her attention to Jefferarri.

Jefferarri leaned his head back in the seat, his eyes closed. Octavia looked at him from head to toe before focusing on his hand. *By now, he would have grabbed my hand in the past.* She reached to hold his hand but thought against it, placing her hands back in her lap. *Somehow, things had to get back to normal.*

Ego stood by the table next to four other new hires under a tent just outside of where the Busbin home used to stand, checking his gear. Despite the heavy snowfall, the renewed task force could comfortably carry on their work under the large white tent. The tent's fabric walls and strategically placed heaters kept the temperature comfortable. As they readied themselves for war, the sounds of clinking metal and rustling fabric filled the room.

"Hey, guys," Jason said, walking up out of the blue.

Ego and the men glanced at him but continued to work on their gear and weapons.

Finally, Ego spoke up. "All is good, Captain," he said, continuing his adjustments, not looking up.

"Good," Jason said, bobbing his head, feeling the cold shoulder. At that moment, he realized how much his fallen comrades meant to him when it came to brotherhood. He let the cold roll off his back and thought, *maybe they're just nervous.* He remembered his first few runs chasing monsters and mythical beasts as a wet pup.

Jason never could get to know the men personally, although he took pride in some of them. The problem was that he was not involved in the process of hiring these replacements, and The Order tossed them into the fire because of time constraints due to the current situation and their being short-staffed. Since they had a little time before they headed out on another "mission," he decided to engage in some chitchat while they prepared.

"You guys came highly recommended from the top. I want to personally thank you all for being a part of the team," Jason said.

The men kept working as if they never heard him.

"You're welcome," Ego said nonchalantly but still kept his eyes on his task at hand.

Jason's eyebrows frowned, not liking the vibe he got from the four men he knew nothing about. *These men are going to be trouble. I know it*, he thought. He decided to test the situation again. "So, how are you guys liking the job so far?" He faked a smile. "I bet you guys never thought you would be real-life monster hunters when you grew up, huh?"

After a moment of no response, Jason braced his hands upon his waistline. Ego looked up, and his eyes met Jason's. With the look on Jason's face, Ego felt the need to break the apparent ice.

"I'm sorry. We're just a little nervous, that's all," Ego said. "We're just trying to focus so we won't disappoint you, sir. You are right.

Chasing monsters is new to us. And I probably speak for everyone at the table that none of us knew or realized these things existed."

I'm no fool, Jason thought, but he played the role just in case he was wrong. "I understand," he said with a smile. His gaze shifted to the other men at the table, who were now looking at him. It felt awkward. *I need to look more into their background.* "Well, I'll let you all get back to it. Please mingle with the rest of the team and get to know everyone. We are family here," he said, stepping back before turning away.

Dixon stepped out of the car into another familiar scene. Crime tape surrounded the cinder block, one-level home. With the loss of deputies from the incident in the woods less than two miles away, only Coe and Diana sat in their cars.

The snow and wind had calmed down. A few flurries fell here and there, but the forecast predicted a blizzard was coming. The sun stood no chance against the thick cloud cover above.

Blood stained the foot-deep disturbed snow, which was steadily growing. The one thing that stood out from this crime scene compared to the Busbin residence, other than the house still standing, was that there were many more tracks than what occurred at the Busbin crime scene. Coe and Diana met Dixon at his car before they walked with him toward the crime tape in front of the house. Coe was the first one to speak. His body language no longer showed a confident stand.

"This is bad. I knew these people," he said, looking at the house.

"I did too, Coe," Dixon said in a defeated tone. He stood next to Coe, briefly glancing at him.

"You want to talk about the outside, or do you want to see the inside first?" Diana asked. "I've already taken pictures of as much as possible without contaminating the crime scene. I vomited once inside, though."

"I don't think contaminating this will hurt anything. Once the Feds get a hold of it, it probably will never have happened if they have anything to do with it."

Dixon looked around, then asked, "Is it that bad in there?" Diana's silence told him everything he needed to know.

"'Bad' is an understatement," Coe added.

Dixon stopped at the crime scene tape. He smelled the iron in the air from what he expected to be a bloody scene inside the house. He turned around to the outside of the home. Something in the distance caught his attention. "Well, what's going on out here?"

"There are at least two different sets of tracks. The ones to the north over there are the same as the ones back at the Busbin's home, except bigger, which stopped over there and never came up on the house. But at some point, the tracks went back into the woods."

Dixon followed the blood trail from the shattered window to the first prints.

"Something dragged somebody out to the bigger one," he said, pointing at the tracks from the window that met up with the bigger tracks. "This one gave that one the body." He turned to Coe and asked, "Any bodies left in the house?"

Without a word, Coe shook his head.

"Violeta?" Dixon asked.

"She's not inside," Coe responded.

Twice as much blood trickled out of the front door. Dixon looked over at a footprint that was in good shape.

"That print almost resembles a canine's," Dixon said as he pointed.

CHAPTER 27
THE TASK FORCE

FOUR HIGH-POWERED FLOODLIGHTS illuminated the tree line, emanating from four large trucks parked beside the Busbin's former home, now a heap of charred rubble. The lights beamed through the minus-4-degree windchill and wind-blown snow that brightened the tree line but struggled to pierce beyond the trees as if the darkness had denied entry. The woods held a devious curse. A weatherproof, military-type camping tent stood about ten yards behind the trucks. Two RVs were parked, one on each side of the tent. One was the command center, and the other was for the task force transportation. A van parked next to it contained supplies and the drone. Snow piled on top of everything in the vicinity. The last truck was to hold the captured Flesh Eater if the mission was successful. They had used the same truck to hold Jimmy when they captured him four days ago.

"The Order wants us to bring the creature back alive," Moody told his crew. He stood in front of his men, finishing up his briefing. "And I'm cool with that, but I need all of you to return and go home. If it dies, it dies. If that means all of you come back in one piece. Remember to follow the game plan 'cause when we follow the plan and have one another's back, we are the best, and nothing on this earth can escape our clutches when we sink our teeth into our mission. Jason has already drawn out and gone over the plan. Go get 'em and be safe. Dismissed."

"Yes, sir!" all the men said in unison as they sprang out of their seats.

Anna walked in with her arms folded as the men filed out of the tent. "The wind is picking up out there," she warned Moody. "This is a death sentence. That thing out there is getting bigger and bigger the more flesh it consumes."

Minutes later, Jason and his crew entered the woods, leaving the heavy snow and wind behind with the help of some protection from the trees. The air within the darkness had a heavy, static feeling.

They wore special helmets with night vision shields and radios linked to the command and one another. The headgear also came with heat detection vision to pick up any heat signatures from anything living. Cold air outside of the woods was biting, and the snow was already over a foot deep. The further the men stepped into the woods, the more the ghostly, unnatural darkness made everyone uncomfortable. The deeper they entered the unknown, the more attention everyone paid to their six. They held their weapons in the ready position, but the flashlights on the rifles did not cover as much ground as they were supposed to. It was as if the shadows overpowered and consumed the light.

Jason constantly glanced back, checking behind him. The farther he walked, the more he felt a prickling sensation of goose bumps on his skin. He noticed he could not see his comrades' flashlights in the distance. The forest absorbed all the light within it.

I've been on many hunts, but this feels different, he thought.

His eyes kept seeing something move just out of sight of the beam of his light, but whenever he shined the light in that area . . . nothing was there. A quick switch to night vision, the same result. His breathing and heart rate accelerated. Goose bumps ramped up on his body. Now, a familiar smell of rotting meat hit his nose. "Keep an eye out for anything. And watch your six," he told his men through his headgear.

Again, something moved to his right just out of view of his beam, but nothing was there when he directed his light in that area. *No need to try any other vision mode*, he thought, knowing the result would be the same. Suddenly, however, the air got colder, and the wind whistled around the trees. Just above the whistling wind, he heard a brief sound echoing from the distance that sounded like a dog. But it did not sound like a regular dog or a wolf's growl. It had a distorted sound that repeated like a broken record.

Something moved slightly to his left. He bounced the light in that direction and hissed, seeing a man hanging from a tree by vines. The elements had frozen his body, and something had feasted on his flesh, leaving huge chunks missing. Whatever had done this hung the body up to taunt them. The torn clothes that hung off his body let Jason know it was the deputy missing from earlier today. Two little yellow eyes above the swinging body peered down at him. The light panned up to reveal an enormous owl perched on the branch of the hanging body.

Crunching sounds to the left of him caused him to adjust his weapon and light in that direction. He caught the end of something, but it bounced away from the weakened light. "I see something," he spoke into his headset. The scent worsened the more he advanced. He quickly rotated between night and heat vision . . . still nothing. Therefore, he switched back to the standard view.

"Be careful," Anna warned.

A scream from a distance made him stop in his tracks. He frantically swung his rifle and light beam around. "What was that?" he nervously asked himself. A few seconds later, a second wailing sound erupted from the trees. "Fuck," he said. "Somebody, talk to me!"

"All vital signs are still active," Anna responded in the helmet. "Watch your six. The drone is picking up nothing on the radar from above."

That means something else is out here screaming, he thought. A screech from a closer proximity that vibrated through his body was too close for comfort this time. Now, he heard something moving in the trees above, and as he swung his rifle and the light up above, clusters of snow fell to the ground. Something bumped him on the back of his head. He turned quickly, with his finger tightening the trigger on his rifle, ready to unleash.

"A vital sign just flatlined," Anna stated through the headset. "I repeat, a lifeline flatlined."

Jason shined his light down to the ground for a quick look at what hit him, and what he saw buckled his legs. It was the headgear on the head of one of his comrades. Blood stained the snow around it like a fresh sponge. He raised his assault rifle and the light with his head on a swivel. Everything moved fast, causing a blur in his vision. *This is a poor plan—a bad idea. We need to regroup. Nothing good can come out of this*, he thought. "Man down! Man down! Fall back *now*!" Jason yelled his command into the headgear.

More screaming erupted from a distance, followed by automatic gunfire. More gunshots followed as more screaming ricocheted through the woods.

"No! No! Nooooo!" the scream tapered off in the distance.

Jason lost his sense of direction. None of the trees looked the same to him anymore, as if they had moved. His fight or flight kicked in . . . and he took off. "Abort mission! Abort mission!" He rushed through the woods, bobbing and weaving the oncoming trees, fallen limbs, and bushes.

"Abort mission!" Anna's voice resounded from the headgear. "We're losing people left and right. Get out of there!"

Suddenly, Jason felt chased. Sounds like twigs and branches breaking got louder, indicating something was coming closer and did not care to hide it. He wanted to unload the clip in his rifle behind him as he ran but feared hitting one of his own in the process. He continued to run without knowing where he was headed.

"Anna, pop a flair! Pop a flair!" Jason begged with exhaustion. "10-4!"

A wail bellowed behind him, and he knew it was safe to shoot whatever it was. He pointed the rifle behind him as he looked back for a quick step of two . . . and that's when he saw it closing in. Its dark eyes were blacker than the surroundings. Even with the little light that hit it, he saw large, jagged teeth with thick, yellowish spittle being slung from its mouth. He squeezed the trigger, letting the bullets fly as they may. The creature let out an ear-splitting shriek.

He saw a glimpse of two flairs rocket through the sky. He changed course with a slight turn to the right, hoping to return safely to the campground. Suddenly, the creature yanked the gun out of his hand and tossed it at him, just grazing his helmet. Then a sharp pain ran down his back as he finally raced out past the tree line into the floodlights of the campground.

The creature stopped short of the tree line, then poked its head out of the cover of the shadows into the floodlights and let out a deep, bellowed shriek in disappointment. Its head was at least ten to twelve feet from the ground. Jason could not see its face clearly with the swirling snow and the distance, but the little he saw was like a vision from hell.

Ego and three other men aimed their rifles and fired at the creature, but the beast stood there, nearly unfazed by the few bullets that hit it while it surveyed the scene, letting out another bone-chilling screech. Then it stopped when a man in a dashiki-caped hoodie poncho walked out from behind the tent and toward it. The poncho cape flapped in the wind, showing the only other clothing he wore basketball shorts. He seemed unbothered by the frigid conditions as he walked through the snow.

"Get back," Jason said as he ran past the four men. He covered his damaged ears, shielding them from the automatic weapons of his four comrades.

The men ran back with Jason for cover, fighting the increasing strength of the high winds whipping up the snow. Anna and Matt ran out of the RV and instantly noticed the man. Moody stepped out of the warmth of the tent and tried to focus. He saw the man too, as the figure walked toward the running men headed back toward safety.

"Who's that?" Matt asked, chattering from the cold.

"It can't be," Anna said, feeling the familiar presence.

Jason stopped in front of the hooded man, nearly sliding into him. "Jefferarri?" he gasped as his eyes widened, looking up at him taller than he remembered.

The creature thundered louder than before, causing everyone but Jefferarri to cover their ears. Jefferarri returned the favor with a howl directed at the creature as his eyes lit a bright reddish hue under his dark, flapping hoodie.

"Jefferarri," Anna said to herself, but just enough for Matt to hear.

Dazed, Matt stared at him. "It can't be," he said as he looked at Jefferarri in puzzlement, but joy overwhelmed his confusion. A quick smile twisted his lips. With so much going on at once, it was hard to enjoy the unexpected reunion.

Ego, who trailed behind his comrades, saw Jefferarri, but then lost his balance and fell. Jefferarri quickly snapped his head toward him, smelling the familiar scent.

"You," Jefferarri said just above the howling wind.

He snatched Ego up so quickly that Ego dropped his rifle. Ego's heart pounded against his chest, threatening to break out, and his breath rushed out of his mouth like a smoking train stack.

"No. I watched you die on that mountain in Carolina!" Ego cried, unknowingly admitting to the crimes from being so frightened.

"I knew it," Jason said. "I knew something was not right about you, motherfucker!"

"Let me show you how to kill, bitch," Jefferarri seethed, opening his mouth to rip a chunk out of Ego's neck.

"Jefferarri, wait!" Anna pleaded. Her eyes filled with emotion from seeing him. "We need to know who was responsible for what happened in North Carolina."

Jefferarri pulled Ego's face closer to his as they exchanged breaths. Jefferarri groaned and bared his teeth. His shoulders rose with each breath he took.

"Jefferarri, *please*," Anna begged.

He tossed Ego at Anna's feet, causing the snow to kick up against her and Matt. The ground knocked the breath out of him. Jason rushed over and quickly zip-tied Ego's wrists behind his back.

"We need to get out of here," Moody woofed , keeping his distance from Jefferarri. "We can't do anything in these conditions, and I've lost enough men today. Let him do what he does—hunt!"

"Go get him," Jason said to Jefferarri as he and Anna picked Ego up from the snow.

Jefferarri turned toward the woods, sniffed the air, and smelled danger coming. "You all better leave. Something is coming—and it's hungry."

"Everyone to the RVs on the double," Moody ordered.

A helicopter had landed about fifty yards behind the trucks. Nobody paid it any attention because they were used to seeing helicopters landing all the time. Eugene was not feeling well and was unable to tackle the weather conditions. He struggled to breathe, and his chest and throat were sore. This weather had snuck up and taken its toll on him.

"I'm sorry I can't make it with you," Eugene said. "I feel like I'm letting you down," he said in a hoarse voice, followed by a painful cough.

"I appreciate everything you have done to this point. It's my fight now. You get some care, and I'll catch up with you soon," Octavia said before grabbing his hand. "Go find Roseline."

"I got him," Calvin said. "He'll be all right. I know a place about a hundred miles from here that will take good care of him. I'll drop him off before I gas up."

"Thanks, Calvin," she said. She kissed Eugene on the hand, then opened the cold door and jumped out. Jefferarri had previously exited the helicopter moments before it landed. She quickly closed the door and high-stepped through the snow toward the camp.

CHAPTER 28
THE FIGHT

EVERYONE FLED TO the RVs as quickly as possible. Everyone, that is, except Jefferarri, who watched Jason help people in one RV, and Anna helped everyone else in the other RV. From behind the tent and RVs, cracking and rustling noises from a distance caught Jefferarri's undivided attention. A tree crashed across the only road leading into and out of the condensed area, blocking all vehicles from entering or leaving.

"Jefferarri!" Octavia called. She was bundled up in her heavy coat with her scarf and hood flapping in the wind. The snow around her was almost knee-deep.

Jefferarri's focused eyes were directed at the familiar voice, and he saw Octavia high stepping in his direction between the last couple of people rushing to the RVs. *What are you doing, Octavia?* he thought before he bared his teeth at her. "You need to leave *now!*"

Her voice cut through the howling snowstorm as she declared, "I can help you!"

"No!" his deep, booming bark resonated through the crisp, wintry air.

Jefferarri's reaction stopped her in her tracks. The cold ripped through her skin. She knew he disapproved of her hanging around. Her sight was then directed behind him.

"Jefferarri!" Jefferarri's grandmother's voice, Margaret, called from the woods. The voice was slightly distorted, sounding like it came from a megaphone. Everyone heard it. "Save me! Come, save me, Jefferarri!"

Jefferarri snarled at the wood line. One eye opened wider than the other. His furrowed eyebrows cast a shadow over bright red, glowing eyes.

"Jefferarri!" the voice of his grandfather, Clifton, called to him in a distressed tone. "It's hurting me," he said in a sobbing tone. "Please, don't let me die again."

Jefferarri bellowed out at the wood line direction.

"Don't let me die again, Jefferarri," Margaret's voice said in more distress.

That did it for him. A recount of seeing his grandmother's helpless face as Burly held her bloody, decapitated head replayed in his mind. The anger built in his gut. He pulled the hood back off his head before racing toward the trees. His teeth and canines slowly pushed out of his gums, causing them to bleed. His jawline pushed forward, and his ears moved up on his head. He grimaced as his joints popped, sending waves of pain through his body.

Jefferarri sensed something different and smelled the powerful stench that cut through the cold air before he turned around. It was partly familiar but not entirely the same. A scream of agony brought Jefferarri's attention to its direction. He slid across the deep snow like tires on a wet road, twisting his body back to the people rushing in the RVs.

An enormous figure had a man in its jaws, ripping the man's body apart. The creature swallowed the man's innards without chewing. The door to the RV closed, leaving the man to suffer his fate alone. Another creature jumped on top of the second RV. The monster tried to keep the door from closing as the people inside struggled to keep the beast out.

"Octavia!" Jefferarri called, rushing back to the RVs. He did not see her, so he assumed she had made it inside.

The creatures noticed Jefferarri and gave him their full attention. The one on the RV jumped off and stood next to the second one. The two monsters briefly forgot about Jefferarri as they wrestled over the bloody, lifeless body before it snapped in half at the lower torso.

The floodlights' glare made it difficult for Jefferarri to see, but he could feel his transformation taking hold as he closed in on the two. The creatures eyed Jefferarri rushing in and left the mangled body in the snow. They rose from all fours to a bipedal position. Jefferarri stopped about twenty yards away when he realized who they were.

The fur had practically covered Jefferarri's body, and his teeth and canines were fully developed. "James? Jamie?" Jefferarri said, confused.

The Twins had been missing all this time, molding into these half-life, zombie-appearing, flesh-eating creatures. The Wendigo's curse had transformed them. Both twins' bodies looked withered. Fur and gaping holes and deep claw marks in their bodies exposed pieces of ribs and dark innards. Their cloudy-white eyes resembled those of the blind and reflected no light.

The tallest twin on the right stood about nine feet tall. His head had the features of a wolf, but the skin and muscles on the left side of his face dangled off the exposed skull. The right side had deep claw marks, exposing the skull as well. His top teeth and canines overlapped his bottom teeth.

The other twin stood at around eight feet tall. Something had ripped the left side of his body to shreds. Dark meat protruded out from the insides, showing extensive damage. His transformation did not go as far as his brother's did. He had less fur, and his head was still more like a human's. He bared his short, sharp teeth in his crooked jaw.

In full transformation, Jefferarri now stood about eight feet tall, with piercing human eyes and razor-sharp teeth. He unleashed a harsh rumble that reverberated for miles. His shaggy black mane flowed down his back in a V-shape to his waist. His protruding snout and pointed ears gave him the head of a wolf. The broad shoulders and chiseled muscles resembled that of a bodybuilder. His short, glossy fur reflected the bright lights. Jefferarri bared his teeth at his foes before dropping to all fours and charging toward them.

The Twins and Jefferarri clashed in the middle, with all three tumbling in the snow. The constant wind carried away the torn flesh and fur as teeth and claws swiped from every angle. They sounded like a pack of wolves fighting in the wild over supremacy.

Jefferarri quickly clenched his claws around James's throat and choked-slammed him into the cold, hard ground. James yelped as his back smacked the icy ground, causing snow to explode upward. Jefferarri grabbed the muzzle and lower jaw to rip them apart, but the smaller twin, Jamie, jumped on his back, sinking his teeth into the back of Jefferarri's neck and clawing at his face. Jefferarri wailed in pain as Jamie tried to rip away his flesh. Jefferarri abandoned the twin on the ground to shake off his attacker from his back. He twisted and turned, trying to get Jamie off him, but James now tackled Jefferarri, knocking both of them to the ground. Snow flew everywhere from the impact of the fall.

The people in the RVs fixed their eyes on the battle unfolding on the two HD monitors in each RV. Nine people, including Octavia, Matt, and Anna, stood in the first RV. Deep down, everyone was nervous, and fear filled the RV. They hoped that Jefferarri could pull off the victory and they could get out of this funk alive. However, Jefferarri looked outmatched, causing a deflated silence.

"C'mon, baby," Octavia said, breaking the silence. "C'mon!" She slammed her hand on the top of a chair.

The same mood filled the second RV, with seven people also glued to two monitors. Moody sat at the desk keeping a watchful eye, and Jason guarded Ego, who sat in the corner.

"Command, come in," Moody said with desperation, trying to reach somebody back at the Command Center at the Compound. "Command, we need reinforcements and rescue. Over!"

Jason's eyes darted back between the screen and Ego. His finger rested firmly on the trigger, itching to squeeze it without hesitation. Many of his comrades died at the hands of Ego's actions, but the need to find out the truth outweighed his desires. He wanted justice for all involved.

Back outside the RVs, Jefferarri and the Twins fought in the snow with teeth snipping and claws swiping. Jefferarri grabbed one twin on his arm and bit into his forearm, ripping chunks of flesh off the bone. Blood black as tar poured from the wound, staining the color of the snow below. This caused Jamie to release his grip from the back of Jefferarri's neck as it shrieked in pain, and Jefferarri took the opportunity to sling him across the snow onto the back section of the RV where Moody huddled. The RV rocked and slid a few feet, leaving an enormous crater from the impact.

The people inside the RV stumbled off balance as the RV violently shook. The monitors flickered for a quick second. Jason was unfazed, keeping his eyes locked on Ego.

Jefferarri let out a fierce growl from deep within as he shifted his focus on James. Visible mist pulsated from Jefferarri's breath, which evaporated in the breeze. Drool mixed with a black mucous soaked his bottom jaw. Blood flowed from the back of his mane and colored his back, dripping onto the snow below him. It was painful, but Jefferarri had no time to cry about it. He galloped at James, and James leaped at Jefferarri, who snipped at his neck but missed. James raked his massive claws across Jefferarri's chest, exposing the muscles under the skin. Then he clamped down on Jefferarri's shoulder but quickly released after Jefferarri bit and ripped off his ear with his teeth, uncovering the black meat and skull where the ear used to be. Now, Jefferarri clamped onto

James's throat, tearing it from his neck, then tossed James away from him. Black blood poured from James's neck as he staggered backward, gasping for breath.

Jefferarri spat out the flesh to the ground and rushed him, ripping his bottom jaw away from his face. Now, James fell to the snow, clinging to life. Jefferarri ripped out James's black heart to finish him.

He tossed the heart at the whimpering twin, Jamie, then walked toward Jamie on all fours, snarling with a sinister grin. In Flesh Eater form, the Twins had no compassion for anything other than to eat, but the Twins had a connection. James held his wound tightly as he stood up, his eyes filled with rage. Jefferarri's growl echoed through the forest as he charged toward him, claws at the ready. In a matter of seconds, Jefferarri tore Jamie to shreds. Fur and flesh disappeared with the wind into the dark. The Twin yelped with no way to escape.

After a moment, with his chest and shoulders rising with each heavy breath, Jefferarri stood back to look at his handiwork.

Black blood drained from the wounds across Jamie's body as he slid down the side of the RV to the ground, leaving a trail of black following him.

Jefferarri looked over his shoulder back at the wood line. He wanted to send a message, so he grabbed the heart off the ground and jammed it into Jamie's mouth. Teeth and black blood flew out of his mouth. Then he proceeded to tear both his claws into his neck and ripped the head from his body.

Next, Jefferarri stood up with the head in one hand and his other hand jammed into the hole where Jamie's neck used to be. His shoulders still rose and fell with every breath. The wind caused his mane to wave. His lips raised, showing his black-and-red-stained teeth. The cold air aided his wounds, speeding up the healing process. After a few seconds, he slowly turned his head and looked over his shoulder back at the woods.

He turned and tossed the head and the body far toward the woods. Ignoring the pain in his body still healing, he threw his arms back behind him and leaned forward to bellow the brashest growl ever that lasted every bit of ten seconds. The woods responded after a few seconds of silence.

It did not take long before the response came. The trees began to sway side to side, sending the snow off the branches to the ground. Something echoed the same noise back to Jefferarri as he did just moments ago, but with more oomph behind it. Jefferarri adjusted his eyes to the top of the swaying trees and saw the figure jerking like a monkey, causing the tree to move. Then the creature jumped out of the tree and landed in plain sight of the floodlights.

The floodlights revealed the tall, emaciated creature. Tall and deformed, with a humanlike head and gaunt cheeks, it gawked at Jefferarri. The dark eyes were set deep back into their sockets, barely visible. Only a few clumps of lengthy hair hung from its head. Its raw lips, which appeared to have been wasting away for some time, displayed black gums and spiraling, jagged teeth three to four inches long. The bloodstained jaw hung down further than usual as its foggy breath quickly inhaled and exhaled with every wheezing breath. Pieces of flesh hung from the bottom canines with blood still dripping from them. The powerful stench from the creature, directed by the howling winds, made breathing almost unendurable. Even hunched over, the beast stood every bit of ten to eleven feet tall. The ash-gray skin pulled tight around its torso, exposing every bone. Some appeared broken or abnormal. No genitals were present, as if they had fallen off. Black, thick drool dripped to the ground from every orifice. The Flesh Eater moved up and down between all fours and bipedal, primarily using its long arms for support.

With his ears laid back like an angry dog, Jefferarri pounded both fists on the ground like an enraged ape at the unnatural figure. At this point, Jefferarri did not remember why he had the temptation to hunt down the creature. He just knew killing it was his calling.

The creature rose upright and launched toward Jefferarri, kicking the snow and frozen mud behind it as its claws dug into the ground. Jefferarri followed suit and leaped in the air at the creature with his arm back, ready to rip his claws into the beast . . . but it was not to be. The creature's long arms swiped at Jefferarri in midair, knocking him hard into the snow. He yelped as he hit the ground. Jefferarri lay in the snow with five deep gashes across his midsection that bled profusely.

"Hungry," the Flesh Eater said in a weak, scratchy voice. His long, snakelike tongue coiled out of his mouth at his potential meal.

But the dog still had a lot of fight in him. Using one arm, Jefferarri mustered up to his feet. He whimpered in pain as he staggered to his feet, red stains beneath him.

The Flesh Eater licked the torn flesh and blood off his claws. Low moans filled the air from the creature. His facial expression revealed he liked the taste. "Gooddddd," the Flesh Eater said in a ghoulish tone.

Jefferarri propelled himself through the air with blinding speed and snapped his jaws at the Flesh Eater—but to no avail. He had trouble getting past those long, spindly arms of the much-taller and quicker creature. It grabbed Jefferarri and sank its teeth deep into Jefferarri's chest, mauling him like a grizzly bear that left Jefferarri wailing in pain before being tossed to the ground with a massive bloody hole in his chest. A fountain of blood poured from his wounds.

The creature swallowed Jefferarri's flesh without chewing like a Komodo dragon swallows its prey. Then he picked Jefferarri up to take another chunk out of him, but with one last-ditch effort, Jefferarri clapped his jaws around the Flesh Eater's neck. Unfortunately, due to the excessive blood loss, he did not have enough energy to cause any significant damage. Both fell to the ground and wrestled in the red and black slush.

The creature pushed Jefferarri off him, leaving deep gouges from his teeth on Jefferarri's neck, and, in return, sank his teeth deep into Jefferarri's neck. Jefferarri had no energy left to fight. The beast picked him up, helpless as a newborn babe. The creature fed off the flesh of his neck as tears flowed from Jefferarri's eyes, and he wailed. He felt the end was near. His eyes dimmed from the red hue to a look of dark death, and his head fell lifelessly. The Flesh Eater punched his claws in Jefferarri's chest and ripped out his heart before tossing him away like a rag doll. Snow fluffed on top of him from the impact.

The Flesh Eater let out a victory roar as he lifted the heart over his head and squeezed it like an orange until it popped. Sprinkles of blood dotted his face and ran down his arms. "Hungry," he said, before moving toward Jefferarri to feast on his corpse . . . when a sudden rustling from inside one of the RVs grasped its attention. It moved and climbed on top of the RV, examining the structure. "Hungry," he continued.

It hopped down and shook the RV until it started to rock side to side, then fell hard on its side. He jumped on it and clawed at the door until it was gashed to threads. The people inside panicked. The Flesh Eat peeked into the RV and saw the terrified people in distress. Shots rang up out the door, striking the creature in the shoulder and face, but it was as if he did not even feel it.

Quickly, he reached into the RV and yanked out the shooters. The gun fell to the ground, and it started shredding the clothes off the unfortunate man with its claws that cut deep into the crying man as the creature continued to rip away his clothes. The man's blood splattered everywhere. The Flesh Eater bit into the naked man's thigh like biting into a barbecue rib. He rotated the man like corn on the cob.

Octavia leaped out of the other RV and charged toward Jefferarri's body, but the gusting wind caused her to stumble after a few steps. Her mindset was in a different place. She was not herself, and her chest burned from the pain Jefferarri suffered.

The creature sniffed the air. It smelled her unique essence and immediately became intrigued. "Hungry," the Flesh Eater said, hopping off the turned-over RV, leaving a huge dent and letting the mangled body fall back down into the opened door.

Octavia's eye rolled back, the searing pain in her chest sending waves of agony coursing through her body. The air around her seemed to thicken, suffocating her senses, as if every breath was laced with the acrid scent of burning. She strained to tap into her powers, but the intensity of the pain made it impossible to concentrate.

The creature crawled over and stood over Octavia, ready to devour her. Red saliva dripped from his jaws, leaving a trail of white vapors gliding in the wind. The smell of the creature made her gag. She looked up and saw it, its teeth bared and coated in blood that dripped onto her back.

"Get away from her!" Jason pointed his gun at the creature and gained its attention.

The creature looked over at him. Its eyebrows flared, and a crooked smile stretched across its bloody face. It looked back down at Octavia, but she was gone. He searched for her and saw Anna quickly guiding her back to the RV. Before it could give chase, a popping noise from Jefferarri's body caught its attention.

Thick, foggy vapers rose from the sizzling sounds of melting snow around Jefferarri. Four men of the task force created a barrier between the creatures with their guns aimed forward as the people tried to cram into the remaining RV. The hunched creature abandoned its pursuit to feast on the curse of starvation and focused on the new developments before him.

The sound of something or someone struggling to catch their breath came from the foggy mass lit up by the floodlights. The popping sounds were accelerating as the creature took a step forward . . . waiting.

"C'mon, Octavia," Anna said. "Pull yourself together. There is nothing you can do now. We gotta survive." The RV was full and left many outside who could not get in. Climbing into the other RV was useless since the Flesh Eater had compromised it. She looked around, and the only option was the trucks. Anna pulled a tired Octavia through the snow to one truck with a floodlight on the back. Matt trailed behind them as best as his old bones would allow. Before Anna and Octavia jumped in the vehicle, they looked back toward the creature and the foggy mass.

They saw a faded shadow outline moving within the mist, pushing up from the ground. The popping stopped, and the shadow disappeared. The breathing and snarling sounds were so deep with bass that they vibrated through everything nearby.

A moment of silence blanketed everyone. Even the howling wind seemed to cease. Then a massive white werewolf's head reached out from the mist and bellowed a deep, bloodcurdling moan from the nearly nine-foot-tall beast, making the Flesh Eater step back.

Jefferarri had pearl-white eyes, the ones Roseline had warned Octavia about, and a snow-white shaggy mane with matching fur on his face. He had a larger snout aligned with deadly razor-sharp teeth. Saliva blew out of his mouth like a T-rex during the seven-second blast from his muzzle.

Jefferarri took two steps out of the dissipating mist to reveal his much taller, thicker stature. His mane still ran down his back to form a V-shape on his lower back that waved in the wind. His rippling muscles showed through his hairless chest and torso. Blue veins ran like rivers under his albino skin. Fur thinly covered his lower body but was thicker in the pubic area. His thick legs bent back like a dog with large, wide feet.

"Level five has arrived," Anna said quietly.

The Flesh Eater screamed to match the decibels of Jefferarri's growl. The two walked a half circle, one sizing the other up, then clashing in the middle. Off the bat, it was a relatively evenly matched fight compared to the first one.

The Flesh Eater ripped his claws across the tough skin on Jefferarri's chest, only to leave deep scratches but not open wounds like before. Jefferarri backhanded the Flesh Eater, knocking him on his back. Cat quick, he quickly sprang up and jumped on Jefferarri's head, biting and clawing at anything he could. Blood flowed from the wounds, and pieces of fur from his mane disappeared in the wind. But Jefferarri tossed him on the ground, ripping off a piece of his ear. He pounced on the creature, swiping his claws across its face, ripping an eyeball from its socket, and causing deep gouges on that side of the face. The eyeball slid, hidden under the slushy snow on the ground. The Flesh Eater wailed in pain, fighting to get up. It gouged at Jefferarri's eyes, but Jefferarri bit off three of its fingers, then spit them out to the side. He used his body weight to keep the beast down. Then he pulled open his mouth and tore its bottom jaw away from the Flesh Eater's face. Tossing it to the side, he then reached over and ripped out its tongue.

One voice behind another, the Flesh Eater cried out for help in the many voices of its past victims. Now, Jefferarri sat on top of the creature, tilting his head from side to side like a dog curious about a noise. Once the voices stopped, Jefferarri curled his lips, then stabbed his claws into the Flesh Eater's chest and yanked out its beating heart. He hopped off the creature, leaving it to flop in the crimson-stained snow. He dropped the heart at his feet and stomped it hard. The creature's heart burst under the weight of Jefferarri's weight. Now, the Flesh Eater stopped moving. Jefferarri dropped to all fours to examine his handiwork. He sniffed as his eyes investigated the lifeless body.

Finally, he placed one massive foot on the creature's heaving chest, feeling the warmth of its body beneath his touch. With a triumphant growl that echoed through the air, he raised his head towards the expansive sky. As the sound carried on the wind, he could sense the raw power coursing through his veins, a surge of adrenaline that brought new life to his battered form. The scent of blood and victory mingled in the chilled air, a heady combination that fueled his primal instincts. Slowly, he felt the wounds on his body start to close, the pain subsiding as his natural healing abilities took hold. As if by some unseen magic, his ear, once marred by a missing piece, began to regenerate, the missing flesh growing back with remarkable speed.

Now, he swiftly whipped his head around, the sound of his movement cutting through the tense silence. His piercing gaze fell upon the four men of the Task Force, his lips curling back, revealing his formidable teeth. The men, filled with terror, tightened their grip on their rifles, the metallic glint reflecting off their trembling hands. Jefferarri moved gracefully to the side, his agile form on all fours. With his head held low and ears pulled back, he remained attentive, his eyes fixed unwaveringly on the men, watching their every move.

CHAPTER 29
THE BOSS FIGHT

JEFFERARRI RUSHED THE men before they got off a shot. He grabbed two men at a time and mauled their bodies to pieces. Blood coated his face and mane, already black with the Flesh Eater's blood. The other men took shots at Jefferarri from what they thought was a safe distance, striking him in the arm and side. Jefferarri bellowed out at the men before charging quicker than the men's eyes could follow in the swirling snow. Before they knew it, Jefferarri had mauled them in the snow as their terrifying screams tapered off, along with their lives.

"Get in," Anna directed Octavia into the truck and slammed the door behind them. Anna peeked over the high seats as the spotlights lit up Jefferarri's fur with a bright glow.

Matt cautiously pulled open the creaking door of the truck, positioned to the right of Anna and Octavia. As he turned to glance back at Jefferarri, a shiver ran down his spine. The sight was mesmerizing, but scary at the same time. Jefferarri's howl pierced through the air, echoing into the vast expanse of the freezing sky. A swirling mist, reminiscent of smoke from a burning train chimney, billowed out from Jefferarri's mouth. With a mix of apprehension and urgency, Matt swiftly slid into the truck, feeling the cold metal of the door beneath his palm, and forcefully slammed it shut.

The creaking sound of the door broke through the silence, instantly capturing Jefferarri's attention. His ears perked up, twitching with curiosity. As he lifted his head, a faint scent wafted into his nostrils, causing him to inhale deeply. Sensing the tension, Anna swiftly lowered herself back into the seat, her finger pressed against her lips, signaling Octavia to remain silent. *Please don't make a sound. Our lives depend on it*, she thought looking directly at Octavia.

Jefferarri slowly stalked on all fours, like a lion on a hunt. He moved toward the trucks with a low, rumbling groan. But sounds from inside the upright RV immediately gained his interest. He leaped atop the RV, scaring the people inside and causing more commotion. He walked around the roof, examining the RV, before clawing at the top like a cat on the carpet, creating large gouges in the metal. Jefferarri could hear the frantic voices of people, which only motivated him to work harder to get in.

Suddenly, with a thunderous crash, Jefferarri forcefully tore a massive sheet of metal off the roof, the growling sound reverberating through the air. His razor-sharp claws mercilessly tore through the face of one unfortunate occupant, causing a chilling scream to fill the cramped space. As he withdrew his hand, he cautiously peered into the small hole in the ceiling, feeling a rush of anticipation. Inside the RV, the air was thick with the scent of fear and perspiration, the cramped quarters suffocating. Jefferarri's eyes scanned the overflowing mass of people, their bodies pressed together uncomfortably. Gracefully, he descended from the ceiling into the snow, his footsteps creating a low rumble, and he embarked on a silent exploration of the RV, meticulously searching for any vulnerabilities or gaps to get in.

Above Jefferarri, an owl glided through the sky, its wings silently cutting through the air. With a sudden burst of agility, he leaped up and effortlessly snatched the owl out of the air, tearing it apart with a savage fury. As the wind picked up, the feathers from the owl scattered and danced in the breeze, before he discarded the remaining carcass onto the snow.

Dawn began to settle in the sky. Jefferarri stopped and raised his head toward the wood line as his ears twitched. Something was tearing through the trees. Jefferarri took a deep breath. He twisted his neck to pop it to be ready for whatever came out of those trees.

A burst of fog rushed out of the woods into the lights. Trees fell behind its path. Gradually, the white fog took on the shape of a gray, towering figure. As the form materialized, large, oversized antlers formed at the top of the mist. They looked like dry-rotted tree branches that measured about forty to forty-five feet across.

Next, a head formed, but not just any head. The head looked like a deer skull with a long snout that had cracked and weathered over time. Small horns formed in front of the antlers, along with an enormous, gaping mouth full of jagged teeth. Only a few discolored muscles and tendons attached the bottom jaw to the top.

Then the neck materialized. Large spikes ran down the back of the neck. Loose skin did very little to cover the rotten muscles and chipped bones. Dark tissues in the neck oozed a dark substance, just like the creatures Jefferarri had slayed before. The shoulder, arms, and torso formed next as the fog continued. The upper body was mainly a rib cage covering wilted, black pumping organs. Some pieces of dark guts protruded out of its torso.

Brownish skin flapped off its arms like rotten bandages on a mummy—patchy fur covered portions of the dead skin. When the fog cleared, it revealed the creature's full stature. It sat back on its hock as a dog would, leaning forward on his arms. Five-foot-long nails protruded out from the tips of its bony fingers. Instead of feet or paws, it had large, black hooves. A dull, purplish glow pulsated from the left side of its chest.

The towering demon rose, reaching the height of the surrounding trees. Its deafening roar echoed through the air, mimicking the thunderous bellow of a colossal, flesh-eating dinosaur, causing the snow-laden branches to tremble violently. The radiant glow emanating from its chest intensified. Wisps of fog seeped from its sinister, obsidian eyes, while its skeletal form bore the rough texture of aged tree bark. A sinewy, razor-sharp tail gracefully swayed through the air behind it.

"The Wendigo," Anna said, looking over the backseat. She watched the tree-tall monstrosity take form and tower over Jefferarri.

"It's a spirit," Octavia followed up. "It's different."

"Yeah," we got to find a way out of here. Even if we could hide from Jefferarri, this situation is different."

"We've got to help him," Octavia spat.

"What?!"

Jefferarri leaped off the RV, hammer slammed his fist into the ground, and then bolted furiously toward the Wendigo. He switched randomly between all fours and bipedal. His ears laid back, and his lips rippled backward, baring his teeth with deep, guttural snarls.

The Wendigo's towering form lunged towards Jefferarri, its massive claw slicing through the air with a sharp, whipping sound. The agile beast narrowly avoided the attack, soaring through the air with grace. Jefferarri swiftly landed below the Wendigo's chest, his claws gripping onto its bony ribs for leverage. The Wendigo retaliated, swiping at Jefferarri, causing strips of its own skin to flutter away in the wind. Jefferarri skillfully evaded the demon's vicious claws, sinking his own sharp claws repeatedly into the creature's neck, reminiscent of a dog digging fervently in a backyard. The monstrous Wendigo appeared unaffected, violently shaking Jefferarri off its back, sending him crashing to the ground. With lightning reflexes, Jefferarri leaped out of harm's way as the Wendigo raised its colossal hoof to stomp at him. The impact of the hoof meeting the ground sent a shockwave through the snow, causing it to erupt violently. The Wendigo emitted an ear-piercing screech as it attempted to snap Jefferarri in two with its gaping maw, but the agile beast swiftly dodged the attack, seizing hold of one of the creature's antlers and forcefully pulling its head towards the ground. The Wendigo's high shrill piercing cry echoed through the air, filled with a mix of agony and fury.

"I've got to help him," Octavia said again before she rushed out into the arctic air.

A gust of frigid air hit Anna in the face. "Octavia!" Anna called. She reached out to her, but it was too late. "Octavia! Un-fucking-believable!" Anna slid out to chase her.

Anna watched Octavia struggle against the inconsistent speed of the snow and wind whipping around her. Her eyes traced the towering demon's form, illuminated by the floodlights before she trailed after Octavia.

The Wendigo swatted at Jefferarri again. This time, the tip of two of its claws slashed across the side of the torso and below the hip, deep into his muscles. Jefferarri wailed in pain like a wounded dog. The Wendigo jabbed his sharp, pointed tail at Jefferarri's torso but caught the wiggly beast in his injured thigh. He picked Jefferarri up by the tail, bringing him close to his salivating mouth to devour. The Wendigo's long, serpentine tongue rolled out of its mouth like a snake.

Desperately struggling to survive, Jefferarri's hands frantically scratched at the slimy, wiggling tongue. The Wendigo's serpentine appendage constricted around him repeatedly, suffocating him like a merciless python ensnaring its helpless prey. Agonizingly, the sound of his gasps for air blended with the sickening squelch of his own blood gushing from the wounds. Each constricting grip amplified the searing pain, leaving him no respite from the tightening grip of the demonic tongue.

"You can't take him away from me," Octavia seethed. Her eyes rolled back, and her body trembled as her powers came into play. She continued speaking in a foreign tongue. Suddenly, the Wendigo dropped Jefferarri on his head, leaving him helpless. His wounds cut deep into his muscles, limiting his movement. The wounds on his body were shrouded in a mysterious mist, courtesy of the Wendigo, disrupting his normal healing process.

Anna ran up behind Octavia. Her breaths came in quick gasps as she stood so close to the monster that her knees threatened to buckle beneath her. Something prevented her from getting too close to Octavia, like some force field or invisible shield.

The Wendigo threw up his hands in self-defense to block her spell that burned at its skin. It recoiled as her spell hit it again, feeling like boiling water was poured over its skin. Bites of fog blew from the back of the creature like a gust of wind. The Wendigo leaped and swung its claws at Octavia . . . only to run into an invisible wall around her. He swiped at her several more times again, with no success. The demon tried to grab Anna, but Octavia quickly covered her with the same force field.

Another blast of her spell sent him back, tripping over one of the fallen trees. It fell back into the tree line. Snow and fog rose from the impact. Then it immediately jumped up and bellowed its displeasure with an earth-shaking screech.

Jefferarri's wounds started to heal as the fog around it left, and he yelped as he stumbled onto all fours. He snarled and attempted to move toward the creature, but the pain still had a grip on him, causing him to sit and lick his wounds.

With a mighty leap, the Wendigo sailed over the two women, landed next to the two RVs, and turned the damaged one on its side. With one hand, it picked up the RV and slammed it down on top of Octavia and Anna. It repeated that act until the RV tore apart, and the gas tank burst into flames, forcing the Wendigo to abandon it. The demon did not like fire. As the bodies fell from the RV around them, Octavia and Anna stood unharmed.

"Go!" Octavia barked as another spell hit the Wendigo. It put up its arms to block it, but the force savagely slid it back into the snow. Octavia's hair turned as white as the snow in some spots as the force field around them weakened.

Anna had to reveal the side of her she never wanted anybody to see when she realized the surrounding wall was collapsing. Her life depended on it. The skin under her face rippled and contorted as she spoke in her unknown tongue. She released the beauty that held back her actual image and power. Her face cracked and peeled like weathered paint, and her body twisted out of her tall, supermodel physique to a potbelly half-covered with long, saggy breasts. Slowly, her nose grew more prominent, and her body stretched her thermal suit to its limit.

Octavia blasted another spell at the demon. It fell on its side, howling in pain. Now, cold and weak, Octavia dropped to her knees, still trying to hold the line. Her chant was quickly fading. Anna broke from the force field, limped over, scooped fire from the RV wreckage into her hands, and then walked toward the demon.

"Come here, you son of a bitch!" Anna gritted through clenched teeth.

The alpha rushed at her. She blew into the fire, igniting it into a bright torch that flickered and danced in the alpha's direction. The demon wailed as it covered its eyes from the flames. Its fur burned. The Wendigo rolled and twisted on the ground to extinguish the fire.

"I'm not done with you," Anna said and blew the torch of fire at the demon again.

The Wendigo quickly leaped out of the path of the flames and grabbed a broken log from a tree on the ground. It flung the log at Anna, grazing her, causing her to fall hard to the ground and leaving her disoriented. As she fell into the snow, the tree hit Octavia's weakened shield. The log smashed into the upright RV and then the truck behind it. The sound of metal twisting and glass shattering filled the air as the log crashed into the back of the vehicle, knocking out the light.

The frantic people in the RV got more rattled. Screams of pain escaped the RV. Arctic air blasted through a large hole created by the log and knocked out all the power, including emergency power, so they could not see what was happening outside.

Taking advantage of Jason overseeing the concern of others, Ego head-butted him. Then he maneuvered his way to the hole in the side of the RV and leaped out of it.

"Shit," Jason said as he shook off the cobwebs and slowly stood up, looking for Ego.

"He went that way," one of the bloody occupants said, pointing at the hole.

Jason finessed through the people toward the opening and noticed some moaning, injured people and two dead bodies leaning against the desk and wall close to the opening. Once he dropped out of the opening, he saw Anna struggling, so he gave her a hand. He would never see Anna's the same ever again.

"Thank you," she said, then wobbled back to Octavia.

Jason looked around for Ego. He did not see him, so he trailed behind Anna to Octavia.

Matt watched through the back window in fear of the truck. Ego ran toward the vehicle, looking back to see if he was being followed. Matt checked his gun and dashed out into the cold as fast as his old bones would allow.

"Stop!" Matt said, with his gun aimed at Ego. He leaned against the truck to help with his balance against the wind.

Ego stopped and raised his hands before he turned around. A fake smile formed on his face.

The Wendigo rushed toward Anna and Octavia, prepared to enjoy a tasty treat. With his wounds healed, Jefferarri sprang into the air and attacked the alpha's left eye socket with his claws. A black, tarry liquid oozed out as it scratched and clawed at Jefferarri when he knocked the beast to the ground. Then Jefferarri sprang up on the Wendigo's head and attacked the other eye with the same bloody result.

Once more, the Wendigo knocked Jefferarri to the ground. Unable to see clearly, the Wendigo swatted at the ground, hoping to strike Jefferarri, and covered his eyes to protect them. His body slowly dissolved into the fog that drifted back toward the forest.

"Jefferarri," Octavia shouted in a weak and exhausted voice.

Jefferarri's ears flickered, and he turned toward her, Anna, and Jason, who had his gun pointed at the Wendigo. He snarled at them, baring his teeth as he stood in a crouched position.

Jefferarri, I know you are still in there. Octavia telepathically sent the message to him, but she was not confident it would work, as Roseline had warned her earlier.

Jefferarri took a step back and shook his head. He did not understand why he heard the voice in his head, but he understood what was being said. By his actions, Octavia knew she had him. It took a lot more energy than usual, but she connected.

Jefferarri, rip his fucking heart out! she told him. *The light—kill the light in the chest.*

Jefferarri looked up at the Wendigo, then back at Octavia. He let out a grating roar, then launched himself at its chest. He punched through the weakened alpha's chest between the ribs with his claws and quickly followed up with the opposite hand. With a determined expression, Jefferarri tugged on the icy heart until he wrenched it out of the chest. The Wendigo scratched and clawed at Jefferarri, but it was too late. Covered in the black, thick ooze, Jefferarri fell to the ground with the Wendigo's heart bouncing off the top of him. The Wendigo wailed as its body completely dissolved into the fog, which drifted back into the forest.

Immediately after the Wendigo vanished, the harsh weather quickly dissipated. The wind calmed, and light snow flurries began. The rock-iced heart continued to pulsate a yellow hue.

Exhausted, Anna wobbled over to a small flame in the burning rubble and scooped some fire in her palms. The flame burned between her palms as if attached to a candlewick. She blew her breath across the flame, which leaped fifteen yards to the heart. Jefferarri quickly jumped out of the way. The heart lit up like a barn fire. Jefferarri yelped and rushed from the flames. Like the Wendigo, he was not a fan of fire.

They stood and watched the now-two-story-high blaze crackle and pop, not knowing Jefferarri had circled them for a strike. He stood up behind them, ready to pounce.

"Look out!" Matt warned the trio of the impending sneak attack.

They turned around to face the towering beast with bared teeth and flared eyebrows hovering over them.

"Oh shit," Jason uttered, jumping back. His eyes widened, and his breathing accelerated. His muscles tensed up. Remembering what the predator did to his comrades, he squeezed the automatic trigger, striking Jefferarri in the side of the gut with several bullets.

Jefferarri yelped and ran back about ten feet on all fours. Blood flowed out of his wounds for a second, but it did not affect him and deter him from wanting to rip his teeth into them.

"Get back!" Anna said. She blew into her hands, guiding a torch of flames that roared toward Jefferarri.

Jefferarri quickly dodged the flames, running out of its reach, then galloped back toward the wood line. He stopped in front of the wood line and rose on his back two legs. His flared nostrils and hostile glare made Octavia's heart race as their eyes locked for what felt like an eternity. His attention snapped to the sky as he heard the sounds of helicopters approaching from a distance. Not understanding why, he knew it was time to go. Jefferarri looked down and saw a bullet drop out of his wound into the snow next to the other slugs that had done the same. He felt his wounds healing and moaned in relief. With an ear-piercing howl, he disappeared into the woods on all fours.

"Well, I guess we know what level five is now," Matt said, pushing Ego to Jason.

Jason grabbed Ego by the neck and slung him to his knees. "You're more trouble than you're worth."

"I recommend you get any information out of him now before we make it back to the Compound," Anna said as she slowly reverted to the beauty everyone was used to seeing, which eased anyone's mind except Matt, who had seen her actual shape several times by now.

The sun teased through the clouds, and the closing sound of the helicopter in the distance brought smiles to their faces. Octavia shivered from the cold and her lack of energy. The black in her hair was nearly gone.

"You're going to be okay, Octavia," Anna said. "Help is on the way. We are safe now, and Jefferarri is gone."

"Jefferarri is dead," she said. A tear rolled from the corner of her eye.

Matt nodded in agreement as he looked into the wood line.

CHAPTER 30
IT'S NOT OVER

"**H**EY," VERA SAID, walking into the medical room where Moody lay in the bed. "How are you feeling?"

Moody's eyebrows jumped as he took a deep breath. A slight smile crossed his face. White bandages wrapped around his torso and his left arm. Wires ran from his body to live computers and machines that surrounded the head of the bed. He could not move because of the soreness in his muscles from being bounced around in the RV.

"How long have I been in here?" His voice sounded a bit scratchy.

"You have been in and out of consciousness for twelve days. The recovery team found you bleeding out. I wasn't sure you were going to make it. Luckily for you, mister, no vital organs or arteries were damaged."

Vera gawked at him with relief that he was alive and in awe of his ability to survive. She couldn't deny the reason that she was present to watch over his care was due to her attraction to Moody. Vera had not been in a meaningful relationship since she'd been a part of The Order's research team for the past eleven years. And she could sense a twinkling brewing between them.

"I feel like a Mack truck hit me." He paused to catch his breath, then continued. "Like it ran over me twice."

"You'll survive," Vera said. "I saw it was pretty rough out there in Hopkinton."

"I'm thirsty," Moody said before clearing his throat.

"I'll tell the nurse to bring you something." She walked toward the door to summon a nurse.

"Okay, thank you."

"Man, I saw the footage of the events that night from the RVs and the trucks. I don't want your job. And Jefferarri . . . I have never seen a Lycan like that. The thing about this job is when you think you know everything . . ." she said. She shook her head and continued, "You find out you don't. You know, I told them the only way to kill Jefferarri was to sever the head from the spine. They only listen to me when it's something they *want* to hear."

Moody remained quiet, thinking back to the mayhem that nearly ended his life. The face of the Flesh Eater and its enormous presence made him squirm. *Its skull head, the fangs and claws,* he thought. Those things would forever haunt him.

"Did Jefferarri get away?"

"He did," Moody replied in a whispered tone. "You all are going to try to capture him, aren't you?"

She sat in the recliner next to him with a half-hearted frown. "I think the world would be better and safer if we confined him here at the Compound."

Moody remained quiet and thought, *That's not the reason.*

"Keep it a buck with me, V," he said. He moaned as he attempted to shift to a more comfortable position.

A nurse walked in with a large, plastic, 32-oz cold drinking mug with a flexible straw. Vera took the water and flexed the straw into his mouth. He drank the water, taking breaths between each draw.

"Do you need anything else?" the nurse asked.

"Ah, we should be good," Vera said. "Thanks."

The nurse nodded and walked out.

After he had drunk most of it, Moody waved the mug away.

"You would not bring him here just for that," Moody said. His voice sounded stronger. "You are going to do the same thing to him you did before and stick him with needles."

"Wait, wait, wait," she said with a smile. "I thought you despised him. You didn't like him. A change of heart?"

"Hell no," he said aggravated. He slowly adjusted again for comfort. "We humans have a problem with trying to control everything. And somehow, that always seems to backfire on the world."

Vera looked at him for a moment. Suddenly, her work phone rang, breaking her out of her gaze. She checked the number, then answered it with a sigh. "Yes," she said. Suddenly, her eyes narrowed, and her lips puckered. "How long has this been going on?" She listened as she walked away from the bed. "I'm on my way."

She turned to Moody and pointed, "You, mister, we will finish this conversation after dinner."

"What happened?" he asked. His eyes fixed on her.

She rolled her eyes, not wanting to hear the response to the answer she was about to tell. "J-C149 is acting erratic. I'll be back soon. Get you some rest."

He shook his head and twisted his lips. He kept his thoughts to himself and watched the short woman file out the door.

Octavia sat on the side of the aluminum frame twin bed facing the wall. Her salt-and-pepper locs hung all over the place, with dark circles around her eyes. She looked close to tears as the sniffles came between every few breaths. Finally, a single tear rolled down her cheek before she wiped her eyes.

They have been monitoring her at the Compound since they took her and the rest from the Busbin's place. She sat behind a glass wall, much like the one at the medical center but with studio apartment amenities. Armed female guards, tense and alert, kept watch outside as cameras tracked her every move from sunup to sundown. Octavia made the guards nervous. Sometimes, she eerily stared at the guards, making their flesh crawl.

Officials and visitors checked in at a desk near the wall, with a guard present. Although her powers couldn't penetrate the thick glass, a panic button was available at the station as a precaution. It would release a mist in The Chamber, instantly putting her to sleep.

They claimed to need tests and make observations. The Order feared her. They knew now her powers reached well beyond the voodoo realm, and they desperately wanted to control her and her abilities, just like everybody else. Proper tests and observations would have shown that she had begun a deep descent into a dark state.

Despite The Order already knowing about her unique abilities, they continuously fed Anna the same lies about "tests and observations" while she sat in her glass cell across from Octavia. She wasted her time by drawing pictures on an easel. Most of the poses of Octavia's were her sitting in The Chamber. She dared not to draw any pictures of Jefferarri or any other monsters encountered at Hopkinton because they would undoubtedly use it for their ill-intent advantage . This kept Anna's sanity at peace and in check. Pictures were scattered across her bed and floor.

She looked over and witnessed Octavia slowly becoming unrattled. It ate her up inside that she could not help the girl who possibly saved many lives not so many days ago. Through all the years of internal loathing for her, she now greatly admired Octavia.

Movement out of the corner of Anna's eye caught her attention. She glanced at Octavia strolling over to the glass wall in her white gown. That cold, dark stare she did every few hours of the day like clockwork, each time appearing more sinister than before. The three guards avoided eye contact with her, and two of them kept their backs turned to her while the other faced Octavia but kept her eyes glued to the floor.

Her eyes met Anna's, past the guards. Anna cracked a nervous but friendly smile. *What is going on in that head of yours, Octavia?* Anna thought. *You scaring me.* Anna placed her hands in front of her chest in the shape of a heart. "Stay strong," she said, where Octavia could read her lips.

Octavia cocked her head with a twisted smile.

"We going to be all right," Anna moved her lips slowly.

Octavia quickly shifted her gaze to the guards, who were still indifferent to her presence, before turning her attention back to Anna. She nodded, then walked back to the other side of the bed. *If she gets out of this, I fear the worst,* Anna thought.

Roseline neatly packed the last of her clothes into her suitcase before zipping it closed. She slid the suitcase off the bed to the floor onto its wheels and rolled it out to the balcony, where another matching burgundy and gold suitcase stood. She looked down at Eugene, napping in the chair with Jefferarri's puppy in his lap. His size 14 Monarch sneakers rested on the outside of each foot. She eased her way downstairs and sat in the chair across from him. The puppy wagged his tail and made a popping sound against Eugene's arm, jarring his eyes open.

"How are you feeling?" she asked.

"I'm good," he replied. "You ready?"

She rolled her neck from side to side to loosen the kinks. "In a few minutes," she said.

"Okay, just let me know," he replied with a smile.

A moment of silence came between them. Eugene squeezed his eyes shut, then opened them wide to stay awake. His hand ran back and forth on the puppy's side, who enjoyed the attention.

Her eyes caressed the man before her, whom her heart had grown fond of. How did this man sneak into her heart out of the blue?

"I appreciate your help," she said.

"No problem. I don't mind." His eyes closed for a pause, then reopened.

Her eyes roamed around the room. *I'm going to miss this place*, she thought. Then her eyes panned to the floor, followed by a deep sigh.

The puppy raised his eyelids and looked at her. He quickly jumped down and then placed his paws on her lap. She rubbed his neck, causing the puppy's head to tilt to the side, enjoying being rubbed. For a moment, her breathing halted, remembering Jefferarri's head tilted the same way back at the house.

"I really hate what happened to those two," she said, releasing her breath. "At one point, they were like puzzle pieces that connected perfectly. She complemented him." She squeezed her lips together for a second, then continued, "He fought off the demon the best he could. Even when he knew it was gonna catch him." She sighed heavily, letting her head drop as her eyes focused back down on the puppy.

Eugene's tired eyes peered over at her, soaking in and understanding her emotions. She had his full attention.

"And he did it for her. He did it for love." She felt her throat closing up. She continued, "I know some would have called it selfish." Her eyes met Eugene's. "Do you think he was selfish?"

He cleared his throat and sat up a bit. "He never gave up. This may be a terrible analogy, but people fight cancer every day . . . because they love life and want to live for a long time. And in many cases, for the sake of their loved ones. So, no, I don't think he was selfish. I think she was worth the fight. And I think that's what she wanted."

She wiped away the tears that were rolling down her cheeks, one by one. "I was so concerned for her well-being that I overlooked what was important to her." Her nose flared up as she sniffled. "The Order just used and abused them. Chewed them up and just spat them out," she said. Her voice got a little rougher.

"It's what the government does," Eugene added his two cents. "I've regretted bringing her to The Order for a long time. I thought I was helping her. Thinking it was the best place in the world for somebody like her. I never knew then the bullshit I was truly involved with. Jefferarri too, but they already had their sights on him. Later on, I found out what they were doing. I let him down . . . I let his family down." Before he knew it, his eyes had welled up with tears.

"Well, there's nothing we can do about it now, I suppose. I just hate I can't see her. Do you know how long it will be before we can?"

He shook his head before he answered. "I have no idea."

"They are not going to hurt her, are they?" she asked with concern.

He bent his head downward and scratched his fingers across the back of it. "I honestly don't know."

"That poor baby," she said.

A few minutes of silence enveloped the two while the puppy rested beside her chair. Eugene reflected on the recent events back at the ranch and how Jefferarri towered over him. The smell and the predator vibe radiated from his body. *My heart was racing in my chest faster than it ever did. I was sure to die that day if it wasn't for Octavia. Hard to believe that the little boy I once held in my arms had grown into a killing machine.* Then he remembered that Roseline claimed to have been in Octavia's shoes.

"Back at the ranch, you mentioned that you were in her shoes at one point. What did you mean by that?"

Roseline raised her head and sighed. "When I was a little girl in Africa with my papa, we visited a market on the outskirts of Ghana. While my papa was shopping for fruit from Mama's list, he taught me to pick the best mangos. I loved mangos. Suddenly, something told me to look to my right. Like I was being forced to look that way. And that is when I saw him." Her eyebrows jumped, and the corners of her lips rose. Then she continued. "A little boy couched down by one of the fruit stands was eating papaya. I could tell he was hungry by the way he ate." She cracked a bigger smile. "His clothes were ripped up and dirty like he had been lying in the mud for days. Before I knew it, he turned his head to me as if he knew I was looking. Well, that's how it felt at that moment. He had the most beautiful gray eyes and pecan skin I've ever seen." She crossed her arms over her chest. "We locked eyes briefly before my dad diverted my attention. By the time I looked back over there—"

"Let me guess, he was gone?"

She laughed, then continued. "Ade. He . . . was standing next to me. About three feet away behind me. He was tall like my daddy, but I could tell he was young like me."

"How old were you?"

"Thirteen. I think. Yeah, thirteen. My papa spoke to him calling him a young buck," she said with a giggle, then continued. "My dad didn't play about boys, but for some reason, Papa was cool. He even brought him two melons before we left. I woke up the next morning, and some flowers were on my porch. My papa and mama were clueless about why flowers were there. I looked down the road, and that's when I saw Ade again crouched down beside a tree looking at us."

"Let the crush begin."

"We used to meet at the tree for a while without my parents knowing."

"Was he homeless?"

"Nope. He lived with his grandparents in a nearby village. They were a poor family. He didn't speak much, but the closer we got, the more he opened up to me. I think it took about three weeks before the first time I heard his voice."

"Wow."

"I left my parents at an early age once he got on his feet. I was about sixteen. A year or so after that, I discovered that we could communicate telepathically. Ade worked for a big-time man, running a small numbers racket for a while. He was a runner for him and got paid really well. One time, the man pissed him off, and Ade killed him. A villager told the authorities that Ade tried to hurt him. The police didn't care and let him go. We started a little farm on the outskirts of the village after that. The older we got, the more I saw. No need to tell you what you probably already know since you know Jefferarri. Ade and I are the old story of Jefferarri and Octavia."

"I understand."

"I loved Ade and dealt with him for twenty-something years. But once his eyes turned white, I lost all connection with him. The white eyes meant his soul was gone, so I had nothing to connect to. Ade even came at me to kill me—something he never tried before. He never remembered who I was. Luckily, I could get away when an angry mob came with guns and fire."

"At your age, that must have been a terrifying experience."

"People started disappearing from the village. Men, women, and children. The bones and half-eaten bodies of people and animals were scattered everywhere." She paused for a moment, then continued. "They got him. They finally got him."

"How?" Eugene asked.

"I wasn't there, so I don't know the details, but they separated the head from his body. The more the rage grows inside and the older they get, the harder to kill."

Eugene played with his beard, remaining silent to soak it all in. From his experiences with Jefferarri and her words, he imagined the horrors she and the people of Ghana had been through. *Did she know her lover was killing all those people and did nothing?* He dared not to ask that question.

"Love will make you do and accept things in its name," he said.

CHAPTER 31
THE ORDER NO MORE

VERA RUSHED OFF the elevator before the doors completely opened. She could hear the banging reverberating up the hall from J-C149's pen. She felt the vibrations rumbling through her body. The closer she got, the louder the noise and the stronger the throbs. She swiped her badge at the door and ran into the chaos beyond the doors.

"What happened?" Upset, Vera asked some people before she took two steps past the doors.

Three techs, one Puerto Rican named Paola, rubbing the back of her neck, and two Black men, Rontrell and Delvis, watched from the safety of the observation room above the pen. Rontrell had his hands clasped over his face, and Delvis sat with wide eyes, watching J-C149 run around the pen. He ran into the lift door and beat it violently with his fists and arms. He acted like a trapped animal desperate to escape. The pounding beat against everybody's eardrums.

"I don't know," Delvis said. "He just started flipping out!"

"Did anyone stare him in his eyes or something?" Vera asked. "No."

Two-and-a-half-inch steel bars cap the twenty-foot-high, thirty-by-forty-foot pen. A large hydration station flowed from the far wall of the observation window.

"Maybe he has grown tired of being couped up," Paola said. "He wants to be free."

"Okay, everyone, just relax," Vera commanded, talking more to herself than her subordinates. Exasperated sighs flowed from her mouth before she pressed her lips together. She watched her hard work unravel before her eyes. *We were making good progress, J-C149. Don't make me put you down.* She swallowed hard after that thought.

Suddenly, everyone jumped when the emergency alarm blasted throughout the facility, and the warning lights flashed.

"What now?" Vera retorted, rolling her eyes. "Today just keeps getting better and better," she joked cynically.

"What's going on?" Bill said, stumbling out of the restaurant and bumping into one of the armed guards running by. Bill fell on his butt, and a sharp pain jolted up his back. "Hey, hey, what's going on?"

"Sorry, sir," the armed guard said after recognizing Bill. The soldier tried to help him up, but Bill refused the offer. "Something has breached the perimeter on the north side, sir. That's all I know. Excuse me," the armed guard said before running toward the northern gates.

Bill slowly got up. The throbbing veins in his neck showed the struggle of getting up off the cold concrete and the annoyance of his blue three-piece Lazio suit capped off with the white shirt and black tie touching the ground. Random shots and screaming made Bill crouch back down. A bloodcurdling howl from a distance rattled the restaurant windows.

Jefferarri! Bill crawled back into the restaurant, struggling through the door as people rushed out.

Bill stood in the center of the restaurant next to a pillar full of plants at the top. Screams and gunfire pierced the walls and windows. His head tilted, and his eyes narrowed as eight armed guards backpedaled past the window from the north wall, letting bullets loose as if their lives depended on it. Then they turned and ran. Jefferarri landed in view right in front of the window on the sidewalk. His body stood too tall to see above his torso through the windows. In his right hand, closest to the window, he held a dying guard. Jefferarri's claws pierced through his body, and blood and gore splattered on the windows and spilled onto the concrete.

Paralyzed in place, Bill stared with wide eyes locked on Jefferarri. His heartbeat increased and pounded in his chest. *Holy shit!*

A woman's scream blasted from behind him. His head jerked around to the wide-eyed young, white girl screaming like in an '80s horror movie. She stood behind the register. *You fucking bitch*, Bill thought. Now, he felt eyes on *him*. He slowly turned his head back to the window, and Jefferarri had his wet nose pressed against the glass, staring at him. Jefferarri's teeth bared in a sinister smile. His eerie white eyes pierced through Bill's soul.

"Fuck," Bill said. He held his hands up and took a step backward.

Jefferarri tilted his head, then smashed the dead body in his grasp through the window. The force was so great that shards of glass cut Bill on his face and arm from way across the room as the body flew past him and slammed hard against the wall next to the screaming woman. Jefferarri rushed in, reached over the counter, and slashed his claws across Bill's throat, nearly decapitating him. Then he tossed him hard over the counter across the room. Bill's limp body slid across the broken glass on the floor before slamming into the wall below the window. Now, Jefferarri turned to the young woman, but she was gone. He looked down behind the register ... but nothing.

Four guards rushed into the observation room. Two stood guarding the door as the other two walked in.

"Dr. Vera," one guard said. "We are here to move you and your staff to safety."

"Why? What's going on?" she asked with narrowed eyes.

"You don't know?" the guard replied. "A large werewolf creature is attacking us."

"A werewolf creature? Like *this* one?" She said, pointing down to J-C149, wreaking havoc on the doors.

The two guards looked. Their eyes widened, and brows creased. "Not sure, ma'am. We did hear the name 'Jefferarri' once or twice."

She smiled as she looked down at J-C149. *It's time to prove to these people that my work is successful.* She turned to the guard. "Where is the werewolf now?"

CHAPTER 32
CHICKEN COMES HOME TO ROOST

JASON AND TWO armed guards knocked on Mr. Haskins's door to his home on the west end of the Compound. His hammer fist banged furiously on the front door of the high stone-designed porch. Mr. Haskins's furrowed brow met Jason at the door. He adjusted his glasses as distant gunfire touched his ears, followed by a vicious growl.

"What's going on?" Mr. Haskins asked.

"We are under attack!" Jason said as calmly as he could.

"Attack! By whom?"

"Jefferarri."

Mr. Haskins sighed deeply, then said, "The chickens have come home to roost."

"Sir," Jason said, "we need to move and get you to safety ASAP."

They hustled Mr. Haskins out to the Humvee, which was waiting in front of the house. They immediately rushed off to the east side of the Compound. Jason sat in the back on the passenger side with Mr. Haskins. The gunfire got louder, overtaking the engine sounds of the Humvee.

"Incoming!" the guard in the passenger seat yelled.

Before the others knew what happened, Jefferarri leaped on the Humvee with such force from the left that the Humvee tilted on two wheels, then eventually rocked over to its side. The driver's window shattered, and the Humvee slid on its side before stopping in the middle of the road.

The impact of Jason's head hitting the door frame caused a ringing in his ears and made it difficult for him to focus his blurry eyes. His ears heard the muffled sounds of men crying, gunshots, and growls. Mr. Haskins rested on top of him, dazed. *God, my fucking head hurts.* He adjusted his body in a better position to breathe with Mr. Haskins's weight on him. Mr. Haskins's body placed a lot of stress on him.

"Heyyy," Jason called out in a weak tone.

He heard muffled voices that came from inside the vehicle. He adjusted his head to get a better view inside the Humvee. The voices slowly became clearer.

"—hold on," a voice said from inside the vehicle.

Suddenly, the driver's door swung open. As Jason's vision cleared, he saw the guard rise out of the opened door and start shooting. Hot bullet shells dropped into the vehicle, with a few hitting Jason. Warm blood splashed on Jason as soon as the shooting stopped. Suddenly, the guard's body flew out of the door. His gun dropped into the Humvee on top of the still body of the guard in the passenger seat. Jason shook the head of the guard, but it felt like a heavy rock.

"Fuck."

The Humvee rocked before Jefferarri's enormous head cast a slight shadow into the cabin. Blood covered Jefferarri's face, and his mouth was agape, showing red-stained teeth. Both his claws gripped either side of the door frame, and his claws shredded the seats as he went after his target. Jason felt around for his weapon but to no avail.

"Jefferarri," Jason whispered in fear.

Jefferarri's ears twitched, and his head turned to the side before a howl rumbled inside the cabin of the Humvee. He rushed out of view and flipped the Humvee back to its wheels, juggling the trio inside.

Mr. Haskins gave a slight moan as his eyes twitched. Jefferarri took on heavy gunfire from automatic weapons, grabbing his attention away from the Humvee. Some bullets grazed his skin and caused hair from his mane to float to the ground. A few bullets penetrated him, causing him to yelp and raise his arms over his face from the stings. Jason's weapon gleamed in the dim light as he picked it up. After inspecting it, he raised the gun and aimed it directly at Jefferarri. He swallowed after the thought of getting mauled by him if he pissed it off, so he just aimed at him in case danger turned back his way.

Jefferarri launched into the air, landing thirty-five yards at the four shooters, ripping three apart with his bare claws and teeth. The fourth one had cowered away, only to get run down and mauled brutally. Jefferarri ripped the coward's spine from his back and threw it, then turned his head over his shoulder and saw Jason carrying Mr. Haskins on his shoulder. He looked at the building and instantly became drawn to it.

A banging echoed through the empty Research Building, followed by a deep, deep roar that made Jason's heart race. Adrenaline surged through his veins as he hastened his pace, his footsteps echoing in the large lobby. Panic set in as he frantically searched for his badge, his eyes scanning the ID pad for the elevator. The path ahead was obstructed by two escalators, hiding them from Jefferarri's view. Each passing second felt like an eternity as the sound of Jefferarri's approach intensified, causing Jason's breath to quicken. The elevators offered no indication of floor levels, only up and down buttons. Impatiently waiting for the doors to open, Jason could hear the growl getting closer and closer, sending shivers down his spine.

"Come on, come on, come on!" he begged the elevator to open. He looked toward the escalators. *If I took the stairs, Jefferarri would clearly see us, and we'd be dead in seconds. Maybe I can drop Mr. Haskins on the floor to save myself.*

Jefferarri crept through the lobby and looked up at the moving escalators. He rose to his hind legs and sniffed the air. He could smell the fear, so he dropped to all fours and followed his nose around the escalators.

Jason turned to dash toward the stairs when he heard the elevator chime. He heard Jefferarri huff as his claws tapped the linoleum floor, getting closer. Finally, the elevator doors opened, and Jason rushed in. His heart pounded so hard that it almost burst out of his chest. He jabbed at the basement buttons in front of the open doors.

Jefferarri eased from around the corner of the escalators and spotted Jason and Mr. Haskins on the elevator. Jason dropped the old man to the floor as Jefferarri's eyes met his. Jason grabbed his automatic gun off his shoulder and readied it. Jefferarri launched at the elevator but slipped on the floor, where he had almost no traction. He belly-flopped to the floor. As the elevator doors began to close, Jefferarri sprang up and launched at the elevator doors again, only to repeat the same action as his hands and feet slipped from under him. The doors closed just in time, with Jefferarri slamming hard into elevator doors, causing the lights to blink.

As the elevator descended to the lower level, the banging from above vibrated through the elevator shaft. He set Mr. Haskins's back against the elevator wall and repeatedly slapped his face to wake him up. As Mr. Haskins started to come to, a blast from above shook the elevator car, and some of the ceiling fell on top of him. When Jason looked up, he saw the corner of the elevator door poking through the ceiling.

"Oh fuck." Jason turned to Mr. Haskins and gave him one hard slap. "Wake the fuck up!"

The elevator halted. Mr. Haskins opened his eyes and looked up at Jason.

"Mr. Haskins, we've got to move!"

Jefferarri landed hard on the roof of the elevator car, followed by a snarl.

"What's that?"

"That is Jefferarri."

"You got to be shittin' me!"

The elevator chimed, and the doors opened. Jason guided Mr. Haskins to open the door when Jefferarri punched through the ceiling. Debris flew down to the floor.

"Move it, move it," Jason ordered.

The doors closed, and they heard Jefferarri fall through the roof.

"We in the basement?" Mr. Haskins asked.

"Yes. Quick, which way?"

Jefferarri violently banged on the closed elevator doors.

"Which way?" Jason asked in a more demanding tone.

The hallway split two ways—right or left. Mr. Haskins pointed left, and they were on the move as fast as Mr. Haskins could move. They made it to the last door down the hall.

"Scan," Mr. Haskins said, pointing at the pad.

Jason waved his badge across the pad, but no dice. He tried again with the same reaction. "I don't think I have clearance."

"I left my badge at the house."

"What now?"

They heard the snarls from a distance. Both looked toward the sound.

"We need to take the stairs down to the lower level. I can use my handprint to get us in," Mr. Haskins said in a jittery tone.

"Bet. Let's move."

Moments later, they reached the lower level and found a tall bronze-colored door.

"Sir," a voice came from the distance, accompanied by the sound of jogging boots.

Two armed guards jogged up to Jason and Mr. Haskins. Blood covered their faces, hands, and uniforms.

"Y'all good?" Jason asked, happy to see them.

"Yeah, we're good," one guard answered.

"We were on our way up to the observation post where Vera and her people are," the other guard said.

Mr. Haskins placed his hand over the scanner. The scanner read his hand and said, "Welcome, Haskins." Mr. Haskins led the men into the lab, but one of them wailed in pain. Blood flew past the men. When the men turned around, they saw Jefferarri dangling one guard in the air with his claws piercing his back. Jason and the other men aimed their guns at Jefferarri, who, in turn, ripped the man in two. Blood and guts sprayed everywhere, including on the men still standing.

Jefferarri's resounding snarl boomed in deafening decibels. Jason and the other guard fired at him, stinging him with bullets. Jefferarri rushed forward, grabbed the other guard by his head, and bashed it into the floor until it turned to mush. As the doors started to close, something caught Jefferarri's attention. He knocked Jason out of the way, blocking the door from closing before slipping in. Then the door closed behind him.

Jefferarri turned to face the door as it closed behind him, the sound echoing through the vast room. He looked around the large room with the red-tinted lights. He went from four legs to two as he strolled down the center of the walkway. Glass cylinder tanks filled with yellowish fluid lined each side of the room. Some tanks were empty, but the others hailed creatures that favored different levels of Jefferarri morphed one way or another. Most looked deformed, while the others appeared normal compared to Jefferarri. He continued to walk through the lab, hunching and looking side to side at each cadaver on display.

His ears twisted as he heard a noise paddling about. He sniffed the air and then dropped to all fours to continue hunting. Halfway down the room, the cylinder tanks ended. Now, different tanks aligned the walkway toward the back. The tanks were on their sides, each with different types of cryptids. Tubes ran into their mouths, and a clear fluid filled the tank. Down at the end of the room stood a large, opened curtain that moved a little. Jefferarri bared his teeth and moved swiftly past the curtain.

Behind the curtain stood a large glass container with thick black bars. Two enormous lights hung from the ceiling facing the container.

Inside the container was something different from the rest. A winged creature stood on display. A tan-skinned, menacing-looking creature with sharply pointed ears and a leathery bat wingspan of fifteen feet stood roughly eight feet tall from head to talons. It had long, jagged teeth and the nose of a bat. The tag on the tank read, "Cristian."

Jefferarri's ears twitched. The sound of breathing alerted him to the proximity of his prey, and he readied himself for the attack. He could not see beyond the glass container because the back of it was a solid black color, but he knew he was back there. He could smell the fear. Climbing on top of the container, Jefferarri used the bars to hoist himself up and looked down at Mr. Haskins, who had his back against the container. Drool hit him on his shoulders and his face. He rubbed his fingers across it and realized . . . It had found him. He slowly looked up at Jefferarri's bared teeth like he was a nightmare. As he looked on in shock, his eyes grew wider and wider, and his legs began to shake, causing him to slide down the container.

The doors opened behind Jefferarri, catching his attention. At the door, Vera stood with J-C149 by her side. J-C149 snarled at the sight of Jefferarri. *Lord, have mercy. He is huge. But all I need him to do is obey my commands to prove the success of my project. I couldn't care less who wins. I can make an army of either of them.*

"Kill him," Vera said, pointing at Jefferarri.

J-C149 slammed his fists against the floor. Then he rushed down the walkway toward Jefferarri.

Jefferarri hopped down and waited, standing upright. J-C149 leaped into the air and swiped at Jefferarri. Jefferarri nimbly sidestepped and slashed his claws into J-C149's side, eliciting a cry of pain. The crash of J-C149 into the container echoed throughout the room. Blood flowed effortlessly from its wounds to the floor. Jefferarri mauled J-C149 on the floor, then stopped. Jefferarri smelled J-C149 while he whined in discomfort. He was no match for Jefferarri on this level.

Jefferarri sniffed J-C149 before snapping his head back in confusion. The familiar scent made him step back. He smelled his blood in him. Jefferarri slammed his fist into the tank in a rage. A hairline crack developed at the impact spot. He hit it again, and the crack grew longer. Jefferarri looked down at J-C149 and glanced at his wounds, which had slowly healed. An armed guard rushed past Vera and began shooting at the two Lycans, striking the glass multiple times until the container gave way.

Jefferarri rushed at the guards, who turned and ran. Vera hit the button to close the door, but it did not shut fast enough. She could hear Jefferarri's growls intensify as he slid past the door, causing an unsettling shiver to run down her spine. Claws ripped through her back and severed her spinal cord in three places. Blood spilled, and chunks of flesh and guts littered the floor. The cowardly guards were long gone. Jefferarri dragged Vera's mangled body across the floor, leaving a bloody trail behind her.

He raised her hand to the scanner, but the door did not open. He tried again, but the same result. Getting frustrated, Jefferarri slammed her body hard against the wall with a resounding roar. Both her shoes flew off. He picked up the hand and tried a third time. This time, her palm faced the scanner. The door opened. What Jefferarri saw made him snarl and take a step back.

Cristian the Elder stood at the door with Mr. Haskins's decapitated body sucking the blood from where the head used to be. The pupil of his eye glowed an icy blue. His wings were tucked under his arms. Cristian's body structure brimmed with vitality, and his muscles pulsated beneath his weathered skin, a stark contrast to the once skeletal frame that resided within the confines of the container. Jefferarri looked past Cristian and saw J-C149's headless body as well. The bars on the container busted outward at the top.

Cristian flew at Jefferarri, knocking himself on his backside. In this weakened state, his claws and talons could not do more than scratch Jefferarri's skin's surface. He needed more blood, and Jefferarri was his next meal. Jefferarri ripped his claws across Cristian's face, leaving two deep gouges at an angle across his face, and then he bit into his left wing. Cristian let out a cry as he escaped from Jefferarri's clutches.

Cristian quickly realized that the Lycan outmatched him. He needed more blood to feast upon to build up his strength again. He flapped his wings to escape the larger killer. His wings caused a strong wind to draft behind him. Jefferarri chased him down the hall and out to the open hallway. Cristian took off up the damaged elevator shaft. Jefferarri grabbed Cristian around his leg and rode him up the shaft until he came out of the missing door caused by Jefferarri earlier. Jefferarri slipped down his leg as Cristian crashed through the window, and Jefferarri leaped out of the broken window behind him. He grabbed his talon but did not have enough to hold on to. Jefferarri's claws cut the skin of the talon as Cristian snatched it away, leaving Jefferarri crashing down to the ground, landing on the back of his head. He slowly rolled over to all fours and looked up at the dizzy image of Cristian hovering a safe distance above.

As Jefferarri's vision quickly cleared, they locked eyes before Jefferarri leaped into the air at him. Cristian moved to the side fast enough for Jefferarri to miss him. *I will see you again when I'm at full strength*, Christian thought. With disgust, he narrowed his eyes at Jefferarri, then flew away, his wings too weak to keep him airborne for much longer.

"Jefferarri," Octavia called from a distance.

Jefferarri snapped his head toward her as she stood at the broken window with Anna and Jason. His breaths came in ragged gasps, and he knew he couldn't push himself any further that day. He snarled at them before taking off to the north end of the Compound.

"Jefferarri," Octavia called again.

"Will you please tell her to stop calling him?" Jason said in a panicked voice.

EPILOGUE

DIXON STOOD OUT on the sidewalk in front of the sheriff's office wearing a pair of dark shades. A brief grin crossed his face as he removed the shades to rub his eyes. His red eyes complemented the dark circles around them. He yawned as he waved at the old 1968 Ford truck, honking the horn as it passed by. Despite the lack of crazy weather or agents running around, the continuous nightmares would not let him enjoy the calm after the storm. However, Hopkinton's climate returned to normal for February. Snow had not fallen in a week, and the sun was on full display this early morning.

Coe pulled up in front of the office in his patrol car. There had not been much conversation between the two since the snowstorm ceased. He got out and greeted Dixon. "Morning."

Dixon nodded at Coe and asked, "How are you feeling this morning?"

"Shit, I'll be straight if it stays like this." Coe lit a cigarette, then continued. "If only I could wean off these fucked-up dreams, I'd be good."

"Yes, indeed," Dixon agreed, not wanting to mention his sleeping issue. "Let's hope it does. Are you going to run for the open position?"

"I'm still thinking about it," Coe said, lifting his chin with a smile and a raised eyebrow.

"You would do a fabulous job if you do."

"Thanks," Coe said. "Welp, let me get out and show my face. Gun range later? It's been a while."

"Sounds like a plan to me. Five thirty?"

"Yep, yep," Coe said before taking a drag of his cigarette. "See you there. Have ya money ready."

"Really? You want me to take your money *again*?" Dixon joked, followed by a laugh.

Coe shut the door and rolled down the window. "There was something in my eye last time. I'm winning my money back." He put the car in drive and rolled forward.

"We'll see," Dixon said, pointing at Coe as he drove off. He replaced the shades on his face with a smile before walking into the building.

Octavia was finally reunited with Roseline and Eugene. Watching Octavia go through withdrawal was a painful experience for them to witness. Her body acted like a possessed person. Her eyes developed dark spots. She spoke in a weird language and pounded her head against the wall or floor until it bled. The smell of death overtook her as well. Despite her immense power, Octavia still yearned for healing and guidance from an elder. With unwavering support, they journeyed back to Haiti, where a sense of rejuvenation awaited her. Healers took her away from the people she loved until she came back around.

As the sun-kissed shore embraced them, Roseline sat tranquilly, her eyes fixed on Eugene, their bond as strong as ever, as he skillfully cast his fishing line into the sparkling turquoise waters. The gentle breeze carried the faint scent of salt and sea, mingling with the earthy aroma of the nearby foliage. Lost in the pages of "Never Again, No More 6: Karma's Payback," Roseline immersed herself in a tale that mirrored Octavia's own journey of recovery.

Until Octavia returned, they would be right there under the radar, waiting for her. But from time to time, she couldn't help but wonder what the dark side of Jefferarri was up to.

In the scorching heat of a July summer, three rednecks reclined lazily around a crackling campfire in Tylerville, North Carolina. The air was thick with humidity, causing beads of sweat to trickle down their foreheads as they passed around ice-cold cans of beer and indulged in the occasional puff of a joint. Behind them, nestled by the serene lake, three tents stood shoulder to shoulder, their vibrant colors contrasting against the backdrop of lush greenery. A tantalizing aroma wafted through the air from their fresh catch sizzling over the open fire.

"I shole am hungry," Bud said, groping his stomach. "We coulda been ate."

"Why we eating so late anyhow?" Jack asked. "It's almost ten o'clock at night."

"Hush yo' mouth," Billy said. Being the biggest and the oldest, Billy gained the beta males' respect. "The fish was biting so we stayed a little longer. Nobody was complaining when we were out there catching up the damn water, now, were you?" He crossed his arms and stared at his companions.

"Well, shit, Billy. We coulda been cooking some while we fished," Jack spat.

"You two are a bunch of bullshitters," Billy said before putting down his can, followed by a long, deep burp. "Make shole nothing crawl or fly in my beer. I gotta drain the lizard."

"You mean the earthworm," Bud cracked.

Billy walked into the dark forest beyond the flickers of the fire.

"It shole is quiet out here tonight. I can't hear shit," Bud said.

"Yeah," Jack agreed. He rubbed his arms and scoped out the surrounding scene.

"You ain't scared, are you, Jack?" Bud laughed. "Hey, Billy, Jack out here scared!"

They could hear sticks breaking in the darkness. Jack and Bud both looked in the direction that Billy walked.

"Billy?" Bud said as he cut his eyes over to Jack with a smile. "Billy," he called a little louder. Now, the look on his face changed. His brows furrowed, and his lips puckered. He stood up and faced the direction Billy walked.

"I don't like this, Bud."

"Billy!"

"Boo!" Billy said, scaring the two. He laughed uncontrollably. His two friends jumped. And Bud soiled his pants.

"I got you, you nitwits," Billy continued to laugh.

The two individuals came to a sudden halt, their gazes fixed on Billy. In an instant, their eyes widened, displaying sheer terror, while their mouths hung open in disbelief. Their pulses raced, causing their hearts to beat rapidly, as their breaths became shallow and rapid.

"Billy?" Bud said.

The two friends took a cautious step back, their gazes fixated on the space above his head. A low growl pierced the air, causing Billy's heart to momentarily stop. Slowly, he turned around, his body trembling. Jefferarri's presence was overwhelming, causing Billy to lose his balance and land hard on the ground. The flickering flames of the fire cast a dim light, revealing Jefferarri's formidable figure standing at a distance. Drool dripped menacingly from his sharp, uneven teeth. His eyes, as white as glistening pearls, gleamed with an eerie reflection of the dancing fire. Without warning, Jefferarri lunged forward, pouncing on Billy.

THE END

NOTE FROM THE AUTHOR

Thank you kindly for your interest in *Fall of the Order*. I intended to challenge myself in a different genre. All characters' names are purely fictional. Much of this story takes place in New Hampshire and North Carolina, but I have altered the setting of most locations and the backstory of some cryptid folklore for the benefit of this fictional story. I hope you all loved reading this story just as much as I enjoyed writing it.

WWW.BLACKODYSSEY.NET

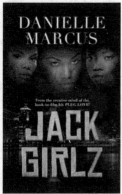